CLOSING DISTANCE

CLOSING DISTANCE

» » » » » » » » » » » » » » » »

Jim Oliver

G. P. PUTNAM'S SONS NEW YORK

G. P. Putnam's Sons
Publishers Since 1838
200 Madison Avenue
New York, NY 10016

Library of Congress Cataloging-in-Publication Data

Oliver, Jim.
Closing distance / Jim Oliver.
p. cm.
ISBN 0-399-13767-X (alk. paper)
I. Title.
PS3565.L475C5 1992 92-9648 CIP
813'.54—dc20

Printed in the United States of America
1 2 3 4 5 6 7 8 9 10

This book is printed on acid-free paper.
∞

ACKNOWLEDGMENTS

Drs. David Greenwald and Bruce Saidman
Medical Oncology Associates, Kingston, PA

Dr. Ted Feinstein, Philadelphia, PA

Robert Berghaier, The Philadelphia Zoo

Much appreciation, affection, and respect to my editor, E. Stacy Creamer, for her on-the-mark suggestions and generous offer of the use of her own title.

And to my agent and friend now, Kay Kidde of Kidde, Hoyt & Picard, my gratitude for grabbing me up and insisting on the best.

To my tried-and-true friend Patricia A. McBroom, for her awing observation at some moment of discouragement:

"But Jim, writing a book is like rowing to England."

I.

At seven in the evening on a Saturday in May near the center of Philadelphia, Pete Flowers, thirty-nine for several weeks yet, single for several years now, stretches out as much as he is able in his old, oil-needy swivel chair. The heel of one of his sneakers rests gently on the desk corner, atop several outgoing invoices. He has been sitting watching the light through the back window of his florist shop shift from apricot to rose for some time, wishing he could stay thirty-nine, thinking up implausible, last-minute excuses he might give his parents to get out of having dinner at their house in an hour.

"When the sunset turns to crimson, I'll go up and shower."

He thinks that he will call his very Catholic parents and say that he just received a plea from Mother Superior at Our Lady of Consolation School. She must have a hundred and nine white corsages for the graduating girls. By midnight.

The Cardinal's personal secretary called. His Eminence is in the mood for lime blossoms. A lot of lime blossoms. Key Lime blossoms. No. Persian Lime blossoms. Direct from Persia.

Pete stands. He sighs. He walks toward the front of his flower shop, turning lights off, turning lights on, changing here and there the positions of objects—an onyx bowl, a malachite vase. He looks for dust on his shelves.

He checks the gauges on the glass-fronted coolers. He speculates on the salability of the flowers inside them come Monday. Spoilage is a central issue in his life.

» » »

In the hall outside his apartment, he stops and listens for disturbing sounds from the third-floor apartment of his tenant, William Petranek. The silence disappoints him. He never hears disturbing sounds from up there. Mr. Petranek does not violate the terms of his lease.

» » »

He stands in his kitchen, one floor above his shop, staring at the sweat beads on the outside of the glass of wine he has poured. During his adult life, he has never been invited to his parents' house on a non-holiday Saturday night. His mother's phone invitation: "We want you to come over for dinner Saturday," not "Would you like . . . ?", not "Do you have plans for . . . ?" And, fully aware that he would have preferred doing something with his friends to dinner with his family, he had not hesitated to say yes.

"Something is up," he says to the very clean, white Formica doors of his cupboards.

What was particularly curious about this dinner, besides the choice of day, was his mother's pointed exclusion of her six granddaughters. To Pete's knowledge, his mother—who treasured all children and especially this nattering, prepubescent clutch—had never asked that they be left at home in the care of sitters. How could they be in the way with all those rooms in his parents' house to swallow them up, and stolid Carmen, the housekeeper, to ride herd?

Nor was Pete the only one annoyed with this break with routine. His sister Bea, the youngest, telephoned him in a snit the day the invitation was made, furious because her mother-in-law, The Ogress, was "too busy" to take her two girls Saturday night. Where would she find a sitter? Even their older brother, Stu, was nonplussed. He hadn't openly objected, but had gone so far as to tell their mother that his two would be disappointed to have to miss dinner with Grams. Liz's reply was uncharacteristic: "The adults never get to be alone."

Mary Alice, the eldest sibling, called the invitation "abnormal." She dropped her commitment to a Friends of Rittenhouse Square dinner without so much as a "But, Mother . . ." on the strength of some shift she sensed in Liz's intonation.

"And her with her *au pair* girl for her kids," complained Bea of Mary Alice in one of many calls to Pete this week. "And not even offering to let me drop my two off at her house. I'd even drive all the way to Paoli with them."

» » »

In his bathroom, waiting for the shower water to warm, Pete stands at the mirror with a thermometer in his mouth. He examines his face, evaluating the ravages of his thirty-nine years. His brown hair is shot with gray, but it is thick; the skin around his eyes is crinkled by crow's-feet, but is still elastic. His eyes are clear. He has good teeth. His one major flaw, a port-wine birthmark in the shape of the state of Delaware extending from his left earlobe to his shoulder, does not seem as dark and offensive to him as usual. He thinks he is basically nice-looking except for the birthmark. There are times he thinks he is good-looking.

He sees a white hair in his moustache.

"Have we come to this?" he mumbles in the mirror.

He plucks it out.

"We have not."

He reads the thermometer. 97.7. He prods the lymph nodes in his neck.

» » »

He stands in the double doorway of his bedroom closet.

His suits are all dark and American cut. His shirts, laundered, folded, medium-starched, are predominantly button-downs. He decides on a white one in deference to his mother, who thinks men look their best in white shirts, but he cannot decide whether to dress up or to dress down with the rest of his outfit. There is no family dress code for dinners, but because the occasion is ostensibly special, he chooses dark, Italian-cut trousers instead of khakis or jeans, and loafers as a statement of the casual attitude he intends to bring to this dinner.

"Something is up," he says, buckling a black, lizard-skin belt.

Pete does not subscribe to Mary Alice's scenario for the evening, which calls for their father to rise at the end of dinner, to lift a glass of moderately priced champagne to his assembled children and to their spouses, and to announce his retirement as CEO of Grand-mère's Meat Pies. Stu, who sells stocks and bonds and is also their father's primary business confidant and part-time financial adviser, would certainly know if there were retirement plans. Since Stu shared almost everything he knew with the other siblings, he would not likely have kept any such plans secret. Nor does Pete see merit in Stu's theory of the dinner: that since their parents have been talking for several years about the need to get their children together to discuss their estate, tonight's after-dinner conversation will pertain to wills and to dispositions. Pete cannot imagine his father's revealing the extent of his worth to their mother, let alone to Bea's Anthony, Mary Alice's Hal, and Stu's Alexa, "that plastic gold digger," toward whom it nearly kills him to be gracious.

Bea has convinced herself that Phil and Liz will tell them that they are selling the family house on Pine Street, the house the four children grew up in, to move to a condo in a high rise on The Square. Pete believes his parents will die in their house, that, as their bodies begin to fail them, they will install an elevator, that they will hire pushers for their wheelchairs when their arms have gotten too weak, and then teams of porters to carry them to wherever the sunlight has moved among those many high-ceilinged, high-windowed rooms.

Nor can he imagine his father retiring from Grand-mère's Meat Pies. It was unthinkable that he would sell the company; unthinkable that he would fail to go in on Saturdays and Sundays to check production lines and to fuss about refrigeration, he who has not in forty years read a book if it did not chronicle the life of some famous American entrepreneur, he who has not entertained a discernible hobby and whose capacity for relaxation is measured in the time it takes to read *The Wall Street Journal* each day and the four monthly trades which relate to the creation and sale of his "Grand-mère Family of Flavors": chicken, beef, pork, Fruits de Grande Mer, and vegetarian.

"Something is up," Pete says again, plumping the pillows on his bed.

» » »

He sits on the couch in his living room. It is a twenty-minute walk to his parents' house. It is now twenty-five minutes before eight. He thinks his brother and sisters are correct, that their parents have made some important decision affecting themselves and, apparently, their children. There has not been a meeting of the family to discuss specific issues in the thirteen years since Bea and Anthony did not show up for their enormous wedding at Our Lady of Mystery Church. The Flowerses, minus Bea, had gathered in Monsignor DiDomenico's stuffy private office, without Monsignor DiDomenico, and had ultimately decided to go ahead with the reception at Blue Rock Country Club, bride, bridegroom, and wedding notwithstanding.

"Divorce!" he says to the ceiling fan.

He stands.

"That's silly," he says to the stereo.

His parents are sixty-four. Divorce at their age doesn't make sense. Certainly they have had problems. Who hasn't? Certainly they are very different people with very different needs. What couple isn't? Pete has always assumed that they love each other. Who would think that they didn't? All those years—forty-how-many?—to raise four nonfelonious children, run a business to prosperity, and survive the death of one of their kids on a city street.

Yet, his parents are diametric opposites, emotionally and cerebrally. Their great expectations for their lives cannot vaguely match. They are not physically affectionate in public, even around the family, limiting their touchings to forearms and shoulders. Do they fuck? Pete wonders. Do they peel each other's clothes off and pound the bed springs into China? Do they lie together on their backs afterwards, hips welded, sweat trickling into their eye sockets?

» » »

When he was twenty-two, Pete moved from his parents' house east of Broad to a small apartment in a high rise west of Broad, a move of some ten blocks in which he saw great geographic significance even though from a friend's living room window on the floor above his own he could see the roof of the house he grew up in and, in certain lights, its verdigris weather vane that was shaped like a fish. For the way he felt from his new distance, he might have moved to Panama or to Peru. And despite anxious misgivings, his parents did not once drop in on him or call. Stu, newly married and house-poor in Swarthmore, called to wish him well and to invite him out to a Phillies game and a dinner of hot dog. Mary Alice, the oldest and then twenty-eight, called from Atlanta to say that her second abortion had gone OK and that she was leaving that city for a job in LA, where she would be giving up men and/or sex. She would decide when she got there. Bea, still at home, called complaining that she did not like living there so much anymore, that she missed having Pete around the house—including the rude noises he used to make on the third floor above her—that Daddy was an arbitrary tyrant and that she had met a cute Italian boy with great buns whom she intended to date if he asked her out. No matter what Daddy said.

Pete called home during those first weeks, reaching his father once—"How's it going?"—and his mother twice—"Are you doing your laundry? Do you want to drop it off?"

Thinking that his parents, Liz at least, would visit unexpectedly with some housewarming gift or another, he kept his small space in perfect order. His ashtrays sparkled; his trash did not accumulate; he washed his dishes as he used them; he never invited anyone to stay the night. He hid his collection of pornographic paperbacks—three books strong—first in the clothes hamper, then, considering his mother's preoccupation with laundry, in a lidded porcelain casserole and, finally, because the casserole was new and she would want to examine it as soon as she saw it, under his bed, only to worry that she might look under there for dust woozies.

Six or seven weeks after his move, on a visit to his parents' house, in a pique, he whined to his mother that she and Phil never came by to see his place.

"Sweetheart," she said, "you haven't invited us."

» » »

The Flowerses' house was a four-story brownstone on the south side of Pine Street. Boston ivy crawled up its Italianate, reddish-black stone facade. English ivy snaked up the rear. The house was more forbidding than inviting. His mother said she spent years thinking about ways to "gentle" the facade's aggressive look, deciding in the end to hang the front windows with fragile, white Belgian lace, a different pattern for each floor, a decorating coup which only slightly dispelled their home's attitude of stern and rather gloomy indifference to its public.

Behind the Pine Street house and connected to it by bricks and by hallways was another building the family called the "Back House." This three-story structure of no clear architectural inspiration contained the Flowerses' dining room, pantries, and kitchen on the first floor, Bea's, Stu's, and Mary Alice's old rooms on the second, and Carmen's apartment on the third. Pete and Cliff had had the third-floor rooms of the Pine Street house. Their parents' room and the library were below them, the hot, bat-ridden attic above. The boys could call out to each other in the night and not be heard in other parts of the house, even by Carmen, who slept little and lightly when she did.

A magnolia, planted at the jointure of the two houses, dominated the garden. It had grown above the third floor and out over the years of the children's lives to create a thick, dark canopy in the center of the garden lot. The magnolia's roots had lifted some of the stones of the terrace, making tent shapes of them. No one ever talked of repairing this damage. When it rained in mild months, someone opened the French doors of the dining room, the better to hear the drops hit the dry, leathery, copper-colored leaves which collected under this tree in all seasons.

» » »

His ring at the door is answered by Carmen, his parents' housekeeper since the birth of Mary Alice in 1944. Carmen has bathed and diapered each Flowers child, bandaged its cuts, blotted its tears, and cheered its return into battle. Yet she has retained throughout their lifetimes a discreet distance from them, a stance which still annoys Pete. She is all devotion to her first duty, the smoothing of his parents' lives.

Although she could wear halter tops and bikini bottoms if she wished, such is the strength of her job security in this house, Carmen chooses black or navy blue dresses exclusively, always with white aprons, bibbed or cut at the waist, which she changes soon after they become soiled. She can go through three or four a day. They are picked up on Mondays and delivered, starched and on hangers, on Fridays by McFee's Cleaners. On the street, and when she leaves the house carrying her overnight bag the evening before her day off, she dresses like a lawyer. Where does she go? Pete often wonders.

"Pete, hello," she says, shaking his hand. She closes the double mahogany doors behind him and gives him a warm, tight smile. "They're all upstairs, except for Stu and" (slightest of pauses) "her." She has not liked Alexa since Alexa's daughter Megan told Carmen she did not have to mind her because her mother said she was only a maid.

"And I have your wine cooling in the kitchen," she says, starting down the dark gray carpeted hall, waving him along with one quick toss of her left hand. They pass the living room and the "parlor," her slick satin dress smacking against her bony, nylon-stockinged legs, into the Back House, past the long dining room, its doors closed as always until they sat at meals. "I need you should taste something for me," she says as they pass through the butler's pantry. "I haven't made this dish in so long."

The kitchen, a vast room painted hospital white, is one of two rooms in the house that have not undergone major renovation in his lifetime. Carmen likes the kitchen the way it was when she took it over. Along its walls, intruding, are several state-of-the-art appliances: a monolithic, black-and-chrome, upright, two-door freezer/refrigerator, a Swiss eight-burner gas stove, and an avocado-colored trash compactor. On a counter is a microwave oven with push-button controls Carmen has refused to learn to operate save for its capacity to defrost. These machines stand out in this clean, plain, otherwise old-fashioned room. They have been foisted on Carmen and she has accepted most of them grudgingly for their functions, preferring the forms of her zinc double sinks, her clunky plank table initialed with paring knife points by each Flowers child and by bands of their friends who once shared her soup lunches and sugar cookies as large as their faces. The table's surface has also been gouged by her own cleaver in the butcher of God knows how many pieces of beef, fish, and fowl over four decades of daily use.

She has opened and recorked a bottle of California chardonnay and put it on ice in a bucket on the plank table. She has polished a stemmed glass and set it out. There is a small, pressed linen napkin next to it.

He pours the wine. He crosses the expanse of sea-green, minutely cracked terrazzo, his leather loafer heels tap-tapping on the immaculate tiles, to where she stands at the counter, the back of her shiny black dress to him, wooden spoon held out.

"I haven't made this since Mary Alice was in college, twenty years, anyway. Imagine it on smoked bluefish, a lot cooler than it is now, if you don't mind," she says, extending the spoonful of pink sauce out at her side, her back still turned.

He smells the sauce. His adenoids tingle at an effusion of horseradish cream on the spoon. He detects a tartness he cannot identify, acidic, not citrus. He notices her draw the back of her hand very quickly across one cheek, wiping something away.

"I don't remember this," he says. "It's wonderful." Something is up. "What's it for?"

"Smoked bluefish. I told you," she says, having moved to the sink. Carmen begins to make clatter now, pushing pots about roughly. Unnecessarily, it seems to Pete.

"You'd better go up there now, Peter," she says. "They're waiting on you. And take your ice bucket with you. There's no wine upstairs, and I don't have time tonight to be chasing up and down."

On the landing of the back stairs, he thinks that she has not called him "Peter" since his brother died.

» » »

The thick, mauve carpet runner on the second-floor hall leads, at some distance, to the library at the front of the Pine Street house. Off this hall, behind him and across from each other, are Mary Alice and Bea's old rooms, and ahead, the only original guest room and his parents' room. All the doors to these bedrooms are closed, as they were always in their childhoods and adolescences so as to protect their mother and those of her friends with fragile sensitivities from the awful clutter and chaos within the children's rooms.

Each Flowers child became a collector. Many of the objects of their accumulations were left in these rooms as the children moved out and their rooms were redecorated. Behind these doors, hidden away now in the bottom drawers of antique bureaus, in shoe boxes tucked into the corners of the top shelves of closets, remain the best-of-the-best of these collections, what could not be parted with long after the rest had gone to the trash. Covertly, these treasures are examined now by the six little girls who are their grandparents' most frequent sleep-over guests: Stu's stones and rocks picked up from Camden to Saint Croix; Bea's imitation jewels, some of them 250, even 300 carats of wide-ranging color and sophistication of cut and polish, which the little girls hold against their ring fingers when the sun is just coming up and the house is silent, and, in front of mirrors, hold against the sunken spot between their clavicles, imagining gold and silver chains attached; Pete's baseball cards, in which his nieces have no interest, lie tissue-wrapped, appreciating in his room in a cracking, cast-off, leather valise that once belonged to his father; Mary Alice's marbles, certain prized aggies and steelies wrapped in rusting gauze, decades old, all won in keen, knee-scuffing competition on the streets within blocks of this house; and, the largest collection extant, on the third floor across from Pete's room, in a never-converted-to-a-guest-room bedroom, Cliffie's boxes of glass-framed butterflies, his jars of mummified cocoons and chrysalises, their abdomens long since eaten out by other metamorphoses, collected along the Schuylkill below the South Street bridge and smuggled in from the islands with Stu's rocks and stones, boxes which no one in the family, except for the little girls who had never known this dead uncle, can yet bear to open.

From the library he hears the laughter which has been the family glue: Bea's cackle and her husband Anthony's bray, his father's "huh-huh-huh-a-huh" and his mother's descending soprano "Ooooooooooh, Lordy!"

"Wait! Wait!" Mary Alice is saying. "That's not the end of it! *Then* she told her mother that she could goddamn well wheel herself right off the *dock* for all she cared!"

"Oh, Mary Alice, she *didn't!*" cries his mother. The

laughter rises up, even Mary Alice's quiet husband Hal letting his chortle ring above Anthony's hoots and Bea's strangled gasps for breath. Pete waits for a moment in the hall to give Mary Alice full play of her story. They are all out of his sight, in the sitting area on the left side of the library. Ahead of him, on the wall he faces, are books, books older than any of the siblings, books going back to their mother's childhood and books bought during each of their own childhoods, the best-sellers of their adolescences and their adulthoods, as well as editions of esoterica relating to Liz's interests in linguistics, ornithology, and medicine. One more cannot be squeezed between the others. Her acquisitions of recent years are stacked sideways on the tops of rows of other books and on tabletops and on the floor in corners and along the walls.

He makes his entrance as the laughter subsides, placing his ice bucket and wineglass on the floor among some stacks of books, for they all rise: the men, except for Anthony, offering handshakes and the women hugs and Anthony both, as does Bea, engulfing him in the azure folds of her large dress and in her flabby upper arms. Their mother looks tired or is missing some stage of her makeup. She hugs him a second or two longer than usual. Mary Alice, sleek in a tan chiffon little-nothing he imagines set Hal back the cost of a first-class plane ticket to the West Coast, offers him a cheek to buss and whispers in his ear, "He hasn't said a word about retirement," and, in a normal voice, says, "You get handsomer every day," then, sotto voce between her costly, clenched, and even teeth, "We'll talk."

And they all sit on the matching flowered sofas which face each other and on side chairs around their mother's burled maple coffee table, piled usually with books, cleared for this occasion. And there is a tiny silence as each decides whether to talk or to wait for another to speak first. At that point Stu and Alexa walk in and it all starts again, the standing and the handshaking and the hugging. Pete has witnessed a hundred of these family greetings. Nothing changes. Stu hugs everyone except their father, with whom he executes a double handshake. Alexa, Stu's pale, red-haired, wheedling wife, gets a hug from Liz and from Anthony, an arm's-length shoulder clutch from her father-in-law, a closed-mouth smile and head dip from Bea, a tooth-some smile from Mary Alice followed by the priggish little hand wiggle she saves for polite circumstances when nothing will not do (Liz winces), and a bear hug from Mary Alice's husband Hal. Mary Alice reacts to Hal as if he had just touched snot. Because Alexa is near him, Pete gives her a hug, too. She pulls back slightly as he puts his arms around her.

Phil takes drink orders. The group resettles, spouses with spouses, Liz and Stu the centers of two conversations that have begun.

Stu is the first son, the second child after Mary Alice in this family of tight chronology. The Flowers children follow Mary Alice, forty-six, at two-year intervals: Stu, Cliff, who is dead, Pete, then Bea, the baby at thirty-eight. Mary Alice, Stu, and Bea each have two daughters born at two-year intervals. These six girls—ten to thirteen years old—have formed many of their considerable attachments to each other through their grandmother's insistence on frequently "borrowing" the ensemble for weekend sleepovers at the Pine Street house.

Among the siblings, it is Stu who most enjoys having everyone together. It is he who plans events throughout the year and who shepherds the siblings and their families all back to the house on Pine Street for Thanksgiving and for Christmas, and to his own house or to Mary Alice's for other obligatory holidays, chiding any who try to avoid these get-togethers by pleading prior commitments. Rarely seen out of his tie and his heavy business brogues (the same model in four colors), never known to have gone an entire day without shaving, even when he had his tonsils out at age thirty, Stu lives a two-sided life. His bedroom closet's stock of arranged-by-weight-then-by-color Brooks Brothers suits and regimental striped ties is belied by the contents of the walk-in closet down the hall, stacked with long, thin boxes which the family claims contain copies of every board game published in the Western World, and, crowded together below the board game shelves, on the floor and in corners, resting like clutches of dinosaur eggs, are footballs, Wiffle balls, basketballs, racquetballs, volleyballs, and, in stacks, rolled-up nets, tall and short, for volleyball and badminton, and his own net for tennis for days early or late in the season when he wants to play on public courts and Swarthmore has taken in its nets or not yet put them out. Near them are the narrow, brightly colored accoutrements of skiing, and green rubber swim fins and face masks and snorkel tubes, enough for all members of his family, though Alexa will not go into the sun except for compelling social reasons.

His car trunk holds the overflow. When he accelerates or takes a tight corner, clanking sounds are heard from the collisions of baseball bats stored there in all seasons. He has stashes of paper strips of legal pads in each family meeting place. He can organize a game of Fictionary in minutes. He is the only male member of the family for whom all six granddaughters clamor.

"Alexa thinks we ought to sell it," he is telling Bea and Anthony and Phil of the house in Swarthmore he and Alexa have owned for sixteen years.

Bea raises her eyebrows and shifts her expansive hips on the couch. She does not gain weight above her throat. She sits now watching Alexa quizzically, her long chestnut hair drawn straight back from her face and rolled in a tight chignon with no stray hairs falling from it. She wears light, exacting makeup on skin without memory of acne or anticipation of middle age. Her wide-spaced, nut-colored eyes have long lashes. Her nose is cleft between her nostrils. Her upper lip line repeats the arch and angle of descent of her eyebrows, and it is this feature which states her face's symmetry. If anyone in the family is beautiful, it is Bea.

At eighteen, against her father's wishes, she began to date Anthony, an apprentice plumber from South Philadelphia whom she saw first from the rear as he threaded pipe in front of the next-door neighbor's house. The sight of Anthony bending over his pipe horse, his melon cheeks just contained in worn, cut-off jeans, dispelled forever her dreams of academe and stirred in her the beginning flush of what would within weeks become unrelenting lust. She wrote her name and telephone number on an index card, gave her sheeny hair ten fast static-infecting brush strokes, rolled her staid Catholic girls' school skirt up three turns, and in two minutes was back inside, having bestowed on him the card and her best approximation of the smile of a world-class whore, and revealed, beyond intimation, the sure promise of titillations to come.

"But *I* maintain, what's the point of selling it after all that work, to buy something just like it?" Stu says.

Alexa, who wants to live in monied Gladwyne, turns from her conversation with Liz and says to Stu, "We *need* more space, is the point."

"Space?" Stu says, appealing to Bea, whose South Philadelphia row house would fit inside Stu's west wing with space to spare. "We don't use what we've got."

"I'm talking about *out*side space," Alexa says impatiently. "The girls *love* horses." She turns her attention back to her mother-in-law.

"You've got a great house," Anthony tells Stu.

Alexa shoots Anthony a brief glare.

"It's got some of the best pipe welds on the East Coast," he says.

"Hear, hear!" Pete says, applauding Anthony, who does all family plumbing.

Bea squeezes her husband's thigh. She leers over at his lap. "Speaking of good pipe," she says.

Anthony's plumbing business cannot support an office. When he is out on jobs, Bea takes his calls and schedules his work. Her passion for Anthony and the jealousy it has spawned have increased in proportion to her weight gain. Somewhere between sizes twelve and fourteen she began tearing up phone messages from women who sounded young and had home plumbing problems. When she grew to a sixteen, she rejected women who sounded young and were calling from offices. At size eighteen going on twenty, it is unlikely that any woman whose voice does not sound like a man's will have her call returned by Ferraro Plumbing.

"You know," his mother says, apropos of nothing, "I've been thinking about getting another dog."

"I loved Strindberg," Mary Alice says.

"I hated Strindberg," Liz says.

"Mother! Why?" says Mary Alice.

"I'd rather not say."

"How could you hate Strindberg, Mother?" Bea says. "He was the cutest dog we ever had."

"I'll tell you why," Phil says. "Whenever your mother had guests, he would go around humping their legs."

"He was tenacious," Liz tells Hal and Alexa. "You couldn't even shake him off. Part boxer. And strong. One afternoon when my friend Mona Wilcox was here, I went out to the kitchen for a minute to get us some coffee and when I got back, Strindberg had her down on the floor. I don't know how long they were there. She didn't even cry out. I was mortified."

Bea takes out a cigarette and taps the filter end on her thumbnail.

"When are you going to quit smoking?" Liz says, suddenly irritated. "You're the only one in the family who still smokes."

"Mother, I have enough on my mind, thank you very much," Bea says.

"You should go to a hypnotist," Alexa says. "*I* would, if *I* smoked."

Liz sits back in her chair.

Bea raises one eyebrow at Alexa. She lights her cigarette.

"You have to want to quit," Bea says, "or it doesn't work."

"Don't you *want* to quit?"

"I enjoy *every* cigarette I smoke, Alexa."

"Eeeeeeuuuu," Alexa sneers.

"Who asked you?" Bea mutters.

Pete sits back into the cushions of the couch. Stu asks Mary Alice about her girls. Hal and Phil talk about sales trends. Next to Pete, in a low voice, his mother says quietly to her hands in her lap, "I don't know. I don't know. Nobody asked me if I wanted to or I didn't want to."

He leans toward her. "What?" he says.

She looks around the room. She sees that Pete is looking at her. He thinks he sees fear in her eyes before she flashes him one of her comfortable, familiar, motherly smiles. In control.

There is a crackling sound from the intercom in the wall by the library doors.

"The table is ready," Carmen's voice announces.

"Not a moment too soon," Bea growls, stubbing out her cigarette.

Liz stands. "I should say. Well, shall we?"

They all rise with her. Liz leads the way through the library's double doors and to the left, down a short hall to the wide main staircase, which is circular and carpeted, as is the floor below, in a deep pile of a color that is neither blue nor gray, Pete thinks, nor indigo at night. His mother leads the family down the curved staircase that has no boards that squeak and, in its center space, a long crystal chandelier. Stu and Alexa descend behind Liz, and the others follow, Pete and his father last. Liz says she has seen a bay-breasted warbler in her garden. She waves one hand in the air as she descends and tells them that this foolish bird has no abiding interest in Philadelphia, preferring Panama and Canada. With each step down, she walks into a new pattern of the chandelier's refracted light. Small, round rainbows pass across her skin and over her pale blue silk dress.

"I need to talk with you," his father whispers behind him. "Can you have lunch with me Monday? At The Garden?"

"I think," Pete says, trying to remember what he has pressing at the store.

"One o'clock," his father says.

"OK," he says.

Near the bottom of the stairs, he realizes he cannot recall ever having had lunch with his father. He has a wisp of a recollection of himself as a child at a meal shared with a grown man in the daylight in a room with colored windows and green-black drapes. Where was that? Not in this house, where there have never been colored windows, and not with his father, he thinks. Not in a school. Where then? Did he dream those green-black drapes?

» » »

The oak-paneled dining room glows in amber tones and flickers from shadows of candles on the sideboard and more candles spaced down the center of the long table. Carmen places the last of the dessert plates in front of Pete. Anthony, next to him, having just downed a pound and a half of lamb and three of Carmen's double-baked potatoes, is the first to lift his dessert fork and to pierce the thick wedge of pecan pie she has given each of them.

"This is super pecan pie, Carmen," Stu tells her, prizing the tines of his fork through a nut half.

"Sweets for the sweet," Carmen says. She pushes the butler's pantry door open with her hip.

As the door swings closed behind her, Bea says to Liz, "That woman has been lying to me for twenty years."

"Carmen has never lied to you, Bea dearest," Liz says.

"Mother, trust that I am a passing good cook and clever enough to follow simple instructions. I've made her damned pecan pie fifty times if I've made it once, and mine *never* tastes like this. Antny, be honest. Do you love my pecan pie?"

Anthony looks at his mother-in-law at one head of the table, and at his wife across from him, his narrow, bladed nose and cheekbones prominent in the light of the candle in front of him. He wipes his heavy moustache and places his napkin on the table.

"It sucks, Bea."

"Anthony!" Liz says.

"Could you be specific, my angel?" Bea asks.

"It's dry."

"Yes. You are correct. It sucks because it's dry. Carmen's leaving something out of the recipe."

"You're cooking it too long," Liz tells her.

"Mother. It's dry when I *under*cook it. There's an ingredient missing, I'm sure of it."

"Mine always turns out," Mary Alice remarks.

" '*Mine* always turns out,' " Bea nanners back. "You are so perfect, Mary Alice. I am not surprised."

"It's because it's a family recipe, Bea," Pete tells her. "And you're adopted."

"Do you know that I believed that?" she says. "For years?"

"She did," Liz says. "She used to come to me and ask me."

"And what did you tell her, Mom?" Stu says.

"I told her she wasn't, of course."

Stu looks stricken. "You mean you *lied* to her?"

"Mother, make them stop!"

"Bea," Stu says, "Dad told me all about your adoption on my twenty-first birthday. Didn't you, Dad?"

"Yes, Stuart." Phil smiles down the table. "And I told Mary Alice and Pete about it on theirs."

"OK, Brutus," Bea says to her father. "If I was adopted, why didn't you tell me on *my* twenty-first birthday?"

"I tried, Beatrice. You didn't want to hear it."

Pete glances at his mother. Her face is blank. She holds her napkin to her throat. One hand touches the stem of her wineglass. She stares at the candle flame.

"Mom," he says softly.

She stares at the light.

"Mom?"

Just as he is about to reach over and touch her arm, she blinks her eyes. She inhales deeply and lays her napkin beside her untouched dessert. She shifts about in her seat. Her leg bumps Pete's leg.

"Excuse me," she says. "Is that part of you?" She taps her foot on the carpet. "I can't find my . . . my, you know . . . alarm."

"Your buzzer?" Pete says of the small button built into the floor, which signals Carmen in the kitchen.

"My buzzer," she says.

"In the middle," he says.

"Yes," she says. "There it is. Phil, why don't you pour us some of that hideously expensive cognac that you hoard?"

To Pete's surprise, his father rises immediately. He seldom breaks out his brandy, even at holidays. Pete and Mary Alice raise eyebrows at each other.

Carmen enters through the swinging door.

"We'll have our coffee at the table," Liz tells her. "Anthony," she says, "Bea tells me you got a big contract this week at some new hotel?"

"Hey, Liz," Anthony says, "this is the Big Time. *Everything*'s copper. I mean, we're talking *miles* of copper!"

He begins a gesticulative discourse on the scope of his new project, the types of its pipes, the numbers of its man-hours. Bea beams at him across the table, rapt in his enthusiasm. How big she's becoming, Pete thinks, and how she rails at herself in her phone calls to him about becoming bigger and about what she has had to give up most recently to try to lose, only to launch into long accounts of the custard pastries and yeast breads she has made or is making even as they talk, to follow the roasts and pastas she has prepared for her Anthony's dinners. Like her mother-in-law, she cooks half the day, and like Anthony, she eats half the night. But while Anthony's body spends everything he gives it, Bea's saves and saves.

At the sideboard, Phil dribbles his precious brandy into snifters. He leans down to each one, comparing its level with those of the glasses he has already poured. He gives himself an extra measure, then carries them, two by two, to the table and places them before each family member, pausing at Liz's place when she tugs his jacket sleeve and whispers something to him.

Carmen moves around the table ahead of Phil, lifting empty cups and saucers from her tray and placing them at each setting. She removes dessert plates and forks as she passes. Her brown eyes are impassive in the candlelight; the feet of some of the cups rattle in the channels of their saucers, a sound seldom heard in her service. At the other side of the table from Pete, as she pours steaming coffee from a silver thermos into Bea's cup, her hand shakes. A few drops of coffee spatter on Bea's gold-edged saucer. Carmen's other hand darts up from her side and, in a flash of white linen, blots the drips with the corner of the starched, creased napkin she carries. When Carmen reaches his mother's place, Liz makes a negative motion. She points at her empty wineglass. Carmen returns in a moment to fill it.

Pete watches the faces of his siblings, each of them either looking at Anthony as he reels off numbers of sink and tub and toilet connections or looking at their own cups or snifters glowing warm before them in this embracing room.

His mother, next to him, nods at Anthony's recitation, smiles at the appropriate times, looks concerned when concern is called for. Her right hand rests in her lap. Her left hand cups her right breast. Her diamond glitters at her armpit. She looks away from Anthony and down at the hand resting in her lap for a moment, then up at her husband at the other end of the table, studying him as if she has not seen him in some time. Slowly, she moves her gaze around the table, examining each of her children's faces as if looking at postcards from enviable places.

When she is about to move her eyes away from Stu and on to him, Pete looks away from her because he sees that her face has begun to screw up in a way that frightens him. He coughs. He resettles himself in his chair. When he glances at his mother again, her face is composed. She is looking at him square in the center of his right eye. She has a tiny smile at one corner of her mouth. She leans toward him. She frowns. "You know," she says to him very distinctly and quietly, focusing on his left eye now and pausing, her eyes darting back and forth from one to the other of his, and when he is about to say, "What?" she says to him, "This morning, while I was putting on my makeup, I saw you come into my room. I saw you in the mirror. And I was so startled, I began to turn around and you put your finger to your lips and held up a sign printed on the cardboard like the ones that come with your father's laundered shirts. I could read it. Even in the mirror. It said, 'TELL PETE.' And I said, 'Tell you what?' and when I started to turn around to look at you, you put your hand on my shoulder to stop me, I felt it, and you shook the sign and its letters changed. It still said 'TELL PETE' but now the letters were in sort of childish print. And you turned and walked out. I can't understand how that happened."

He is aware that his heart is beating in his ears and that his mouth is open.

She takes a large swallow of her wine as Anthony winds down on his new project. She turns away from Pete and back to Anthony.

"Isn't that wonderful," she says to Anthony, reaching over and patting the back of his hand. "I am so proud of you."

She picks up her coffee spoon. She taps it on the side of her wineglass.

"Excuse me. Excuse me," she says. She pushes her coffee cup and saucer back. She rests her forearms on the table, one hand grasping her other wrist.

At the opposite head of the table, his father's deep forehead shines, beading, in the candlelight. An artery at his temple throbs. He takes a pull from his brandy. He stares at the carpet.

Liz smiles down the table. Not, Pete thinks, her comfortable, assured mother-smile, but one that is tenuous and wistful. He is startled at what she has just said to him. He watches her, fascinated.

She slides the wedding rings on her finger. Mary Alice exhales.

"We," she says. "Actually, *I* . . . *I* thought it would be a good idea for us to come together tonight to talk about something that is . . . going to happen. That is happening."

There is a rustling of fabric around the table as the family move in their chairs, as they turn to glance at Phil, who does not move, who stares at the carpet.

Carmen slips, empty handed, through the swinging doors into the pantry beyond.

Liz opens her mouth to speak. She closes it.

The table is utterly still. Mary Alice's right hand pinches an earring she has been worrying. Bea, thinking the house will be sold, holds up one palm to ward off the news. Stu frowns, puzzled. Hal looks at Phil, who looks at the floor. Anthony, biting his napkin, looks at Pete, who looks at Alexa, who looks bored.

His mother leans back in her chair. She sits forward again. Her forefinger beats on the table.

"It seems . . . There has been . . ." She makes a hissing sound.

What is going on here? Pete thinks.

"I have done a bad thing," his mother says suddenly. "I have done something that I think I've taught most of you not to do."

She looks to the other end of the table, appealing to Phil, who studies rust-colored, triangular designs in the Turkish rug beneath his chair.

"On Memorial Day, last year, I found an odd stain in . . . my bra." She cups her right breast gently with both hands. Mary Alice bites her thumb.

Liz gestures toward the ceiling in the direction of the library at the front of the house.

"All those books up there," she says. "I could have taught classes on this. And did I call Max for an appointment? I did not. Instead of calling my doctor, I began to do my own wash." She looks at the door leading to the pantry. "I began to save my soiled bras until Carmen's day off. I began not to touch and not to look at my breast," she says. "I would look at the other one and, in some way, I guess I mirrored it in my mind so that they were both the same. So that they were both healthy. . . . That is amazing to me."

Pete and his brother and sisters have never heard their mother refer to her own breasts and bras in any context. They are looking at her now as if she had changed her race. Pete tries to appear normal, just concerned, not horrified. He sees that Stu has covered his eyes with his hand. Alexa idly plucks the petals of a white peony in the centerpiece. They form a small pile on the damask tablecloth.

"One day in the fall, your father said I had something growing on my breast. A sore. I said, 'Nonsense.' He said, 'Call Frommeyer.' I said I would.

"I began to take showers instead of baths. They are quick and you keep your eyes closed during a good part of them."

She lifts her cognac. She drains it off. She coughs. She smiles.

"A week ago I finally saw Max. Two days later, I saw someone down at Johns Hopkins at Max's suggestion. They both tell me that I have, in clinical terms, a poorly differentiated infiltrating ductile carcinoma in my right breast, with cerebral metastases. For those of you who are not readers of medical texts, that last part means that I have waited long enough for the cancer to have spread beyond my breast."

She hunches her shoulders and smiles quizzically.

The table is silent.

"Mother of God," Anthony says softly.

"Now I will tell you what I have decided to do. First of all, I want to be the one to tell my granddaughters about this, and I would like you to have them here for lunch tomorrow so that I can do that. Second, Max has recommended a regimen of treatment that I've decided to go along with.

"I will have what they call a simple mastectomy this Tuesday, across the street at Pennsylvania. I will be there for some days to heal, and will begin radiation therapy right away."

"Is Max . . . ?" Stu says.

"Is Max what?" she asks.

"Is he going to operate?"

"No. He doesn't like to do friends. Dr. Burd, the man I saw in Baltimore, has offered to do it here. Max says he owes him one."

"Mother," Mary Alice says. "What about a lumpectomy?"

"Precious, at the stage I'm in, even a mastectomy is like taking a switch to a gorilla."

She sighs. She looks around the table.

"I know that I've made you all feel bad. Also, I am going to have to leave you in the lurch now because I am very tired right this minute, and I'm going to ask your father to go upstairs with me."

She stands, and Phil stands at the other end of the table, and they all stand, looking bewildered.

Alexa is the first to move. With a purse-lipped smile she walks around the table to Liz and takes her hand.

"Mrs. Flowers," she says. "You *know* that if there's *any*thing that I can do . . ."

"Thank you, dear," Liz says. "There is something. Call me something else."

Liz walks out the door. She stops and says, "Drop those children off at one, do you hear? And pick them up promptly at three. Good night, angels."

"Good night," Phil says, following her out of the room. "Good night."

In a moment they hear Liz say to Phil on the stairs, "Well. That wasn't so bad, was it?"

II.

Irritably, Pete kicks off his green-stained cotton trousers. He throws his shirt into a corner of the bathroom. There is no time to shower before lunch with his father. His hands are green from plant material he has worked with all morning. They have to be scrubbed. He stands at the sink in his jockey shorts, clawing at a slimy bar of soap, forcing it under his nails. The telephone rings. He thinks he will not answer it, then, wondering if it is his father calling about their lunch, he grabs a towel and takes it with him to the phone next to his bed. He picks the phone up with his towel.

It is Bea.

"Meet me for lunch," she says.

"I can't."

"Take the time. I have to talk to you."

"Bea, I'm having lunch with Dad."

There is silence.

"You're having lunch with Daddy?"

"At one. Talk fast."

"He never invited *me* to lunch."

"He never invited *me* to lunch."

There is silence. He imagines her lips pouted.

"Where are you eating?"

"The Garden."

"I love The Garden. . . . I'll just drop in."

"No, Bea. I think this is *mano a mano*."

"Why is he inviting *you* to lunch?"

"Watch it. Because of Mom, I guess."

"You know," she says. "This whole situation sucks. Nobody tells me anything. And now you're having a secret lunch with Daddy."

"Bea, it's not a secret lunch."

"Then why doesn't anybody know about it?"

"Bea, I'm late. I'm not dressed. My hands are sticky."

"What have you been up to?"

"Bea."

"Meet me for a drink later."

"I can't. I'm up to my ass in orders."

"Dammit!" she says. "Who will I talk to?"

"Go visit Mom."

"But I want to talk *about* her!"

"Bea. I've got to go."

» » »

With no time for a clothes crisis, Pete has one, going back and forth between two similar suits, holding red ties against them, then blue ties, then green. His ties are all brightly colored. He buys them regardless of need, usually when his mood needs a lift. He owns few subtle ones. He is perspiring. He wishes he had showered. He wishes he had laid out his clothes in the morning, that he was not having lunch with his father.

» » »

He hurries down Spruce Street, his clothes damp from his rushing and from the humid May day. The hair at the nape of his neck is wet. The skin under his damp leather watchband itches.

Striding toward him near Eighteenth, his chunky arms swinging, dress-shirt collar squeezing his muscled neck, and tie blown back over one thick shoulder, is his friend Paul Levee.

"Hey," Paul says, eyeing Pete's suit. "The dreaded lunch with Dad?"

"God, yes. Where are you off to?"

"I'm meeting my ex. We're having a nonviolent meal in a public place while we fight over who gets permanent custody of Freddy."

"You have Freddy."

"I have Freddy. I'm trying to keep Freddy. Want to trade lunch partners?"

"I'll take Dad."

» » »

He is led to his father's table by a woman in a tuxedo shirt and black tie, whose white apron brushes the tops of her black sneakers. The room—rich, paneled, and polished—is filled with groups of business people.

He and his father shake hands.

The woman who brought him to the table takes Pete's drink order.

"Nice suit," his father says.

"Thanks."

They pick up their menus. His father's face, square like his own, is deeply lined. Pete does not read his menu. He looks over the top of it at his father across from him studying his own menu. He is surprised to see that his father's eyes are a different color than he thought, not the yellow-brown he shares with his mother and siblings, but green. Enlarged through the lenses of his bifocal glasses, his father's irises are a dark, mossy color. Why has he never noticed before? Did he never look at his father's eyes? And his father's face seems to be falling now, everywhere below his eyebrows. He sees that there are pouches of flesh collecting under his eyelids and in his cheeks and at his jaw, where everything had been smooth the last time he saw him. He stares at his father over his menu, wondering at this transformation. How could he have missed on Saturday night the straight lines that radiate outward and down from the edge of his father's lower lip? Forty or fifty lines there and his father only what? Sixty-four?

His father looks up.

"How's business?" he asks.

"It's been good. A lot of weddings and graduations. I need another person. Two people."

"Why don't you hire them?"

"It's a dilemma. It's hard to find creative people who have experience, and I don't have time to train. And Doris. She's a fine designer, but she couldn't teach you how to pull out a Kleenex. . . . How is it at the plant?"

"It hums," he says. "I liked it better when there weren't so many machines. The pies taste as good as then. They even look better. Did you try the new microwave pies I sent over?"

"Not yet."

"I have a machine now that puts marks on the crusts so they look like real human fingers formed them. Hype," he says. "We all stand around and watch the machines over there."

A waiter brings his drink, announces some specials, and departs with a small bow.

"Thank God," his father says.

"Excuse me?"

"I hate it when they tell you their names and that they're going to be your waiter."

He and his father go back to their menus.

"Have the carpaccio," his father says to him. "It's the best."

"I don't like raw meat."

"You always ate funny," his father says. "Not like the rest of them . . . Her seviche is to die for."

"I don't like raw fish," Pete says to his menu.

"Shall we get a bottle of wine?" his father asks.

"What are you having?"

"Maybe a steak."

"Red wine gives me a headache."

"I think that's all in your mind."

"Cute, Dad."

"Bali chicken. That's what I'll have," his father says, pointing at his menu. "Pick a wine."

Once they have ordered and are waiting for their food to arrive, his father fills the silence with small stories of what his brother and sisters have been doing. Pete has heard most of these pieces of news from his brother and sisters, but he lets his father repeat them. He even asks questions now and then, knowing the answers already, to keep the silence at bay. As the conversation continues, Pete begins to suspect that his father knows he has already heard these stories.

When their wine has been poured and their orders of Bali chicken have been presented by a small gang of waiters, his father finally gets to the point. "I'm very worried about your mother."

"I am, too."

"I don't mean the cancer so much," he says. "That is, the operation." He puts his fork on his plate. He touches his napkin to his lips. He says, "She's going crazy, I think."

"What do you mean, she's going crazy?"

"She's getting spooky."

His father, articulate about the intricacies of food mixers, seems dumbfounded by his wife.

"Could you be specific?" Pete asks.

"I don't think she knows it. You shouldn't tell her we had lunch. She'd think we were talking about her."

"I'm sure she'd be surprised if we were not talking about her."

"I mean about this. I mean her behavior."

"What about her behavior?"

"The first thing happened a month ago. Your mother lost her car. One day I noticed that it wasn't out back and I asked her if she had it in the shop. First she said it was in the shop. Later she said she didn't know where it was. She made a joke about it. She told me she had driven to Wanamaker's to go shopping the week before and when she was done, she took a cab home. She missed the car the next day; she couldn't remember where she parked it. One of my employees found it in a parking garage on Twelfth. A hundred and twenty bucks to get it out," he says.

"Dad, she was probably worried sick about herself. You'd forget things, too, if you had cancer."

"Wait," his father says. "Carmen called me at work last Wednesday." He puts his elbows on the table and leans forward. "She said your mother was upstairs in our bathtub with all her clothes on. Eating her lunch. When I got to the house, she was reading in the library. I asked her about the tub and she said she didn't eat in tubs, thank you; she said Carmen must have been into the scotch."

"Could Carmen have made that up?" Pete asks, knowing that she couldn't have.

"You know she hardly drinks," his father says, "Something else: Sometimes we'll be talking and she'll just stop for a minute or two and just look exactly where she was looking when she stopped talking. Once it looked like she wasn't breathing. Her eyes don't even blink. Then she starts talking exactly where she left off, or she'll look at me like she didn't hear what I just said."

"She did that Saturday night at dinner," Pete says. "Have you told Max?"

"Of course I have. I called him right after she had lunch in the bathtub. He mentioned some drug he was giving her. Said it's going to get worse before it gets better."

"That's all?"

"That's all. I think your mother has told Max to keep quiet."

They look at each other for a moment.

"You want to hear another one?"

"No."

Pete leans back in his chair. He crosses his arms.

"Why are you telling me all this?"

"She's your mother."

"But why not Stu? Or one of the girls?"

His father looks out into the dining room. Another diner catches his eye and waves. He waves back. He turns to Pete.

"Stu is not . . . Stu is too close. I mean, when there are business decisions to be made, Stu is extremely good. In some ways, he's better at that than I am. There aren't many men who are better at that than I am. But when it comes to family? He has no objectivity. He's too involved with everyone."

"And Mary Alice? Bea? Why not them?"

"I don't know," he says. He plays with his food with his fork.

"You don't know?"

"No offense," his father says, stabbing a piece of chicken with his fork and pointing it at Pete. "I know you two are close. But I never felt like Mary Alice . . . likes me." His father, embarrassed now, pokes his food again.

"We're not that close," Pete says.

"Could have fooled me."

"But I know Mary Alice likes you. And Bea. If you told her to drive her car into a bridge abutment for you, she'd ask you which highway. Why not tell her all this?"

His father finishes off his wine. He gestures toward Pete's glass and pours more for them both. He rakes the short fingers of a hand through the short gray hairs on the side of his head.

"She doesn't focus. I take that back. She focuses on Anthony. I love her, but she is scatterbrained, you've got to admit."

His father drums his fingers on the stiff linen tablecloth. The hairs between his knuckles are gray.

"Why me?" Pete says.

"What difference does it make?"

"It apparently makes a difference to you."

His father leans toward him, almost conspiratorially. He says, "Why do you want to know?"

"Because you and I never talk. We haven't since I can remember. I'm not complaining about that, by the way. It's just the way we are. But all of a sudden you invite me to lunch for the first time in our lives and tell me something about our family that you decide not to share with the others. I'm flattered. But I'm curious. Why me?"

"Because you never got involved in their stupid squabbles is why. You're so fucking independent. You never ask any of them for advice and they all go to you." He breaks off a chunk of bread from the loaf between them. "And you get things done," he says, buttering it.

His father places the bread and his knife on a plate. "And I want to ask you something," he says. "You don't need to give me any bullcrap to save my feelings."

"All right."

"I want to know why you refuse to come into the business."

"You're still pissed about that?"

"No, I'm not pissed. I'm disappointed."

"You're pissed."

"Don't tell me I'm pissed when I'm not pissed," his father says, annoyed.

"You've been pissed off at me for ten years because I didn't want to join Grand-mère's."

His father's eyes narrow. "OK, I am pissed. I worked my ass off all my life to build that business up for you and Stuart, and neither of you want it. It's worth millions."

"Crap."

"What do you mean, 'crap'?" his father says, squinting now and jutting out his chin.

"Dad, am I going to hear that tired old litany again about your boys letting their long-suffering father down? You built that goddamned business because it was fun for you. There was no other reason. Now that it's done and you're getting older, you want to say you did it for us."

"OK," his father says, putting his palms up. "Have it

your way. I did it for me. I'm asking you now why you don't want in."

"The reason I didn't want in ten years ago isn't the same as why I don't want in now. Ten years ago it was because you were mule-headed; you thought you were the only one with the right answers all the time, and you were tyrannical about it. The only way to survive at Grand-mère's would be for me to have been your yes-man. That's not my style."

"So what's different?" his father asks. "I'm still stubborn. I have most of the right answers. What's the reason now?"

Pete gathers the corners of his napkin.

"I was going to say that I like what I do. And I guess I do. But I've begun to notice that I don't like it as much as I used to." He makes a loose knot in the napkin. "But now the reason has to do with routine. I'm not good at things that don't change."

"Things change all the time at Grand-mère's."

"No. They don't. At least, it's the same product all the time. You just find new ways to make the same things. In my business, I seldom do it the same way twice." He makes another, tighter knot in the napkin. "Hell, I *can't* do it the same way twice. A lot of my customers go to the same parties. . . . And it has to do with lifestyle, too."

"What do you mean, 'lifestyle'? You want to be a yuppie?" his father says, gesturing toward a neighboring group who have spread computer paper over their table. "*Be* a yuppie. You want to be a hippie? Be a hippie. Am I stopping you?"

"No. And that's the way I like it. I decide the hours I work. Or I don't work. I decide who to hang around with and where I hang around with them and I don't give a royal fuck whether you or your Vice President in Charge of Public Relations approve or not. I like that."

His father grunts. He picks up his fork and puts it down again.

"How much do you make a year?"

"None of your business."

His father smiles. "You're right," he says. "I'll double it. No. I'll triple it."

Pete raises an eyebrow. "Maybe you can't afford me."

"I can afford you. How much do you want?"

"Have you made an offer like this to Stu?"

"Of course. He likes being a stockbroker. Anyway, I already pay him to consult on the financial side. That's what I need him for."

"And what would you need me for?"

"I'd teach you to be me. To run the operation."

"As I said, I'm flattered. And don't be insulted, Dad. It just wouldn't work out."

The lunch crowd has begun to thin. Bus people in black and white move about the room with trays. There are faraway clattery sounds of the handling of china in the back of the building.

Pete sits back, his arms on the arms of his chair. His father dips pieces of chicken into the fruity sauce that pools at the center of his plate. He looks sad and disappointed. Pete feels guilty. He looks at his watch.

"About Mom," he says, thinking that his father will not ask him now what he wanted to ask him. "I'll call Max this afternoon and make an appointment to talk with him. I'll find out what he knows and you can let the others know. Will you be with Mom for her operation tomorrow?"

"Sure," his father says, pushing his food around now with his fork.

"The girls will be there," Pete says. "I haven't talked to Stu."

His father says nothing. He looks across the room.

"Do I feel a five-day snit coming on?" Pete says.

His father ignores him. He occupies himself with asparagus.

"Umm. Is this the end of the world?"

His father spears a slice a chicken and a round of asparagus and puts them in his mouth. He does not look at Pete.

"You realize this is one of the reasons I couldn't work with you, don't you?"

His father shrugs his shoulders.

"OK," Pete says. "I'm going back to work. Doris is alone."

"You haven't finished eating," his father says, pointing at his plate of Bali chicken.

"We've covered the agenda," Pete says.

His father flinches.

Pete stands.

"Thanks for lunch," he says. He extends his hand to his father, feeling righteous, and bested. His father, rising halfway out of his chair, takes his hand and says, "Good to see you."

» » »

He stops in the bar at the front of the restaurant. His hands, even his head, are trembling.

"Goddammit and fuck," he mutters. The bartender looks up. He asks to use the phone. He calls information, and then Max's office.

Karen, Max's receptionist, wife, and chief protector, is distracted and doubtful. When he tells her he is a block away, she hesitates. She tells him she will sandwich him between appointments if he comes right over and needs only a few minutes.

» » »

Max's waiting room in the Medical Tower on Seventeenth is nearly filled. Pete is the only male there. Karen puts a caller on hold. Mondays are not easy, she tells him under her breath. "Maybe in a few minutes," she says, inclining her head toward the seating area and going back to her call.

The windowless room is decorated in many shades of gray. He takes a seat on a nubby gray wool sectional between a semi-reclining thirtyish blonde who reads from a magazine balanced on her vastly protruding abdomen, and a woman in a black pixie haircut whose pregnancy is only slightly less advanced. These women shift their weight to the left and to the right to accommodate him. He smiles. They do not. He calculates that if he stands to take a magazine from the low table now just out of his reach, he will disturb a delicate balance of innersprings and body masses. He folds his arms. The sofa and matching nubby chairs that line three walls of the room are all armless and seem more tilted back than ordinary furniture. He leans back like the rest of them. Too far back for his comfort. Most of the seated women are in obvious stages of pregnancy. One of them has fallen asleep. One of her shoes, a spectator pump, is half off; her calves are spread out at an awkward angle. One arm embraces her belly.

All of the women in the room are wearing blue or gray. Two of the women across from him seem focused on his chest. He looks down. His suit, a glen plaid in light grays, blends into this room, he thinks. His scarlet tie speckled with sharp blue figures is the brightest object in sight. He thinks it is the most beautiful tie he owns, but in this fecund arena, he feels suddenly embarrassed by it. He pulls one jacket lapel over part of the tie. A third woman facing him looks into his eyes and down at the tie. A fourth closes her magazine and lays it on the gray Parsons table next to her. Bored, she scans the taupe ceiling panels and the perimeter of the lazy waiting room, resting her eyes, finally, on his tie or maybe his crotch. She lifts her eyes to his, smiles languidly, and drops her gaze down again and keeps it there. He crosses his legs.

All the women shift their weight.

A nurse calls from a doorway beside Karen's office. "Mr. Flowers?"

"Me!" he says, too loud. He stands and several of the women glare at him.

He wants to apologize for butting ahead of them. He wants to announce that he is not a drug salesman, that Max is a friend of his mother's, that his mother is having her breast removed in the morning. He straightens his jacket and tucks in his red tie yet again. He walks across the dove-gray carpet to the nurse who waits. She smiles encouragingly past him to the women who wait.

Max's office is gray, with green accents provided by two imitation plants, a ficus tree with silk leaves and a dracaena with bulging stipules and stems of a color that does not occur in nature.

Max rises from his chair and shakes Pete's hand across his desk.

"Hello, Pete!" he says, sitting immediately and motioning him toward one of a pair of round, gray, upholstered chairs in front of his desk.

Max is thin-faced, gray-haired. He sits at the ready. His elbows are on his desk. One hand rests atop the other. His small shoulders are hunched forward. He stares at Pete over the tops of his red-framed bifocals.

"What can I do for you?" he says, eliminating small talk.

With his arms on the arms of his chair, Pete levers himself up from the depths of its deep cushion. The slanting back of the chair makes this difficult.

"I . . . We're concerned about Mom," he says. "Dad told me today that she's been acting strangely. Saturday night she seemed to almost go into a trance."

Max looks away. He lines up the edges of some files on his desk. He takes the cap off a ballpoint pen and puts it back on. He examines the pen.

"Considering the stress she's under," he says, looking back at Pete, "that is perfectly normal."

"Dad said she lost the car."

Max looks back at him.

"Your mother has cancer," he says. "Sometimes people do strange things when they find out they have cancer." He takes the pen cap off again. He taps the pen point on the file folders.

"Saturday night she told me I was in her room that morning. I haven't been in her room in years."

"Pete, you have to expect that your mother is not going to be herself for a while. This is a very stressful time for her," he says. "She has one of the best surgeons in the country. I anticipate no problems with the operation." He pushes his glasses up. He makes tiny taps on his forearms with his curled fingers. He looks at his intercom.

"I don't understand why she's acting weird. Is there something else going on?"

Max scratches his eyelid. He looks annoyed.

"Pete, your mother is getting excellent care," he says defensively. "I don't know what else you expect."

He looks at the intercom again. It clicks. Karen's voice says, "Dr. Frommeyer . . . room three. Dr. Frommeyer, room three."

Max stands. "I'm sorry," he says, extending his hand. "You understand." He doesn't smile so much as pull his lips up.

Pete's arms are trembling. He realizes he has been supporting much of his body weight with his elbows. He pulls himself out of the chair.

"You still running?" Max asks, walking around his desk, smiling now. He puts a hand on Pete's shoulder and squeezes tightly. "You look great, kid. A little tired. I wish I had time to run. No time, you know. I'm sorry to have to hurry off. Mondays. They're a bitch. You understand," he says, steering Pete toward the door with the hand on his shoulder.

» » »

Walking up Spruce Street, perspiring again in his suit in the damp heat, unsatisfied and angry at his interview with Max, Pete stops outside the deli two blocks from Max's office.

"Goddammit," he says. "Fucking doctors." He turns and stalks back down the block toward the Medical Tower. He stops again at the thought of having to wait again in the gray room of blue and gray waiting women. He turns back toward the deli.

The dank smell of urine hangs in the phone booth at the side of the deli. There is no directory. He has no change, only ten-dollar bills. He stands in the sun outside the phone booth. Sweat drips at his sideburns. His cotton shirt begins to stick to his sides.

Inside the phone booth, and without change to make a single call, he realizes he cannot remember Max's number. Standing as close to the open door of the booth as he can, he calls information and makes a credit card call to Max's office two blocks away.

"Karen, this is Pete Flowers. I have to speak to Max again for a minute."

She pauses. She sighs. "He's with a patient. Would you like to leave a number?"

"Karen. Interrupt him. This is important."

"He's with a patient."

His shirt front is wet. The sweat beads above his eyebrows begin to run down to his eyelids. They itch.

"Listen to me," he says, taking a breath. "Someone has peed in this phone booth I am in. It is goddamned hot in here and I haven't got time to play around. Put him on!" he orders.

There is a silence, then a small click and staccato sounds of violins playing dissonant music.

He steps backward toward the doorway. He holds the handset as far away as possible. He turns to face the cleaner street air.

He waits a minute. Two minutes. He steps farther away from the handset until the grating violin sounds are weak and tinny, then, fearful that he will not hear Max when he comes on, he moves back into the booth.

He wipes sweat from his forehead. His watchband itches. He tucks the handset between his ear and shoulder and removes his wristwatch. He wipes it on his jacket and puts it in his pants pocket. The violins are joined by percussion instruments. He thinks he will hang up.

"Yes, what is it?" Max says with undisguised irritation.

Pete decides to attack.

"I went out of my way to come in to see you," he says.

"And I don't appreciate the runaround. It is not drugs and it is not stress that is making my mother behave the way she is. Now tell me what's going on."

Max is silent. He sighs.

"Come back over. We'll talk."

"Now, Max."

On the window of the booth, someone has printed with black felt marker in large, crude letters: JOHNNY MANSON DOES IT FOR A DOLLAR.

"Your mother requested that I not discuss her . . . situation with family. I didn't agree with that, but I went along with it. There are some things you should know. The cancer in her breast has metastasized to her brain. There are two lesions in the frontal lobe. We've begun treating them with a steroid. You can expect that she's not going to be herself for a while."

"What do you mean, 'not herself'?"

"She seems hyper to me. Sometimes she may not make perfect sense."

". . . You're saying she's a little crazy?" Pete wishes the phone cord were longer.

"I'm saying that her behavior may be unpredictable. Maybe not."

"You don't seem to be saying much, Max."

"I'm saying more than your mother would want me to."

There is a muffled sound as Max covers his phone with his hand.

"Excuse me, Pete. I have to be with a patient."

"Max, if Mom isn't making sense, it doesn't make sense for you not to help me understand what's going on."

"Pete, I've got to go now."

III.

The door to his mother's hospital room is open. She is asleep. She lies on her back in the bright fluorescent light. Her chest is covered with layers of bandage. She has clenched the bedsheet and pulled it up to her neck with one hand. Her wrists and hands are bent; her fingers curl down at her throat.

He sits in the chair beside her bed. She frowns in her sleep. The hair, always perfectly coiffed, is scraggly, oily. The corners of her mouth are cracked. Her skin is blotchy and flaky. Her jaw is sleep-slack.

From the hall come the sounds of televisions tuned to disparate channels, the trundle of rubber cart wheels on vinyl floor tiles, and the squeaks of soft-soled nurse shoes. He thinks of his father at lunch two days before, aging before his eyes. He watches his mother's face. It is stripped of the subtleties of her artful makeup and the conscious mannerisms that make her attractive.

She groans. She turns, frowning again, and settles into a new position, hands still at her throat, knuckles curled down, her palms protected. He sleeps that way also. So did Cliffie, fingers curled in at the throat. Is that genetic? he wonders. Can you inherit the positions you sleep in?

Her eyes open suddenly.

"Pete," she says. She feels for the bedsheet, making sure she is covered.

"Do me a favor," she says, trying with great care to push herself up in the bed. Her voice is gravelly. "Pull me up by my good shoulder. So I'm sitting."

He tugs at her arm gently, afraid he will hurt her.

"Get under my armpit. Pull," she says. "I'm not going to break. Now, bring your chair more to this side so I can look at you. I hate my neck, don't you? It's so sore. Why is my neck sore? . . . Well," she says. "Aren't you going to tell me how good I look? Everyone has been telling me how good I look."

"Jesus, Mom. You look like a bus wreck."

"I thank you for your honesty. You know it must be bad when they remove all the mirrors," she says, patting at her head with her good hand. "And Hospital Hair doesn't help."

"That's Intensive Care Hair, Mom. What's wrong with your skin?"

"What's wrong with it?"

"You look like a lizard."

"So much for honesty. Lie to Mother, sweetie," she says. "It just started. An allergy, maybe. They don't know what it is. I have it all over. Everywhere."

She adjusts herself against the pillows and flinches. She looks at her watch.

"I haven't been in a hospital since Bea was born. As a patient. Throw me that robe over there. . . . I still can't look at myself. One of my nurses had what I had. They assigned her on purpose, I'm sure. She said that would change. That I will gradually feel better about it. I accept the notion of change intellectually."

She drapes her robe over her shoulder and the right side of her chest.

"Did your father send those roses or did you sign his name? It looked forged."

"He did. I mean, I signed his name, but he called me and asked me to make up yellow roses."

"They mean 'jealousy,' you know, in the Language of Flowers. Your father is telling me that he wishes it were he who had one breast cut off." She chuckles and winces. "Lordy, Liz, don't laugh. By the way, your friend Bill Payne sent me a card. Thank him for me."

"I will. We're meeting for a drink later. You always said you liked yellow roses," he says, feeling defensive of his father.

"I do like them. And thank you for the violets. They're dear. I'm getting all my favorite flowers."

"From all your favorite Flowers."

"Yes," she says. She glances at her watch. "Almost time," she sighs.

"For what?"

"Your mother has become a junkie," she says. She touches her right shoulder gently with the palm of her left hand.

"It burns all the time. And when they change the dressings, it's like parts of you being torn off. I'm due soon for what they call my Double Whammie. I believe it contains street heroin, and I don't know what else, but it lets me out of this body for a while. For the first time in my life, I understand why people shoot themselves up. . . . Did you ever use drugs?"

"Just marijuana."

"Really? 'Just marijuana,' " she says. "You never told me."

"It's not the kind of thing you tell your mother."

"Do the others smoke marijuana?"

"Which others?"

"Your brother and sisters."

"You'd have to ask them."

"When you children were growing up, you were the only one who would not rat. Each of the others had a price."

"I don't think they did about serious things."

"You are too considerate. Is it still like that?" she asks, sneaking a peek at her watch.

"Mom, would you like it if I went out and asked them to give you something?"

"I'd like it, but they won't do it until it's time. I have offered deals that would mortify you. Is it still like that, I was asking."

"We all go for the laughs at each other's expense," he says, "but that's one of the rules of survival in the family. I don't think any of them would sell out over a vital issue."

"I'm not so sure," she says.

"What do you mean?"

She stares off at the wall for longer than a conversational pause. He wonders if she is having one of her lapses.

"I used to think," she says, turning back to him and rubbing her neck, "that I loved my children equally. I prided myself on that. Concentrated on it. I paid attention to how each of you reacted to the arrivals of the others. I always tried to put my attentions where they seemed to be needed. But when you were all grown up and I had a chance to look at you as adults whom I know, I see that I do not love you equally."

"You mean, at the same time."

"I mean that I do not love you equally. You have all grown up to be different, not only from what I expected, but from what I raised you to be. I find that I love you more the closer you are to what I raised you to be."

"What did you expect me to be?"

"An ax murderer," she says. "Don't disappoint me, Peter. Ah, there. I've made you smile. You haven't smiled since you walked in the room."

"Seriously," he says.

"All right, but don't get huffy. You did ask. Unlike your father, I did not expect you to join Grand-mère's. I thought Stu would. Really, I was sure you would be a baseball player or a pilot. All you ever thought about was baseball and planes when you were a teenager. I was surprised when you went to Wharton School of Business, of all things, and more surprised when you quit Wharton and took off for California. I still get angry about that when I think of it. Dropping out of a master's program to study flower arranging with a Japanese. But that is another subject and has to do with what I raised you to be. Back to what I expected. I expected you to fall in love and marry an elegant, witty girl whom I would enjoy going shopping with and who would make you happy and give you fat babies. I did not expect you to be homosexual. And I don't think I raised you to be one."

He flushes. He has not heard his mother use this word in the context of his own life before. It is a word she reserves for reference to artists and literary figures when their sexuality makes them more interesting.

"You look surprised," she says.

"Only that we're having this conversation. Here."

"What better place?" she asks sarcastically. "For the past year, while I blissfully ignored my cancer on the outside, I have been doing a lot of thinking about it on the inside. And about some other things. My shit has hit the fan and we are in this room because it has. What better place?" she asks. "And for how long have you been thinking about being a homosexual?"

He hesitates. "I don't know."

"Of course you do. I have been thinking about it since you were, I don't know. Thirteen? And I think of that as wasted time. A terrible waste."

"Whoa!" he says. "You don't know what you're talking about."

"I said, 'don't get huffy.' What I am talking to you about is the waste of your time and mine and the family's. All of the time I have spent denying that my breast could be crawling with cancer and all of the time we have ignored together that you are what you are is a waste. I could be healthy. You could have had the support of your family."

"I think you've picked a poor analogy."

"I was not equating our . . . conditions. I was suggesting that we have both lost important time for foolish reasons."

"I don't think you know what it's like to grow up listening to faggot jokes."

"I was called 'Bookbag' most of my childhood."

"It's not the same."

"Two of my dearest friends have not even called me since I told them I have cancer."

She squints. She turns her head, sniffing the air. "What is that?" she says. "That smells like rust. That's rust! Oh Mother of God. Oh Merciful Sacred Heart of Jesus, it's happening again!"

He is on his feet. "Mom?"

She covers her eyes with her hand. "Maybe I can stop it. I think I can stop it maybe I can." Her left leg begins to tremble. "No. Noooooo."

He stands by the bed, trying to understand what is happening. His mother, wild-eyed, goes white-eyed and heaves back onto her pillows in spasms and grunting sounds and a spray of spittle. "Rrrrrrrruh rrrrrrruh rrrrrrruh rrrrrrruh rrrrrrruh." Her entire body arches, impossibly, like a footbridge. In horror, he runs out into the hall to find someone to help.

IV.

He walks through the front doors of Pennsylvania Hospital to the middle of the wide sidewalk. He stands there a moment, deep-breathing the cool, rain-wet May air.

"Jesus. Jesus. Jesus," he says.

After watching his mother sleep for a while, his mind still awash in the implications of her seizure, he left the elevator at the third floor instead of at street level and stood, confused by his error, before a tan Formica nursing station. The elevator doors closed behind him.

Slowly, his IV bags slapping against the wheeled rack he pushed before him, plastic tubes swaying to his own labored rhythm, an old, thin man in a thin hospital gown shuffled toward him down the middle of the corridor. The flat soles of his slippers did not leave the shiny beige flooring; they slid, one before the other, in a spent, cross-country ski gait.

"Excuse me," Pete said, stepping back to the elevator door to give way.

The old man nodded. Some of his wispy hairs, the color of his waxed-paper skin, nodded also, a beat behind, and he turned absently in Pete's direction, then stared at him. Then he suddenly averted his face, staggering slightly, his rack of clear and opaque liquids smacking as he shifted to his right and hurried away at the same slow, pained, and labored pace, his withered, bony buttocks exposed through the vent of the gauzy, flowered gown.

Pete pressed the Down button. The elevator door opened immediately. Concentrating to make sure he pressed the button for the street level, Pete was disturbed by a new thought. As the elevator descended to the lobby, he began searching for the key to the memory that had begun to nag him. As he crossed the empty lobby toward the spare and spotless front doors of the hospital, he remembered a room at the shore years ago, large and spare and contemporary. Which shore? He remembered being naked on his hands and knees on a hard platform bed in the languid light of pre-dawn, looking down, at the younger face of the old man who shuffled now in the corridor above. What was his name?

Pete breaks into a sweat. He turns left and walks quickly up Spruce toward Broad.

"Jack," he mutters, crossing Tenth Street against the light. "Not Jack. John? No. J something. When was that? A long time. What shore? Long Beach Island. Nineteen eighty-five. Eighty-six. Frakes. Jerry Frakes. Jesus."

He passes a competitor's shop at the corner of Twelfth Street but does not turn to look at the lighted display in the window. He is counting.

» » »

The Shubert Theater has just let out. A crowd of playgoers rounds the corner and hurries up and down Spruce toward parking lots, the men in suits and jackets without overcoats, women clinging to their last opportunities to wear fur. The men hold the arms and elbows of the women and steer them between pedestrians and parked vehicles in their race to get to their cars quickly, to be among the first in line to leave the lots. Several of the women are pulled along faster than their high-heeled shoes allow. The women force small smiles.

By the time he reaches it, the crowd in front of the Shubert has thinned. He passes by quickly, heading toward Locust Street. But just as he walks under the Shubert marquee, the Academy of Music doors open to a trickle, then a surge of coats and suits and shiny leather shoes. Young people move rapidly down the steps and disperse; older concertgoers linger on the sidewalk in farewell conversations. There is a lot of blue hair. Pete walks quickly, hoping to avoid running into friends of his parents' or of Mary Alice's, or Stu's. More than halfway past, thinking he is safe, he hears, "Pete! Yo, Pete!"

At the top of the Academy steps, hailing him loudly and waving, is his friend and ex-lover Bill Payne. Tuxedoed. Carnationed. White silk scarfed. "Wait up!" Bill calls. He does a quick and perfect soft shoe. He Fred-Astaires down the steps, attracting attention, smiling as he descends, dipping and dodging with exaggerated-shoulder dance-step movements through the crowd. He is the tallest person there. He stops in front of Pete, his left arm and left leg extended to the side. He draws both slowly in, dragging the edge of the sole of his black patent-leather pump on the sidewalk until his feet touch. He snaps his fingers, cocks his head, and says, just low enough not to be overheard, "Kiss me."

"Oh, God," Pete says, looking around. "Only if you call me Alice. You have a Friday-night subscription. I thought I was supposed to meet you at your house."

"You were. But Daddums has a Wednesday-night subscription and he had two seats for tonight, but he's only free Friday night. So we traded. I called you at the shop to see if you wanted to go. Doris said you had left, so I called your house and talked to your machine."

"I was at the hospital."

"How's Liz?"

"Don't ask," he says. "Later."

"We have to stop by my place anyway so I can change," Bill says, moving toward the street corner. "After I called you, I tried Levee. He wasn't home. I called Geo. He wasn't home. It was terrible. There I was, alone and dejected in my tiny flat with no one to share the concert tickets, so I decided to find a date. And how better on short notice to find a date than to wear a tux? I said to myself, 'Payne, look as if you *planned* to go to a concert.' Sure enough, I met an impoverished student waif in the lobby who didn't have a ticket. She studies oboe at Curtis. Attractive, if you happen to be a braid fetishist, and perceptive, I thought, until the vulgar brat told me at intermission that I look like her father. I don't, do I?"

"God, no. Listen," Pete says. "Would you mind if we got some food instead of going to a bar? I didn't have time for dinner."

"I could fix something," Bill offers.

"I said I wanted food."

They turn the corner, sidling against the exiting flow of pedestrians, and step off the curb to avoid the congestion at the Academy's Locust Street exits.

"How about Apropos?" Bill asks. "They serve late. More important, I like to look at their bartender. Levee called me at the office this afternoon, by the way. He was not in a good mood."

"Bad day?"

"Not exactly. He's been offered a promotion."

"A good day."

"Well, there's a small hitch. Barnaby-Burnham has a contract to construct an addition to the port at Jidda. Our Cement Queen happens to know his concrete to the extent that they want him to go over and supervise the pouring."

"Terrific. Where's Jidda?"

"Saudi Arabia."

"Jesus."

"Yes."

"But he's Jewish."

"So was Jesus. There's more. Do you know what they do to faggots in Saudi Arabia?"

"Burn them?" Pete says, opening the Academy House door for Bill.

"They cut off their pee pees."

"How rude."

In silence, they ride the elevator several floors with a man and a woman who stand at the side of the car, locked in an embrace, each rubbing the other's buttocks. The woman giggles and slides one hand into the man's pants pocket.

"Did you see that?" Pete says when they leave the car.

"Could you not see it? The guy had a hard-on. And they think *we're* bad.

"Anyway, Levee wants to turn it down, but his boss showed him how he can bank about fifty grand above living costs by the time his part's done. The thought of breezing into town with all that cash has him nearly crazy."

"They don't drink there, do they?"

"Nope. And can you imagine Levee going a year without a joint?"

"This is not a promotion," Pete says. "This is a kamikaze mission. Sending a scotch-swilling Jewish faggot pothead to Saudi Arabia?"

Bill unlocks the door to his penthouse. "I am dying of thirst. Would you please pour me a Naked Lady while I slip into something more normal?" He heads down the hall.

Pete crosses the expanse of Bill's vast living room, passing between two of its three seating areas. His feet sink into several Oriental rugs laid on thick carpeting on his way to the stainless-steel kitchen. The refrigerator holds Ziploc bags of several kinds of lettuce, Bill's requisite two dozen or so Tupperware-lidded containers of walnuts, pecans, pine nuts, and pistachios, sunflower seeds, pumpkin seeds, sesame seeds, and dried apricots, raisins, apples, and, in larger savers, homemade batches of these items mixed with brans and grains, combinations that are all called "gorp." There are eight or ten bottles of the carbonated Polish spring water Bill has brought in by the case and which he calls "Naked Lady" after the blonde with large breasts on the label. Suddenly Pete is aware of breasts everywhere.

Bill's bedroom, the largest of the apartment's three, has

windows facing south and east. On clear mornings, sunlight fills this room for hours. At night, it offers a vista of Old City and Society Hill and, across the Delaware, the lights of Camden and glow of Cherry Hill beyond. He cannot see his father's factory from here.

He puts Bill's drink on the mahogany highboy and sits in a black leather wingback chair across the room. Bill, in his jockey shorts and pleated formal shirt, slaps wrinkles from his trousers and dusts the satin lapels of his jacket. He zips the suit into a plastic storage bag and takes it into his dressing room.

"Are we still on for Saturday?" he asks Pete from inside.

"I think. Depends on Mom. Where are we eating?"

"We don't know that yet," Bill says. He returns to the room carrying a pair of jeans. "Nary and Gora are still trying to find someone to close the store. If they can't, one of them will have to do it. Geo doesn't know if he has a date yet. Thank you for this water," he says, drinking it down.

"Who would be the date?"

"Who knows? Some airhead-twenty-two-year-old-fashion-freak with a Dick of Death," Bill says.

"Named Darryl."

"Or Kenneth. Levee wants to go somewhere fancy . . ."

"Again? You should never have taken that boy clothes shopping."

"I had nothing to do with that. Geo got him started on the clothes kick. Anyway, Gora's in charge of restaurant selection," Bill says, inserting one long leg into his jeans then the other in a series of fluid, balanced movements.

They play racquetball once a week, a game in which they both excel. Pete plays fast and cutthroat, moving in on the ball, hitting hard, racing to place. Bill, taller by five inches and twenty-five pounds heavier, plays in slower motion. His game is all follow-through; his only sharp movements are confined to his neck and head, which snap when he connects with the ball in a jerk that whips sweat from the ends of his black hairs in spatters to the walls and floor. Smooth and prepossessing, Bill operates in two modes, their friend Geo claims, calm and calm.

"I still like to watch you get dressed," Pete says.

"I remember when you liked to watch me get undressed," says Bill, tucking in his shirttails.

"I miss sleeping with you," Pete says.

Bill looks pensive for a few seconds. Then he grins. "Well. Thank you again. But is that all you miss? What about my sparkling wit? My kinetic mind?"

"I still get to enjoy them. Maybe not at four in the morning . . ."

"We made the cum fly," Bill says.

"We did."

Bill sits on the bed. He pulls on a sock.

"You know," Bill says, shaking out the other sock and not looking over, "we could be fuck buddies . . . Guys are doing that these days." He pulls on the other sock.

"We're too proprietary. Don't you think?"

"I don't know. Maybe."

» » »

They sit at their table overlooking the bar, on a level several feet above it. There are no other diners within fifty feet. Two young, well-dressed couples drink noisily together at the bar.

"You call that hot?" Pete says, indicating the bartender. "He looks like my father. No. He looks like *your* father. By the way, I saw you slip that bill to the maître d'. How much for this fabulous view? We could have sat here for nothing."

"Five bucks. That bartender's always here Wednesday nights. He comes on at eleven."

"For the famous eleven-to-two shift?"

"Read your menu."

"You must have yours memorized."

"Bitch."

"I'm having a steak," Pete declares.

"Poison," Bill says. "Eat something healthy. At least eat chicken."

"I want meat. I want overcooked beef."

"Ugh."

Bill raises his hand toward a waiter standing at the periphery of the main group of diners. The waiter nods and heads toward them.

"Sort of cute," Bill says as he approaches.

"Too young."

"Good evening, gentlemen," says the waiter. "My name is Kenneth, and I will be your waiter."

"Where's Geo when you need him," Pete says.

"Excuse me," Bill says. "Is your name really Kenneth?"

"Yes, sir."

"You don't happen to be into clothes, do you?" Pete asks.

"Stop that. Kenneth, bring my friend a gag. I'll have carrot soup and stir-fried vegetable salad. And a Diet Coke when you have time, thank you, Kenneth."

"Jack Daniel's on the rocks. Garden salad, hold the alfalfa sprouts. And the sirloin. Very well done."

Bill makes a face. "I didn't teach you anything."

"Nope. So how is your life?"

"It's all right," Bill says. He places his elbows on the table, laces his fingers.

"Just 'all right'?"

"Yeah. Even keel. That'll change. Daddums is working up to 'a talk.' He's been acting strange. No. He's been acting human, that's what's strange. Sister Woman told me Daddums has been stopping by their house a couple of times a week for maybe a month. She says he plays with the babies. Actually holds them. Says things to them. Do you believe it?"

"This is not the Daddums I knew and disliked."

"It's not. Sister Woman's been putting off telling Daddums she's preggers again. But she blurted it out. He said, 'What wonderful news.' *Tears* in his eyes. Last week he called her and asked her if she and Randy had enough *money,* for God's sake! Monday he called her again and said he had a personal question. This from a man who has never asked her what time it was. What he wanted to know was did she think I could run The Empire. 'Do you think he's got the balls?' was the way he put it.

"Well, you know how Sister Woman hates controversy, but she says she said, 'Daddums, would you ask me that if Billy were straight?' "

"There's something in the water," Pete says.

"What?"

"I just had the same conversation with Phil. Go on."

"Daddums told her that was an interesting question and he would give it some thought."

"What do you think?"

"About The Empire?"

"About the balls."

"I've been giving them a lot of thought lately."

"And?"

"I admit I'm more than a little awed by the prospect of managing fifty-five million dollars' worth of real estate."

"That much?"

"More, if you count what Linda and I have from Mums' estate."

"And I tossed all that away?"

"Maybe not irrevocably."

Kenneth places their drinks.

"So when is the coronation?" Pete asks.

"He's considering retiring. He hasn't done it yet. Hey. You know me. I love to play. Playing is not an avocation with me. It's a full-time job. It requires concentration. Single-minded devotion. But The Empire? Darling man, that's fucking drudgery. Daddums never quits. He's at it all day. Into the night."

"But that's his choice, Bill. Look at my father. He's at that plant day and night, too. When he put on the third shift a couple of years ago, he was like a wild man. Not because Grand-mère's meat pies were going to be in every freezer east of the Mississippi instead of just the East Coast, but because those production lines would be going *all* the time. And do you know what the second thing he did was when he set up three production shifts? He had a bedroom and bath built onto his office in case he had to stay there round the clock. You wouldn't have to run The Empire the way your father does, is the point."

"I've been thinking we should do it together."

"If you and Daddums could just separate out all that ego, you'd be a terrific team."

Bill leans toward him. "I'm thinking about *you* and me."

"You and me run The Empire? Payne, you have gone over the edge."

"Wait. Consider the possibilities. Not only are we both smart as whips, but we have balance: I'm a little impulsive; you're slow to change things. I spend money; you save it."

"I like to work; you like to play?"

"Ex*act*ly. It's perfect."

The waiter brings their first courses.

"Bill, when did you hatch this scheme?"

"You'll be interested to hear that I had a little help. Do you remember about a month ago doing flowers for a wedding at Saint Bonnie's? Bride's name Madalyn Jonsson?"

"No."

"Née Weyl?"

"Oh, God. That was a fucking nightmare. I drove up to Galino's to decorate for the reception as it was burning down."

"Apparently you were helpful to dear Madalyn's daddy not only in finding a new location within a couple of hours, but a new caterer, too. And a good one. I was at the wedding."

"I was lucky."

"Be that as it may. Curtis Weyl and Daddums were roommates at Penn. He's Daddums' best friend. He also sits on the boards of two of our corporations. *And* he's my god-daddums."

"Small world."

"Mmm. He had you checked out."

"What do you mean, had me 'checked out'?"

"Curt Weyl loves my family. He and his wife used to go on vacation with my parents. Linda and I half lived with them when we were kids. Curt has been politicking for a couple of years now to get Daddums to retire. He knows me like a book. He knows that I don't want to run The Empire by myself and he probably knows I'm a little too rash to keep it together anyway, so he started a little talent search to find Billy a suitable partner. So Daddums will feel free to retire to Hilton Head. So they can play golf together every day for the rest of their lives. Your name's on the list."

"How the hell could my name get on a list to run a real estate holding company?"

"For two significant reasons: I wrote you in and they found you out."

"Bill, what are you talking about?"

"Curt asked me a few weeks ago whom I'd like to work with if he could get Daddums to retire. I said you, and he remembered you from Madalyn's wedding."

"All I did was find a fucking caterer."

"We are modest. Apparently Uncle Curt made a few calls and one of the people he talked with was a buddy of his at the Wharton School who did a little work with you years ago on something called ExecuString? A management system he said you *invented?* Is that true?"

"It's no big deal. It's something I put together a long time ago. You know. The right place, the right time. Anyway, it's been eight years since ExecuString came out. The system's been modified and reworked a hundred times. I doubt anyone even uses the original model anymore. I haven't spoken with Dr. Popple in years."

"Well, he hasn't forgotten you."

"Well, no matter," Pete says. "It wouldn't work."

"Why not?"

"I can think of at least three good reasons. For one, it's not a good idea for good friends to work together."

"Ridiculous. Daddums and Curt are good friends."

"Did they sleep together for a couple of years?"

"Who knows?"

"You're fucking delirious, Bill."

"Anyway, what's that got to do with it?"

"Everything."

"Bull. What's your next reason?"

"I like what I do pretty much. I make an OK living. I went into it so I wouldn't have to drive in the stress lane."

"You're a workaholic. And pardon me for bringing it up, but being rich gave you some comfortable options."

"I'm not rich," Pete says, defensively.

"Your parents are."

"My parents are."

"And you will be."

"We don't know that."

"How would you not be? They're not likely to leave it to the Church."

"They could live for another twenty-five years. Besides, I've never planned on their money."

"What's your third reason?"

"It's a crazy idea."

"Thank you. Just crazy enough to work. It's the only idea I've had that's a good solution to Daddums' retirement."

"Why not sell off The Empire?"

"We talk about that at tax time. We don't really want to sell it. We have some very profitable investments that it doesn't make sense to sell. Besides, I don't want to play *all* the time. How much do you make a year now?" Bill asks.

"There is something in the water. None of your fucking business."

"Now, don't go puffing up. How much?"

"Sixty-four thousand last year, after taxes."

"A decent living. Not bad for a single person with no dependents."

"You?" Pete asks.

"It's not an appropriate comparison. It's not apples and apples."

"Hey, I showed you mine. Show me yours."

"Fair enough. Last year The Empire paid me two hundred thousand. I picked up another quarter of a million in profit from an apartment building I sold."

Pete cocks his head. "Four hundred and fifty thousand?"

"Mums' trust pays me fifty thousand annually until I'm sixty."

"What happens then?"

"I get the principal. Mums thought I was profligate. She figured I'd mature by sixty."

"Forgive me for asking, but what's the principal come to?"

"An average state lottery. Two and a half mil."

"So you're managing on about half a million bucks a year?"

"More or less. There's another twenty thousand or so in profits from a distribution center Sister Woman and I own out in Conshohocken. And some dividends from The Empire."

"Not bad for a single person with no dependents."

"Pete, if you would come and work with me, The Empire would pay you what it pays me. Two hundred thousand. And there would be certain stock options that would make you wealthy in a few years, unless we ran it into the ground, of course."

"What would I do?" Pete finds himself saying.

"It's really very easy," Bill says. "You'd do what Daddums and I do. We own a lot of rental properties and a few businesses. We watch them. Sometimes we decide to sell something. Sometimes we decide to buy something. We make tours. We make recommendations. We hire and fire people. We eat out a lot. You like to eat out a lot. There's nothing to it. Think about it," Bill says. "Take a couple months. I won't talk about it unless you bring it up. How's your mom?"

"I have a question. I'm not going to do this. But how did you propose to keep Daddums out of our hair and down on the golf course?"

"You're worried about his interfering? I promise you that he won't, and I will guarantee that. He'd just come to board meetings."

Pete nods. "I'm really very flattered, Bill. But I think you and Mr. Weyl had better widen the talent search. By the way, Mom thanks you for your card. That was thoughtful of you."

"How's she doing?"

"I don't know. She had a seizure while I was with her tonight. A major one. It scared the shit out of me. I ran out in the hall and started grabbing anyone with white on. Until this week, I've never seen my mother not in control. In the hospital tonight she looked so whipped to begin with, and while we were talking she suddenly started jerking all over the bed. Dad told me she's been acting funny."

"What's going on?"

"Her doctor won't say much. The guy's good, but he's a prig. All he'd tell me is that the cancer in her breast has metastasized to her brain. She has two tumors there."

"What do they do? Operate?"

"No. Radiation, and they'll start her on steroids to shrink the tumors."

"Jesus."

They eat in silence for a moment.

"So how are you?" Bill asks him.

"I'm all right. I don't know. I'm all right." He sips his bourbon. "I'm in one of those phases, I guess." He looks across the room. "Bill, do you worry about AIDS?"

"I think about it a lot. I worry about you and our friends."

"Not about yourself?"

"No," he says. "I'll tell you this, but I'm not telling anyone else. I went and got tested. I'm negative."

"You didn't tell me you were getting tested," he says.

"I didn't tell anyone."

"Why?"

"I didn't want people to ask me how the test came out."

"But you're negative."

"I could've been positive."

"I understand that you wouldn't want people to know if you were positive, but why not say if you're negative?"

"It's complicated," Bill says. "I mentioned to you and Levee and Geo about six months ago that I was thinking about maybe getting tested and all three of you said I was crazy. You changed the subject."

"I don't remember that. . . . Why did you get tested?"

"I wanted to know. You should want to know. This isn't 1982, darling most. It's 1990. They've got some good stuff now."

"Excuse me," Pete says, impatient now, "I'm having a little trouble putting this together. Of all of us, you are the least likely to want to look an ugly thing in the eye. You must have been awfully nervous going in for that test."

"Nervous. I was a wreck. I was sure I'd be positive. When you and I broke up, I went bonkers for a while. I slept with a lot of people."

"For a *while?* You've slept with a lot of people for a long time."

"No. I haven't. In fact, I haven't had sex with another person in almost three years."

"I don't believe it."

"Why not? What am I to you, Slut of the East?"

"Bill, you're always taking people home."

"That's your perception. I've taken a few guys home in a couple of years—for cuddling only."

"Are you telling me you're celibate?"

"Yes."

"Why? What about 'safe sex'?"

"There's no such thing. For me. Why did you ask me if I worry about AIDS, Pete? Are you worried?"

"I think about it all the time. And tonight by accident at the hospital I saw this guy in the hall who looked really wasted. He looked like somebody's grandfather. And he seemed to be trying to get away from me. It wasn't until about five minutes later that I realized that that old man is younger than I am. He's Jerry Frakes. I *dated* him a couple of weeks. He's got it."

"Maybe he didn't have it when you were seeing him."

"Maybe he didn't. Maybe he did. But it's not just Jerry Frakes. In the past two years, four guys I slept with have got it. Three of them are dead."

"Who was the third?"

"Gil Monke."

"You slept with Gil Monke?"

"Yes."

"When?" Bill says, putting down his spoon.

"Years ago."

"You didn't tell me that."

"Well, I did."

"No, you didn't. I would've remembered."

"I mean, I slept with him."

"How often?" Bill asks.

"I don't remember. A couple of times."

"You slept with Gil Monke and you don't remember how often?"

"It was a couple of times. What difference does it make?"

"Gil Monke was only the hottest man I ever saw. In my entire life."

"What am I, chopped liver?"

"I loved you. I lusted for Gil Monke. So did you. We used to talk about it. I hated it when he'd say hello to you in the bars. When did you do it?"

"I don't know, Bill. A few years ago. This is not a big deal."

"Did you sleep with him while we were lovers?"

"Of course not."

"Are you sure?"

"I didn't sleep with anyone while we were lovers."

"Gil Monke. Jesus, he was hot," Bill says, returning to his soup. "You never told me about that. How come you never told me about that?"

"How come you never told me about getting tested?"

"Hottest man I ever saw. In my entire life. You been feeling OK? You don't have any symptoms, do you?"

"No. I mean, I don't know. I'm all the time feeling my armpits. I worry about my weight."

"You look a little thinner."

"Do I?"

"Sorry. I couldn't resist. I love to taunt hypochondriacs. You look OK."

"Just OK? I used to look fine. It's a vicious cycle."

"Circle."

"Fucking English majors. When I lose a couple pounds, I panic. Then I binge on pasta and ice cream and when I gain a few extra, I try to lose them and then I worry that I'm losing them."

"You never ate right."

"And I've been getting these little headaches every now and then. Nothing big. I mean, just these little headaches, and when I get one, I'm sure it's starting."

"Probably just a brain tumor."

"Jesus, Bill."

"Sorry. The Devil makes me do it. Go ahead. I'll stop."

"Also, I feel warm all the time and I never have a fever. It's always subnormal."

"You're a cool guy."

Bill puts his palms up.

"You know what I did the other day? I bought full-length mirrors for the insides of my closet doors so I can see my back and check it for Kaposi's."

"Why don't you get tested?"

The waiter returns to their table. They sit in silence, examining the complexity of white, spray-painted ceiling ductwork as he removes their appetizer plates, dusts the tablecloth for no apparent reason, and places their entrées.

"Because," Pete continues when he has left, "what will change? If I had the test and found out I'm positive, I'd still worry about my body all the time. In fact, it would be worse. I'd be depressed. It would be like living with a death sentence."

He cuts into his steak. "Why did I order this?"

"Salad's delish. Maybe you're negative."

"I'm not. I couldn't be. Bill, I can't even remember all the things I did with those guys. Jerry Frakes is the fifth one I was with to get it. That I know about. The odds are not in my favor."

"Pete, I was sure I was positive, too, and I'm not. And I like to get fucked, which is not your favorite sport. Or has that changed?"

"It's not my favorite sport, but I have left my footprints on a couple of ceilings. Including yours."

"Be still, my heart. But that doesn't mean you have it. It's just as possible those guys weren't infected when you were with them. It is also possible that some people may have a natural immunity for all we know. Look, I know I'm pushing testing. It's just that I hate to see you so unhappy because you're in limbo."

"I think I'd rather be unhappy in limbo than frantic in hell."

"What do you do about sex?" Bill asks.

"Do about it?"

"I mean, I know you have sex."

"Do I do it with other people, you're asking?"

"Have you taken up goats?"

"They're not my type. . . . I was having sex in a manner of speaking."

"What the fuck does that mean? How do you have sex in a manner of speaking? Are we talking phone sex or something?"

"Cute. Since Bobby Fox got sick two years ago . . ."

"Three years ago," Bill corrects him.

"Has it been? Already? God. That's another thing. Time is getting out of control. . . . That really took the wind out of my sails, Bobby's getting sick. Not only did somebody I know get AIDS, but somebody I slept with, for God's sake. He was the first one. And I remember saying to myself, We only did it once so that probably didn't count, and it wasn't that we were wild and kinky either. Bobby Fox was not what you'd call a sexual athlete. And I can't remember even whose house we did it in. But what I do remember like I remember where I was when Kennedy was shot was the day Bobby Fox called me and told me he had AIDS."

"He called you?"

"I told you that story."

"No, you didn't," Bill says. "I didn't know he called you. I didn't know you were that close."

"We weren't close. That's why the call was so . . . such a shock. He called me at the shop. I was making a wrist corsage out of peppermint camellias when the phone rang. I can still see the designs in those petals. I haven't liked to work with them since. Bobby asked me how I was and what I was up to. He was always extremely polite. Then he said the reason for his call was that he was contacting all the people he had slept with, and I thought, Oh fuck, it's penicillin-shot-in-the-heinie time, and instead he said he wanted to inform me that he had AIDS. And I was so taken aback that I guess I didn't say anything. Then he said something about he felt it was his social responsibility . . . Imagine. His fucking social responsibility. Let me tell you, I've thought a lot since about the nature of social responsibility. And I hate him for that telephone call."

"What did you say?"

"I thanked him for calling. I'm a polite guy, too. And I put the camellias down and I went upstairs and poured myself a double bourbon on the rocks and I made a deal with God: I would never have sex again if He wouldn't let me get AIDS."

Bill rolls his eyes. "Foolish person," he says. "God doesn't dabble in sleazy sex deals."

"I'm dead meat if He does. The next weekend, I met some delicious trick and our deal got a little watered down. I would never be bottom man again if He wouldn't let me get AIDS. But it was OK there for a while to be top man until it sunk in that that wasn't very responsible on my part, so we amended it that I could be top man only if I wore a condom. But we had to change that because what if it broke, or something? So we cut a deal that I would give up anal sex completely if He wouldn't let me get AIDS. Blow jobs and jerking off were allowed."

"Pardon me for interrupting, Monty, but what's God get out of all this?"

"I don't know. One of his children in purer form? It gets sillier. Around then, all those studies came out about the high concentration of the virus in semen, so we adjusted down to my not giving blow jobs without condoms, then I gave up either getting or giving them. Then came all that stuff about how a little crack in your skin is all it takes for the virus to get in your blood. I quit biting my nails. But I'm in the flower business, and there's no way I can get through a day without getting stabbed by a rose or a wire or a holly leaf or something, and there never seemed to be a time when I didn't have a wound of some sort, so I gave up jerking guys off."

Bill shrugs. "Rubber gloves?"

"Billy, I never had a problem with asking a guy to use a condom, but I cannot ask somebody to put on rubber gloves. I just can't. Sex has finally become such a bother; it's such a source of anxiety that I've given it up. I've been celibate, too."

"Incredible. How long?"

"Not as long as you."

"Is this classified?"

"A year and a half. Two years. I can't remember."

"Well," Bill says. "This is serious. How long do you plan to remain among the Great Washed, I guess we could be called?"

"Until there's a cure."

"I think we are talking a long time, my friend."

"What about you? You're going to go without sex for that long?"

"I don't know about that. I've taken a different sort of vow. I haven't given up sex altogether. But I did decide not to have sex with anyone I don't see a very good possibility of having a future with. I just haven't met anyone in three years with that potential."

"What if you did? Would he have to be negative, too?"

"Obviously I'd rather if he were, but that's not a requirement. He'd have to get tested. I'd need to know what I'm dealing with. I am not going to be infected with that virus. For anyone."

"Must be nice."

"What's that, Pete?"

"To know you don't have it."

"It still doesn't make life easy. Easier, for sure . . . Maybe you should get tested."

"I don't think. I don't know. I don't want to know." He slices a piece of steak. He puts his knife and fork down. "I sort of want to know, but only if it's good news. Getting the test would be easy. I just don't think I could go back for the results."

"Yep. That's the hard part. Maybe you and the Big One could hammer out another deal. You go for the test; He gets the results and sends you a sign."

"Like, an angel knocks on my door, or something?"

"Nah, He'd be more subtle. You're out jogging, maybe, and a begger stops you and gives you a quarter."

"Or he looks just like Rock Hudson and he asks me for one."

"Right . . . You ought to go, maybe. Ease your mind."

"Tell me something. If you found out you had it, would you call all the people you've slept with and tell them?"

"I've never been into S and M."

» » »

Outside Bill's building, they stand for a moment before parting. Thunder rolls down Locust Street from West Philadelphia.

"Come on up and wait out the storm."

"No. Thanks. I think I'll make it home before it starts," Pete says, thinking he would like to stay but shouldn't for some reason.

"Your choice," Bill says. "See you Saturday."

"Saturday," Pete says.

Bill leans over and gives him a hug, one arm around Pete's shoulders, the other around his waist. When he embraces Pete, Bill drops his hand to his buttocks and squeezes. It is a small squeeze, but it adds a margin of intimacy to the hug and it takes Pete by surprise, not that his buttocks were touched by the person who was his lover, but that his body reacts with a quick rush of blood to his groin. Pete turns left and begins a fast walk west, hoping to beat the coming rain. His apartment is eight blocks away. The wind picks up. He wonders if Bill's squeeze was intentional or if it was just an impulsive touch, an innocent accident of parting quickly. And, if it was intended, what did it mean?

» » »

He towels his hair and shoulders dry, then drapes his wet clothes on the rim of the tub. He hopes to get into bed while the rain is still falling. He opens a window in his bedroom wide, the better to hear it, to drift off to sleep to it.

He sets his alarm for an early trip to his wholesaler. He crawls into his king-sized bed, making, as he settles in, his ritual arrangement of the five conventional pillows he keeps there: four of them laid end to end alongside him, one for his head. He stretches out along the pillows, putting a leg and an arm over them. He does not like to sleep alone.

He thinks of the years of sleeping with Bill, Saturdays in the beginning, then long weekends, then weekday sleepovers after being out late. Then occasional nights separated. Then none. Weekdays at his house. Weekends at Bill's.

Their friends picked up their routine. Their families were left to the mercy of answering machines.

For a year and a half or maybe two years, this was their comfortable arrangement. Each was welcomed into the other's social circle. Their casual natures and good looks, as well as their senses of humor—Bill's quick and dry, Pete's quick and appreciative—assured them frequent invitations. They reciprocated during the tenure of their lover relationship with two large parties, which became the stuff of legend.

When Bill first broached the idea of buying a place together, Pete was ambivalent. When Bill began looking, Pete became nervous. Although the condos and houses Bill chose for consideration were acceptable, Pete found fault with them all. He offered no alternates. He did not participate in the search. He had too much work, he said.

He began to spend less time with Bill. He said that his business was growing. Their schedule began to change by small degrees: most of the week together, then some weekdays apart, then only long weekends together, then Friday and Saturday. Then Saturday or Sunday.

Their friends no longer knew which number to call. Their families were weaned from answering machines. Conversation became a burden. Sex flagged. Bill began to sigh. One night over dinner Pete allowed that "this" was not working out.

They talked less. Bill sighed more. Gradually, during

visits timed to avoid each other, their possessions came back to their own homes.

On weekends they saw the same friends. They were kind to each other, even protective. They kept their keys. It was civilized.

» » »

The rain falls in intermittent sheets. Thunder trundles across the Schuylkill.

He rolls, his back to the pillows now.

"You jerk," he says. "You jerk."

V.

The voice of Stevie Figman reading the 5:00 A.M. news begins in Pete's dark bedroom. He wakes at five on days when he has to get up and on days when he can sleep in. If the clock radio goes off, it is a day he must get up.

He often wakes a few minutes before the clock radio clicks and Stevie Figman's voice starts up. During this time he tries to figure out what day it is and if the radio has been set to go off with Stevie's voice or if he can close his eyes and drift off to his next internal clock setting.

What day is it? he thinks. What is the drill? It is Friday: Mrs. Wayne, flower shipment at the airport, wholesale market, bank, payroll, Tri-State supplies order. He rolls over. He sighs.

He imagines that Stevie Figman is in his mid-forties, tall, and overweight. He can picture him dragging on cigarettes; he clears his throat on the radio too often. Sometimes he imagines Stevie with brown hair; sometimes he has no hair. He thinks that someday the phone at the shop will ring and the voice of Stevie Figman will ask him to do all the flowers for his son Stevie, Jr.'s bar mitzvah. It is appropriate that Pete do the flowers. Stevie Figman has woken him up for years. He knows Stevie's politics. Knows that his wife's name is Freda. Freda Figman.

He turns onto his back. He has an erection. He rolls over and hugs the pillows at his side.

When he thinks about waking up to someone else in his bed, it is nearly always Bill, whose long legs and torso he did not like to get up to leave. On holidays and Sundays he would wake suddenly at five and realize he did not need to get up. He would roll over to face Bill, put an arm and a leg over him and pull himself as close as possible. So started the ritual of the slow and pleasant disjointing of his early morning thoughts into dreams.

He misses most the holding on.

He strokes himself a few times and stops. He sighs. He throws the sheet off and moves his legs over the side of the bed. He feels warm. He puts his palm and fingers flat on his forehead. It feels warm to him. He decides to take his temperature.

In his bathroom he leans with his hands on the sink edge, his eyes closed, the thermometer under his tongue. He weighs the pros and cons of running now or running later. If he runs now, he will feel good all day. If he runs later, there will be more men in Fairmount Park, more nice bodies to watch. He decides to run later. He reads the thermometer. His temperature is subnormal. How could he feel so warm and be so cool? He is relieved and anxious. It could be a symptom that something is wrong.

» » »

In the kitchen he places five ten-dollar bills in an envelope, seals it, writes "Mrs. Wayne" on it in neat architect's print, then leans it against the pepper mill. He scans the cupboard doors, fearful that he might have missed one of her taped notes that read like terrorist demands:

> Mr. Flowers
> I must have Comet and Endust and
> Liquidgold. I told you to get B
> vacume bags not C. I need more

rags. You know what kind. Turn
the matress foot to head.

His cleaning woman moves no heavy objects. She instructs him periodically in the turning of mattresses. She remembers all the turns and when the turns have gone full cycle. Her religion forbids that she touch liquor. She interprets this edict broadly to include its containers. She leaves him scolding messages when he forgets to dust the bottles on his bar.

While searching in his living room for the keys to his van, he hears the muffled, measured squeaks of floorboards above him as his tenant, William D. Petranek, paces. He stops. He looks up. He listens. His own breaths hiss through his nostrils. Petranek moves above him, back and forth. The sun is just coming up. Why is he pacing?

He believes Mr. Petranek has taken some of his magazines. When certain issues were not delivered, he suspected the postman, whom he has seen many times having his paper bag lunch in quiet, bushy sections of the park—seen him reading. Seen him removing magazines from their brown mailing sleeves. He suspected the postman until he saw Mr. Petranek one afternoon walking up the stairs from the vestibule with a copy of *Consumer Reports*. His own copy appeared in the foyer a week later. A page about air purifiers had been ripped from it.

» » »

At 5:55 A.M. he is leaving the Schuylkill Expressway and entering Twenty-sixth Street. His van windows are open to the early morning air. There are no vehicles in his rear-view mirrors, none ahead as he speeds along the straight stretch which is the boundary of the Atlantic Refinery. He listens to Brazilian music on the radio. As he speeds through the cool dawn, he thinks he would like to be hurrying to the International Terminal to catch a flight rather than to Cargo City, an unromantic place, to pick up eight cases of short-stemmed double white stocks shipped to him from

Bogotá, Colombia, which he will use to fragrant and, he hopes, startling effect at the wedding of Miss Molly LaBerge to a pushy asshole with a Porsche.

The sky is overcast. Stevie Figman has announced a gray day. All day.

On the long downstroke of the General Platt bridge, he can see the entire airport, its planes positioning themselves, lining up at one of the major runway intersections, ready for takeoff to the south in trails of gray-black exhaust.

For years he has canceled every vacation he has planned. Maybe in the fall, he thinks, turning right onto I-95. When things slow down. He might go someplace outrageous. He can afford it. Madagascar, maybe. Wake up in a rain forest to the wonderful wailing songs of lemurs instead of the nicotine-thickened voice of Stevie Figman. Consume leisurely meals of small, cold lobsters on a quiet veranda at treetop level. But something will come up, he thinks. Something always comes up. A big wedding. A bigwig's house party where his clever designs will be inquired about and lead to yet another house party, another wedding. And he will cancel his reservations at the Hotel Indolence to do the wedding of the season. Would he take vacations if he worked for The Empire? Would he ever wake to hear the indris stretch their sleep-doped voices in the tops of baobabs? Will Stevie's froggy morning voice be the only one he'll ever hear?

» » »

At Cargo City he files a claim that a box of his flowers was damaged in a search for drugs.

» » »

In his shop workroom, Pete, Doris, and Philip, a part-time designer, tie raspberry-colored ribbon into deft bows and attach them to wooden picks. They place three-foot streamers in a darker shade of raspberry on the picks and poke them into Styrofoam blocks on the counters.

Pete does not enjoy the repetitive work of weddings, the tedium of making each table arrangement exactly like the first one he arranged. He looks forward to noon, when Doris's daughters are to arrive. With their mother and Philip they will copy twenty-nine times the one chair row sconce Pete has drawn in colored chalks. He will demonstrate the requisite technique only once, then he'll move on to his own work station to construct the flower tiara and bouquet he has designed for the bride, the palest woman he has ever met. Paler even than Alexa.

Behind them, in the refrigerated holding room, thirty white spheres constructed of white stock flowers rest in their boxes on cool beds of tissue. One will hang over each of the dining tables at the reception at the Barclay Hotel following the intensely color-coordinated wedding of Miss Molly LaBerge to Mr. Donald Schrag, "of Baltimore," Molly's fidgety, throaty mother keeps saying, as if he were titled. The notched ends of the streamers will hang from the flowered spheres, not quite touching the waxy petals of the gardenias floating in clear acrylic cubes at the center of each table.

Philip rakes his shoulder-length red hair back with his long, thin fingers. "Why would anybody want to put fish on a wedding reception table?"

"We're not talking mackerel," Pete says. "These are designer fish. Mr. LaBerge manufactures tropical fish equipment. He's had his factory make clear cubes especially for dear Molly's wedding. Each one has an acrylic partition down the center that will be invisible to the guests. Mr. LaBerge is having special water brought in tomorrow morning. The cubes will be filled with the water and a fish will be placed in one side of each cube. Then we go around and float the gardenias, and just before the guests are to arrive, one of his guys will go around and put a fish in the other side of the cube."

"Why don't they put both fish in in the first place?"

"Because these are male Siamese fighting fish. Each one becomes enraged when it sees another male. It displays its fins and attempts to attack the other one."

"But it can't through the partition."

"Exactly. And Mr. LaBerge doesn't want to exhaust them before they become entertainment for his guests. A little joke on his part. He doesn't like the son of a bitch his daughter's marrying. But he's doing his best to go along with the program. What color are these fish, do you think?"

Philip holds up his bow.

"You betcha. Raspberry!"

Pete wraps tiny plastic water vials in satin. He wires them to the white satin hairpiece he has constructed. He thinks he will wait until morning to insert the miniature *Phalaenopsis* orchids he has bought from a Connecticut grower into the tubes, so small that he will fill them with water with a hypodermic needle. Long-stemmed sprays of the orchids nod in the slow, moist air of the cooler. White, waxy petals with deep raspberry throats.

"Say it with flowers," he thinks. He has been saying it with flowers for fifteen years and has never said the same thing twice so far as he can recall. He has repeated himself in the use of certain material, but not in its arrangement. His pieces are never exactly alike except when they are required to be: centerpieces for tables at weddings when they insist. Otherwise, he always gives them a new presentation, a new "look." He is known for that. They seek him out. They have even changed the dates of their weddings or dinners when he absolutely could not take on one more job without giving them something less than special for their money. They know he will not compromise. They have learned to call well in advance.

Does he like this enough still to keep doing it? Will the time come when new ideas and new looks stop teasing his mind? He can feel that time coming. He can feel it coming because although this tiara is going to take the breath away from some people who care about such things, who appreciate the complexity of its construction, he thinks he does not anymore. The process no longer excites him. Although he will awe them with what he has said in flowers, he is no longer excited to say it.

» » »

"I can't make up my mind," Levee says yet again, smacking the bar with his thick-fingered hand. "Do you know what this is, Pete? This is a fucking golden opportunity. They'll pay virtually all my travel and my living expenses. OK, they're charging me rent for the apartment I'll live in in Jidda. But do you know how much they'll charge me? Guess."

"I couldn't," Pete says.

"C'mon. Guess."

"Three-fifty."

"Seventy-fucking-bucks. Seventy! I can sublet my place here in town for a year and *make* money! Guess how much my boss figures it'll cost me to live over there. A day. Guess."

"Levee, I don't know how much it costs me to live *here* a day."

"I do. *I* do. I have figured this out. Last year, after taxes and all that shit, I spent eighty-four dollars and twenty-four cents a day. To live. Just to *live*!"

Levee sits straight up on his bar stool. He hunches his muscled shoulders and holds the palms of his hands out and up to the ceiling. His blue eyes are wide with astonishment.

"Think of it. I remember people going on about living in Europe on five dollars a day. I'm spending eighty-four a day to live in Philadelphia. Guess how much a day to live in Jidda."

"I don't know."

"Guess."

"Twenty-five, thirty dollars," Pete says.

Levee cocks his head, purses his lips. He takes a pull from his beer.

"Nine bucks," he says. "Just think how much money I

could save. Harley says I could bank fifty thousand dollars while I'm over there. You know how much I saved last year? Guess."

"Paul, I can't guess."

Levee taps his filed fingernails on the bar. "Zilch. Nada. Zero. You know how much I made last year? Thirty-six thou about, after taxes and shit. Guess how much I spent last year? Take a guess."

"Thirty-six thou, about?"

"You bet your hot ass. In-fucking-credible," he says, shaking his head.

"Well, Paul . . . If I could say . . ."

"You can say any fucking thing you want. You're my friend. Hey, if it wasn't for you and Billy and Geo and Nora and Gary, I hate to think sometimes. You want another beer?"

"No. I've got to get over to the Barclay. I've got a wedding there tomorrow."

"What time's the wedding?"

"Eleven. Reception's at noon."

"You've got plenty of time. Josie," he calls to the bartender. "Two more. I need some help with this, Pete. I've got to tell them Monday."

"Levee, I think you should do it."

"Why?"

"Why not?"

Levee puts his elbows on the bar. He rubs his temples with his index and middle fingers.

"It's the traveling," he says.

"You travel now."

"Yeah. But that's not the same. I travel a week at a time at the most. Five, six times a year. This is different."

The bartender delivers their beers. Pete points to his ten-dollar bill lying on the bar.

"It's exciting," Pete tells him. "Don't you think?"

"Sure it's exciting."

"Why wouldn't you want to do it?"

Levee rolls his eyes. He covers them with the palms of his hands and peeks out at Pete through his fingers.

"I'm *scared*!"

Pete laughs. "Scared of what?" he asks.

"You won't tell the guys?"

"I wouldn't do that."

"I'm scared of flying," he says. "I don't think I'll come back."

"But you fly all the time."

"I don't fly all the time. I haven't flown since 1976."

"How do you get to all these places you go to?"

"I rent cars. I drive. I take the train. Last year, when I had to be in California for that bridge pouring, I scheduled vacation time before and after the trip so I'd have three days to get there and three to get back."

"Levee, you drove? To California and back? I didn't know that."

"You think I'm crazy."

"No. I don't think you're crazy. I'm surprised, is all. How come you never said anything?"

"I'm embarrassed."

"What is it about flying that bothers you?"

"Plane crashes. Last year I made a reservation. To Louisville, Kentucky. Some job or another they wanted me to look at. I decided it was time to just get over this. Way in advance, I bought the ticket. A Super Saver. Three or four days before I was supposed to leave I broke out in this weird rash on my chest. Then I got sick to my stomach every time I thought about it. I canceled the reservation and drove straight through. I had to pay for the ticket. Two hundred and five dollars."

"But what's the snag for you?"

"Specifically? Well, it used to be simple. It was just the idea of flying into a mountain at five hundred and sixty miles an hour. Then all that terrorist shit started and I got scared of the plane I'm in blowing up. But the worst thing I think about is me sitting there minding my own fucking business, you know, maybe even reading. Maybe *even* dozing off a little, and the skin of the plane starts peeling away and I get sucked out at thirty-four thousand feet. Do you know how long it takes a person strapped in an airplane seat to fall thirty-four thousand feet into the middle of, say, goddamned Rittenhouse Square? Do you know how long I'd have to think about being splattered on those paving stones? Or impaled on that bronze lady in the pool holding the duck? Jesus."

"You wouldn't think about it. You'd pass out. There's no oxygen that high up."

"Flowers. Really. Do you know what comfort that knowledge is to me? I mean, think about it. It takes time to die from oxygen starvation. You don't just pass out, you fall *while* you're dying. As you're gasping for breath, you see the city of Philadelphia—what?—seven miles under you? Maybe you even see the tiny patch of green water in the middle of it where the duck lady is. Look at my arms. I get chill bumps just thinking about it. Our airplanes are getting *old*. You know what the airlines do with old planes when they retire them? They don't put them in airplane graveyards. They sell them to foreign countries."

"Paul, the Saudis have new everything."

"I can't get it out of my mind," Levee says. "I know there are about a hundred reasons why I should go. And if it was just flying into mountains I had to worry about, I think I could do it because you fly over water a lot to get there. But all this other shit, I mean nuts blowing up planes and old planes falling apart . . . I'm telling you, it makes me crazy."

"Look, Levee. I think you've got to find a way to look at this differently. You're letting it control your life. You've got to play the odds. There are thousands of flights every day all over the world. The odds are in the millions against anything happening to a plane you're on."

"Hey. I know that. I'm a fucking engineer. But I'm beyond analyzing the odds. I mean, this is like . . . sick!

I haven't even told my parents. That part's worse than the flying."

"What do your parents have to do with it?"

"They want me to change my name."

"Your parents?"

"Of course not. Barnaby-Burnham. My company. Jews aren't safe in Saudi Arabia. We're probably not even allowed. They want me to change it to something like Smith."

"Paul Smith. It doesn't sound Jewish, does it?"

"No. I'm holding out for Smithvitz."

"Hard to say."

"I think I'd hyphenate it. Smith-Vitz."

"Yeah. Makes it sort of British."

"God," Levee says, pointing across the bar. "Look at the ass on the guy with the nuthuggers."

"What're nuthuggers?"

"Where you been, Flowers? Bike pants. Green tank top."

"The kid?"

"He's twenty-five. Twenty-eight. My parents'll die. Lennie will die. Rose will silently hold me responsible for his death. I'm going to have to go over and see them. I'll tell Rose first. I always tell her terrible things first. Gives me an idea how to handle Lennie. If her one leg jiggles, he'll just have a small screaming fit. If she puts her fingertips under the front of her dress and moves them like her heart's beating and jiggles her leg, he'll elevate out of his chair and pace around the kitchen holding his head. If she does both of those things and closes her eyes and opens her mouth a little like she's going to throw up, I'll just get in the car and drive home. I won't even tell him. I'll just change my name to Smith-Vitz and make a reservation on El Al."

"Wrong country."

"OK, then. Air Arab, or whatever it's called. The one with the new planes that aren't tired. I don't think I can do this, Pete."

"What'll happen if you don't take the offer?"

"A couple things. I probably won't get any more offers. And I'll feel bad about myself if I pass it up." Levee tosses down a couple inches of his beer. "But"—he grins—"I'll be alive!"

"Why don't you sign up for one of those courses for people who are afraid to fly?"

"I'm afraid to call them."

"Jesus."

"Yeah."

"Hmmm."

"I know."

"How goes the custody battle?" Pete says to change the subject.

"Talk about fucked up," Levee says. "You want another one? Josie! Two more."

"Levee, I've got halls to festoon. Miss Molly LaBerge walks down the aisle at eleven tomorrow morning."

"Where are your employees?"

"They're at the Barclay."

"Josie, two more."

"Levee, I haven't finished this one," Pete says.

"I know you guys think this business with Freddy is ridiculous," Levee goes on.

"No one ever said that, Paul."

"Geo as much as said I was a horse's ass."

"Well, we just don't want to see you throw good money after a couple of lawyers when it seems like it's something you two could work out between you."

"Hey, I love Freddy. And if I take this job in Saudi Arabia, I'm going to be away from him a long time. Maybe even a year. I want it legal that he comes back to me when I get back."

"He might forget you. He's only three."

"He won't forget me," Levee says. "I'm his dad."

» » »

At 10:30, home from the Barclay, where he supervised the placement of Kentia palms and a sea of raspberry-colored geraniums, he glances at his answering machine. There are four messages. He has not eaten. He needs a shower. A small headache is beginning at the middle of his forehead. He feels the glands under his jaw. Do they feel lumpy? He decides to take a shower while some frozen dinner rotates, defrosting, on the carousel tray of his microwave. He starts for the kitchen but thinks of his mother and turns back to the telephone to retrieve the messages in case one of them concerns her.

Bea's voice: "Hello. It's me. Call me when you get in."

His mother's voice, annoyed: "Answering machines are not very satisfying to mothers. Don't bother calling back. I just wanted to tell you about something strange that happened tonight. How much time do I have on this thing? While I was eating my dinner, a nurse came in my room. She didn't even plump the pillows or anything, she just stood at the foot of the bed. I hadn't seen her before and I said 'Hello,' and she said she was Mrs. Manning or Mannering or something and she would be helping me through my illness. She had a very nice voice. Very soft. I liked her right away. She asked if she could sit down and we just chatted for a few minutes. She asked me about my family and she told me about hers. Then she said that if I liked, she would be coming around now and then to talk. Then she stood up and shook my good hand and she said she'd better be leaving so she wouldn't interfere with my Mary Alice's visit, and she stopped at the door and she said, 'Tell Pete to check his tires.' It wasn't a minute later that Mary Alice walked in. Isn't that bizarre? I want you to go out and check your tires."

Bea's voice again: "Where the hell are you? Call me, OK?"

And again: "Pete, can we have lunch tomorrow or something? I have to talk to you about Mother. Call me in the morning. I'm up early."

In his kitchen, he moves icy packages about in his freezer, pieces of dated chicken, strange, foil-wrapped shapes inside plastic bags, assorted mysteries in plastic-lidded containers whose labels have fallen off. Impatient to eat, he takes out one of the NEW! MICROWAVEABLE! packages of Grand-mère's Fruits de Grande Mer his father has sent him. The photograph on the top of the box shows succulent pieces of shrimp and scallops cascading out of forked-away brown crust.

"Hype," he says as he scans the directions for the microwave cooking time.

Later, showered, combed, and bathrobed, his head aching less from the aspirin he has taken, he sits with his tray at his desk in his bedroom, facing the eleven o'clock news. He has transferred the pie from its beige plastic container to a china plate next to which are a linen napkin, silver knife and fork, and a glass of chardonnay. As salt-and-pepper-haired Jim Gardner briefs viewers about a fire in the Northeast, he wonders what Jim Gardner looks like without clothes on. He breaks into his seafood pie. He is surprised to find that it looks like the photograph on the package. The crust is brown and flaky. The filling is thick with shrimp and scallops, even lobster chunks and thready pieces of either fish or crab. It tastes good.

"It's good," he says aloud. "It's damned good." He takes another forkful and tastes crab and a hint of Marsala wine. "I can't believe he did that."

» » »

He sits in a T-shirt in the dark on his living room sofa. He cannot sleep. It is 1:30 A.M.

Above him, William Petranek moves from room to room in his apartment. Pete imagines he might be packing, remembering socks or toiletries or belts, but he never goes anywhere, even for weekends. Since he moved in in January, he has never had a guest that Pete is aware of. A tall, thin man in his fifties, Mr. Petranek arrived with a van from Conran's, everything new, everything black and blond wood and neutral-toned fabric, price tags still attached to his brown bathroom towels stacked in black acrylic waste cans, new rag area rugs in washed-out blues and roses. Except for the lettuce in his bags of groceries, not a living thing among his new possessions. In spite of his rental application, where he listed himself as "single," not "divorced," Pete assumes Mrs. Petranek threw him out.

In the dark of his own colorful living room, tall plants and small trees arch near his windows. Their leaves reflect the street light. His fingers rub the buttons of the stereo remote control. He does not turn it on.

He thinks that his mother will get worse and that she will not get better, that whatever is growing in her brain must also be growing secretly, or with her doctors' knowledge, in other organs in her body. Why should those migrating cells discriminate, after all? And she with her shelves of medical books and lay books about nutrition and health, how could she choose to ignore a lump in her breast, a palpable node growing there month after month for, what? A year? Had she not shuttled all her kids to doctors during all their growing-ups at the first signs of fevers and lassitude? Nothing escaped her vigilance. Could there be a specialist over fifty in this city of doctors who had not had a Flowers child in his examination rooms? Certainly there was not one who had not dined at her table or shared cocktails in her sitting rooms of dark leafy silks and stiff, iris-printed draperies. Yet her own lumps flourished in their garden of her neglect month after month. What could she have been thinking? That they would simply give up their ghosts in the face of her faith in the exercise of mind over matter? Turn and run like the bully of his own childhood whom he knuckle-chopped in the mouth at her instigation?

He is angry at her failure and her hypocrisy. He saw her reading those books; saw the stacks of *Time* and *Newsweek* and *American Health* under her library coffee table. How could you pick one of them up and not find an article on breast cancer these days? How unpleasant could a mammography be? Could that have been worse than fits in a hospital bed?

And his father in his seven-hundred-dollar suits and hand-sewn Egyptian cotton shirts, saying she is getting spooky, sending his kid into battle with Max instead of having it out himself with the doctor in that noncommittally gray office. In that incredible sinking chair.

Forget Stu, he thinks, flicking the stereo on, then off before the sound comes out. "Too involved with the family, my ass," he says, standing, wondering if it is baseball that preoccupies his brother now that the Flyers did not make the play-offs. Or Wimbledon, when is that? Or is it the Japanese stock market that he follows in the night through the satellite dish hidden now from his horrified neighbors behind a stand of scale-ridden euonymus. Is he glued to the screen out there in Swarthmore at this minute? Will he show at the hospital Sunday? In the morning, when there are no American games and it is night in Japan? He hates to hear his mother excuse him—"Stu is very dedicated to his business."

And Mary Alice, the Slave of Fashion, seen more often in the *Inquirer*'s society column than on the fifth floor of Pennsylvania Hospital.

"Well. Fuck 'em," he says, tossing the remote control onto the sofa cushions.

"And fuck Molly LaBerge," he says, thinking that he will feel like shit in the morning at the Barclay Hotel if he is not able to sleep soon.

And what would it be like to be a duke for The Empire? If sex together was so good, does it follow that working together would be as good? There was nothing like that sex, he thinks. Not before. Not since. Maybe once or twice with men he hardly knew or didn't know at all. Sex for the adventure of it. The newness. The chemistry of flattery from men who wanted him over other possibilities; the chemistry of surprise at what he would find under their clothing and what he would feel when they touched him with his eyes shut. And none of them lasted for him. There was no conversation. Or there was too much. Or there was conversation and the sex began to pale the next time or the next. But with Billy it went on and on. Expecting to be bored, he was not. Expecting the next hot body who smiled at him to replace Billy's in his bed, Billy's became the only one he wanted there.

In weeks he'll be forty. Indisputably mature. Clerks have called him "sir" for years. Will it be "venerable sir" after June 26? Should he change careers after his birthday? Get a face-lift? Give himself an extravagant present? Get tested? Go down to Sixteenth and Pine instead of to lunch and let them siphon some blood?

He flushes at the thought of it. And going back. How could he go back? A door opens and his name is called by a man holding a clipboard, his brow ever so slightly furrowed over a smile rehearsed behind the door before it opened. The man beckons him through the door, into the tastefully, no, cheerfully furnished room to a seat on a sofa upholstered in a pretty print with a flourishing plant next to the sofa, maybe a tank of tropical fish, some lively, active species, and hopeful photographs on the walls of children playing, dancing in expectation of full lives. And some small talk as the counselor settles into his chair, no, stretches out in a relaxed way beside him on the sofa.

"Couldn't find a parking place to save my life this morning!" Whoops. "You're a florist, aren't you? All these funerals, you guys must be doing real well." Whoops. "Well . . . Anyway, Mr. Flowers, let's get down to brass tacks. I've got good news and I've got bad news. You're HIV positive. It's *in* you. You've *got* it. AIDS. So to say. As it were. In a manner of speaking. If you receive my drift.

"That's the bad news. The good news is you could live awhile." A gesture toward the dancing children. A wave at the darting tropical fish.

Standing: "Any questions?" A glance at the wristwatch. "Got to be going. A lot of anxious folks out there. Heh, heh. Perhaps you'd like to stay awhile and read brochures?

Got a bunch of good ones here on medication side effects. Take some with ya, if ya want. New one here from the Hemlock Society. Ya know who they are, dontcha? Well, they're not in the nursery business, heh, heh, see ya."

He turns on the lamp on the end table. He punches the Power button on the stereo remote control. The classical music station. Something he has heard before. Acceptable. He stretches out on the sofa, naked except for the T-shirt, and leans back. He crosses his legs. They are lean and muscled from running. His stomach is flat; more than flat, he notices. His ribs show through the muscle there and his wrists look smaller than they did, but they probably are not, he thinks. But maybe they are, and he thinks maybe he will get up and weigh himself but that is just paranoia, he thinks. The clock on the bookshelf reads 1:45. The middle of the night, when you hope you'll think differently when the sun is out.

The walking above him has stopped.

If he knew he had it, would he kill himself? If it were guaranteed? Not that he'd do it the way that woman at Max's building had. A jump from a twelfth-floor ladies' room and her legs had actually penetrated the step-out roof six floors below, actually went through the roof, left her standing there up to her thighs in tar paper and lathing strips. Did her feet shoot through some doctor's office ceiling? Some patient flat on her back with her legs in stirrups waiting alone for her pelvic, bored out of her fucking mind, waiting and counting ceiling tiles and suddenly feet fly through? Jesus.

He gets up. He goes to the refrigerator. He stands with the door open, looking inside. The cold air flows around his ankles.

Mom would kill herself, he thinks. If her mind went off without her. If she thought she had lost it. If books and music and theater escaped her. If conversation came and went before she caught it, she would kill herself. But she would choose something very neat. Something very clean.

She would do it by some elegant design, the Perfect Suicide, thinking ahead to who would find her and how, and how she'd make it as clean and as painless to others as possible. She'd spare all of them the gruesome details except for the making of arrangements and maybe not even that. She'd drive herself—no, take a cab—out to Kirk and Nice Incorporated at night, break into the embalming room through the garage, incurring minimal damage but leaving a generous check to cover repairs to doors and to locks. Choosing a vacant slab, she would go quietly into her good night on designer tranquilizers and fifteen-year-old scotch, having previously arranged with Federal Express to deliver papers detailing who she was, why she was there, and precisely what they were to do with their surprise guest.

He pulls off a stalk of celery and closes the refrigerator door. He returns to his sofa. He wipes a few pieces of grit from the stalk of celery with the tail of his T-shirt. He bites from the root end.

In the morning, when he is head-achey and sleep-hungry, Molly LaBerge will marry a dick-head. Fuck Molly LaBerge. No, let the dick-head.

He chomps off a piece of his celery stick.

His mother has cancer. He could have AIDS.

"Is no easy," he says. He chews.

VI.

Since the ritual murder of their next-door neighbors' sheepdog, Hal and Mary Alice have kept their garage spotlight burning all night. It shines through the trees into their bedroom. It makes strange, amorphous shadows on the walls. In the week since Orestes' body was found hanging upside down by one ankle from a low limb in the woods between their property and their neighbors', Mary Alice has not had a full night's sleep. Hal has no trouble sleeping. He lies at the edge of his side of the bed, his back to her. She lies on her back, her legs spread, the big toe and first toe of one of her feet clamped on Hal's Achilles' heel.

Mary Alice thinks about tomorrow, the day she gets laid. Should her schedule change because her mother is sick?

Getting laid once a week is not much, she thinks. She depends on that time. She needs the release. She needs the heat of it. It's enough. And what difference can it make to Mother? She goes to see her mother at the hospital. She's there as much as she can be. She can't be there all of the time. How could she do that? Bea will be there certainly. What difference will it make if she's not there one day?

How would it change anything? Mother might not even realize. Might not remember. Hadn't she said today that it was Friday? Tomorrow is Friday. Her day to get laid. Her day to get laid again in Baltimore, Maryland. One more

Friday left to get laid there, then we play in New York. Up and down the Eastern Seaboard. Where after New York? Not Boston. She couldn't do Boston with time to spare, since he insisted on the Cambridge Hyatt, which was miles from Logan and she couldn't just jump on the shuttle on a Friday. It was so packed coming back. Couldn't keep the girls waiting. Couldn't ask Hal, really. "Where will *you* be?"

"It's Friday, Hal. My day to get laid."

New York next week. Washington the next. Washington is easy. Philadelphia is the best. Baltimore is next best. Maybe the best. Taking the train, dressed in a chic business suit, looking for all the world like she worked for Chase Manhattan, catching the Bankers at 10:58 out of Philly, arriving in Baltimore at 12:09 to cab to lunch brought to his room with a panoramic view of the Inner Harbor, over which they fucked their brains out with the drapes pulled wide. A shower, then a cab to catch the Senator at 2:56, arriving Thirtieth Street Station at 4:13 in time to catch the 4:20 Paoli Local to pick up the car at the lot at the station to pick up the girls at their dance lessons with perfect makeup and every goddamned hair in place.

She'd call in the morning. If Mother was in bad shape, she wouldn't do it. She'd stay here. What difference will a week make? Or maybe she and Hank could screw each other Monday. Or late Tuesday morning. Before her cystic fibrosis meeting.

The tulip tree branches cast penumbral forms on her Post Modern Mauve by Sherwin-Williams walls.

All of the lovers of her married life were H's. Before Hank, Howie, and before Howie, Henry, who did not like to be called Hank. Hank is the best of the lot, but not as good as Hal was. Not nearly. She squeezes Hal's heel with her toes and feels his heartbeat there. It seems rapid. Did he take his beta-blocker after dinner or forget it again in his hurry to get to his briefcase? Will she wake in the daylight to find him cold beside her? She listens to his breathing and wishes she could sleep again. But if he goes into apnea and his breathing stops for twenty seconds, for fifty or longer? She has counted as high as seventy-seven while she waited, her own breath bated, panicky that his would not start up again.

This family is going to hell in a handbasket. Should she write Stu an anonymous letter? Buy some unbonded paper and envelopes at Woolworth's? Type it on an untraceable machine? "Dear Stuart. Dear Mr. Flowers: I know that you put gin in the morning orange juice your sister Mary Alice hand-squeezes for you at her beach house in Loveladies. I have witnessed your flush-faced, surreptitious trips to the bars in both her houses. I have found your litter of tiny empty airplane bottles in her trash."

Mail it when the train stops in Wilmington?

She'd do it face-to-face. Over lunch. At Le Bec Fin. Mary Alice (Mrs. Harold J.) Flemming, Socialite Do-Gooder, photographed recently at lunch with her brother, Stuart T. Flowers, Vice President of the investment firm Bitler and Morant, in a discussion of his secret drinking.

She'd tell Mother. She'd bring it up casually as they talked about the removal of her stitches or as Mother struggled to remember if this was Bea or Mary Alice or if this was Megan's mother or Enid's. She should wait until they were alone and she was focused. Goddamned drugs were making Mother nuts. Goddamned Max ran when he saw her coming. Goddamned breast cancer.

With her left hand, she rolls her left breast with her palm, then, with her fore and middle fingers, rolls with little circles, feeling a few square inches at a time the width of an apple peel until she reaches her nipple, the tip of which she takes between her forefinger and her thumb and squeezes, pinches. Her right hand slides up her thigh and across her stomach, lifting. She drags her middle fingertip through her cleavage, spreading the few beads of sweat that have suddenly formed there. She lubricates her fingertips with them and rolls her right nipple between the fingertips, and touching the left-hand fingertips in the sweat, too, she does the same with the left nipple, the sensitive one, the one that is slightly larger than the other, not that you would notice, she whispers, squeezing Hal's heel with her toes. He always went for the right one. Always. No matter which side of the bed she slept on. No matter who was driving. No matter if she bound it up with adhesive tape, she'd bet. Why that one? Did he nurse on the right? Was he right-eye dominant? Was his right brain larger than his left? His right ball? If she touched it, would he start in his sleep? Would his dick forget his raft of medications? Wake this once after years of disinterest, suddenly thick with desire?

The tyranny of sex.

Everything had a price. And Pete. Would he have to pay? Did he have boyfriends? One safe one that he saw all the time? She knew all of his girlfriends when he was a kid. She'd known none of the men in his life. Not even the Japanese one he went to Stanford for. Not even, really, Connie Payne's son. She'd been so stupid adding one and one and getting one when she and Hal had sat three rows behind the two of them at Friday Night Subscription. For eight months and fifteen concerts. How could she not have known, the way they looked in each other's direction sometimes when the playing was especially right? Connie had never let on. Never hinted. And we were what all along, Connie and I? Sisters-in-law? My brother her son's lover. What would that make us?

Did everyone know? Was she the only one who didn't know that her brother, Liz and Phil Flowers' son, was diddling Art and Connie Payne's boy and vice versa. Maybe they all knew and no one told her. If Pete did it with Bill, he did it with others and all of those others were doing it with still others.

So handsome. Who wouldn't want my brother Pete? My girlfriends wanted him, for God's sake.

The tyranny of sex.

A branch snaps in the garden. She gets up from the bed and stands at a window in her sheer nightgown, holding back the sheer curtains with both her hands. The garden is lighted. The heavy heads of the white peonies by the pool glow green from the underlit water. Things move only in the breeze. She sits on the wide sill, her arms around her knees. The night air balloons the long skirt of her nightie. It cools her thighs.

If Pete got sick, she didn't know what she would do. And what should she do about Stuart? And Mother? She'd changed her family's diets so that Hal would have no fat. There was no fat in the house. Not even in the freezer. No ice cream. No cheeses. She'd taught Inez to read labels. Inez would go back to France in the fall a proselytizer of good eating habits. No goose grease in her cooking. If she married, her husband would live to be ninety.

Would Hal see sixty? She didn't own a black dress. No widow's weeds in these closets stocked with every color of the rainbow. Buy a new dress, he's always saying. And jewelry. He hides small treasures in improbable places for her to find when he isn't there, or when he is. The price of no sex? She wouldn't marry again. How could she find another Hal? How long would she have him?

Hal begins to snore. He has rolled onto his back, the forbidden position. Thank God he snores. Before the snoring catches and the silence and the counting begin she is in the bed, pushing him back onto his side. "Hal, roll over. Move, Hal, honey. Move."

She takes his heel again between her toes. How long would she have him?

She counts his heartbeats in the dark.

VII.

"God, I haven't eaten here since I was a teenager," Bea says, joining Pete for lunch. She lays her sweater and purse on the empty seat next to her and settles heavily into a caned armchair.

"The Barclay. What a clever idea, Peter."

"Well, not so clever as convenient," he says. "I did the wedding reception you saw all those yuppies in the lobby going to. I thought I'd hang around in case there's a problem."

A waiter appears at Bea's side.

"*Mademoiselle?* Something from the bar to begin?" he asks her.

"André, this is my sister Bea," Pete says. "André is a friend of mine and a very fine waiter."

André bows to Bea. "*Mon plaisir,*" he says.

"Hello, André. A Bloody Mary," she says. "Make that a double. Hot and lemony."

André bows again and moves a step behind her. He raises one eyebrow and purses his lips toward Pete.

"Handsome man," Bea says, clasping the tip of the filter of a long, designer cigarette with her fingernails. "He looks familiar."

"He's a neighbor of yours. Eighth and Christian."

"French?"

"Here in the restaurant. Outside, he's South Philly Italian."

"How do you know him?" She ignites her black enamel lighter and moves the flame slowly to the end of her cigarette. Her eyes never leave his, an affectation she learned from her college friends. She inhales deeply.

"We had a short . . . that's not the right word. We had a brief, torrid affair."

"I'd expect torrid. What made it brief?"

"He wanted to settle down."

"And you didn't?"

"It was too fast," Pete says. "A couple of weeks and he was talking about moving in together."

"Maybe you should've given that one a little more time and thought. Reminds me of Antny. I love big shoulders. But Antny does not have big shoulders."

"You're not complaining."

"I'm not complaining." She sits very straight in her chair. She looks around the room, quiet on a Saturday for lunch. She pats her tightly pulled-back hair.

"Antny brought me here for dinner on our first date," she says. "I remember his face when he got the check. It went white. He tried to look so calm. He called the waiter over and ordered after-dinner drinks. Then he said he was going to the men's room. About a half hour later, his cousin Frankie walked into the dining room all dressed up in a suit. The only other time I ever saw Frankie in a suit was when his father died. His hair was still wet. Frankie said he was in the neighborhood. He hugged Antny, and I saw his fist dart into Antny's jacket pocket. Then he said he had to hurry off to meet his date. I've always liked him for that. Last night at the hospital Mother called me Mary Alice."

"And what did you say?"

"First I thought it was just a slip of the tongue. You know how she always did that when we were kids. Called us everyone but who we were. I just ignored it. Then she asked me if Hal was parking the car and I said, 'You mean Antny,' and she said, real pissy, 'I mean Hal.' And I said, 'Antny brought me, Mother,' and she looked at me real surprised, and then she looked confused and her chin started quivering. Oh, Pete, she never cries. I felt so bad."

He nods. He twirls the stem of his wineglass between his fingertips.

"I've talked to Max twice," he says. "I went to his office and I insisted on seeing him for a few minutes. He was very evasive. He said Mom told him to keep quiet. All I could get out of him is that she's on strong medications, and that the brain lesions are going to cause 'some problems,' as he put it."

Bea flushes. One hand goes to her throat, the other to her face. Her thin wedding band shines in a valley of her finger flesh.

Will she have to have that ring cut off someday? Pete wonders.

"What are you talking about, 'brain lesions'? Mother had a mastectomy."

"Hasn't Dad talked with you?"

"Not about *brain* lesions, for God's sake!" she says.

André serves her drink. He winks at Pete as he leaves. Bea ignores the drink.

"She told us at dinner. Dad said he was going to call you," Pete says.

"Daddy never calls me. What are you talking about, brain lesions, Peter?"

He sighs.

"The cancer in her breast has spread to her brain."

"That's not possible," she says. "I don't believe it."

"It's true, Bea. Max said so."

She takes several swallows from her Bloody Mary. She chokes and touches her napkin to her lips.

"How could that happen so fast?"

"She waited too long, Bea. She said that at dinner."

"What are they doing?"

"They're treating her with a steroid."

"Steroids are dangerous, Pete. They outlawed them at the Olympics."

"This kind can shrink tumors."

"Oh, now they're talking tumors. A minute ago it was lesions," she says. She raps the tips of her long fake nails on the tablecloth. Her eyes fill with tears. "Is Mother going to die, Peter?"

"I don't know what's going on."

"Are you keeping something from me? This whole goddamn family keeps things from me," she says angrily.

"Bea."

"No, it's true," she says tearfully, looking around. "You all treat me as if I'm still eight. I'm a grown-up woman with two children, for God's sake."

She blots the skin under her eyes with her napkin. She examines the napkin for makeup stains. She lights another cigarette.

Pete shifts in his chair. He always protected her when they were children, slipped treats to her when she was punished, defended her rebellious choices—to go to a Jewish summer camp where she would know no one instead of St. Ignatius of Loyola of Stroudsberg, where they all went and where she knew everyone. He kept his arm around her bony shoulders during the confused days of Cliffie's dreadful death, which hung in the big house like sound in a cave. He wants now to hug her again. He doesn't move.

"Bea, I don't know much more than you do," he says. "It's all the same, lesions and tumors. I guess lesions sounds better, is all. They're why she called you Mary Alice. They're making her confused sometimes."

André places menus on their service plates and retreats.

"Can't they give her something?" she pleads, as if he were a doctor. "You know, it's a goddamned conspiracy!" she declares, hoisting her tall, frosted glass and drinking half of it.

"Yesterday after Mom called me Mary Alice, I cornered that nurse, Mrs. Martin? The one with orange hair? I got her out in the alcove by the nurses' station and I asked her point-blank why Mom was acting funny. I asked her if they were giving her tranquilizers or something. You know what she said to me? She said, 'Mrs. Flowers, I'm your mother's nurse, not her doctor.' I said, It's Ferraro, not Flowers, and there's never a doctor around I could ask, so what's going on? 'You'll have to ask Doctor,' she said, and she stepped around me and she walked *away* from me! Aren't these people there to *help* you? I mean, where does she get off walking *away* from me!"

"It's Mom, Bea. She's told everyone to keep quiet."

"Why should she do that? What's the point in making everyone crazy?"

"She doesn't want to make us worry."

"Oh, Jesus," Bea says. She drains her drink and looks around for André. "This isn't *worrying*? I haven't slept all week thinking about her losing her breast. Now it's brain lesions? Excuse me. Tumors. I'd rather worry about it all at once, thank you very much. I'm having another drink," she says, holding her empty glass up to André across the room and making a circular motion in the air with her forefinger. "So are you. Now tell me, is there something else Little Sister should be worrying about? Maybe Mom's having a leg amputated, or something?"

"No, Bea."

"All right then. Explain to me what these tumors mean."

"What they apparently mean is that Mom is not going to behave like we're used to sometimes. Dad told me that she lost her car for a week last month, for example."

"Peter. My mother would not lose a car. She's the most precise person I ever met. That's ridiculous."

"Well, it happened. She went shopping and she left it in a parking garage and forgot about it. For a week. Last Saturday night at the dinner table, she turned to me and said that I had been in her bedroom that morning—carrying a sign. Last night she left a message on my machine telling me a nurse told her I should check my tires. Obviously, something is going on, Bea. Here comes André with the drinks. You ready to order?"

"I'm not hungry," she says.

André places their drinks. He steps back, folds his hands, and says with a slight French accent, "In addition to the menu listings, the chef has prepared two entrée offerings: salmon timbales with a light lemon sauce and angel hair pasta with three caviars. Quite pretty and delicious."

He makes a move to leave and Bea waves her cigarette at him. The ash breaks off and falls beside her chair.

"I'll have that," she says. "And a small salad with lemon only."

"The timbales?"

"The pasta."

"The house dressing is really nice, Bea," Pete says.

She sighs. "OK."

"Do you have soft-shells?" Pete asks.

"It's May," André remarks, with a small smile.

"And the house salad," says Pete. André bows again. His sleeve brushes Pete's shoulder as he leaves.

"How often do you eat out, Peter?"

"More than I eat in. Four, five times a week."

"How can you stay thin on restaurant food? It's disgusting. I gain weight reading recipes in women's magazines."

"That doesn't burn many calories."

She adjusts the collar of her blouse.

"Hot in here," she says. "Why didn't someone tell me these things? Does Mary Alice know about this? Does Stu?"

"I don't know. I haven't talked with them."

"I bet they do. It would be just like them not to tell me." She shakes her cigarette at him. "Her and her goddamned volunteer work," she mutters, stabbing out the cigarette and reaching for her lighter. "And Stu. Always chasing his balls around. Did you ever try to spend an hour alone with him? You have to buy a season ticket to the Padres."

"That's San Diego."

"Oh, who gives a shit?" she says, blowing smoke at him. "Did I tell you I called Alexa last week? Well, I did. I broke down. Mom said I was being 'belligerent.' She's *my* sister-in-law. *I* should be the one to reach out. She said I never really made Alexa feel welcome. No," Bea says, holding up her palm to Pete. "I admit it. I have no problem with that. Eleanor Roosevelt I am not. Anyway, I thought about it for a day. I said to Antny, 'Is it me?' And he said she's a bitch, but I sure wasn't helping matters any. So I decided I'd call her. I can't believe I didn't tell you this. I really bit the bullet. You know those Queen Anne dining chairs they have? Well, it just makes her nuts that she's missing one side chair. Like nine isn't enough? She's even been to New York, looking. Well, I found one. Actually, *I* didn't, exactly, my friend Paolo the decorator did and it was in his basement and I now owe my firstborn to MasterCard for it. You know, you might like him. Well, no, you wouldn't. You like 'polished.' Paolo is not polished. You know what he calls his shop? The House of Elegance, and let me tell you, there's some pretty scary shit in there. Anyway, the chair is elegant and Antny agreed we should buy it. We were going to give it to them for their fifteenth anniversary in August, but I thought to myself, now here's an icebreaker if there ever was one. I figured I'd give it to them early and invite Alexa over for lunch and surprise her with it. So I called her. And she said, 'Oh, Bea. Hello. I'm on a call on the other line. Can I get back to you?' And I said, 'Of course, Alexa,' as sweet as honey. Pete, if I ever get Call Waiting, will you please blast me in the forehead with a twelve-gauge? Well, I waited for her to call back. Then I did the breakfast dishes. And a load of towels, dried and folded. And I invoiced all of Antny's jobs up to the day before so I could get them in the door before the mailman came. Then I called the harpy back. 'Sorry, Bea,' she says. 'I got busy.' Sure. Putting on your weekly application of Treacherous Towhead, I'm thinking.

" 'Alexa,' I said. 'If you're free Thursday for lunch, I'd love to have you over. Just the two of us.' And she didn't miss a beat. She said, 'Oh, Bea, I would just love to, but Megan has an orthodontist appointment at one on Thursday. You are so sweet to ask.' Well, I already knew her Megan called my Joanie the day before, all excited because she'd just been to the orthodontist and she doesn't *need* braces, but I didn't miss a beat either and I said, 'No problem, Alexa. I'm free Friday.' And that lying little powder-faced snot paused just this tiny fraction and said, 'Oh, Bea, I'm having lunch with Mother Friday,' and I had to bite my tongue to keep from saying, 'Oh? In *Ca*nada?' because I happen to know from Mom that Alexa's parents are in Montreal for two weeks visiting Alexa's uncle. But I plowed right on and I said, '*Any* day next week will be just fine, Alexa,' and she said, 'Oh, darn, Bea, the UPS man is coming! I'll have to get back to you.' Pete, either that UPS man was coming between her legs, or he was rappeling up the cliff behind their house, because there is not one telephone within sight of a front window in the entire place. So I said, 'Fine, Alexa. Give me a buzz and we'll do lunch,' and I drove right over to Paolo's House of Elegance and picked up *my* chair. And if the hateful sow ever does show for lunch, I'll let her sit her jealous ass on it! They are getting a magazine subscription for their anniversary. To *Self*."

André places their salads and wishes them bon appétit.

"To siblings," Bea says, raising her glass.

"And to their spouses," Pete says, touching hers.

"Well," Bea says, eyeing her food, "I've always liked old Hal."

She stabs a piece of artichoke heart. "They don't have sex, you know."

"Who doesn't?"

"Hal and Mary Alice."

"How do you know that?" Pete asks, having been told by Mary Alice.

"Mary Alice told me when we went to the shore with them last summer." She pops the artichoke piece into her mouth. "This dressing *is* heaven. Hal can't get it up. His blood pressure medicine. He has to take a couple of things.

It's been that way for years, apparently. If Antny couldn't get it up, I think I'd wither away. Not that some withering would hurt," she says, smacking her side. "I never had sex with anyone but Antny. Did I ever tell you that?"

"No."

"Antny is huge," she says, forcing a large piece of ruby lettuce into her mouth.

"You've alluded to that. How do you know if you've never had anyone for comparison?"

"The girls," she says, chewing and positioning the tines of her fork over a boiled egg quarter. "What do you think we talk about when we get together? Arts and crafts? Uh-uh. My friend Rita Grasso? She said her Al was bigger than my Antny. One thing led to another and we had a contest. You know me. I love a challenge.

"Are you going to eat those eggs?"

"No, Bea."

"Why?"

"I never eat eggs."

"You don't like eggs?"

"I love eggs."

"Saying 'no' to cholesterol?"

"Yes."

"You know," she says, reaching over to his plate with her fork, "they have low-cholesterol eggs now." She snatches up one of his egg slices. Part of the yolk detaches and begins to fall. Her left hand darts out. She catches it in her palm and tosses it into her mouth, adding the white on the fork in her other hand.

"I know how to make this. It's dry mustard, not prepared, and a tiny bit of balsamic vinegar. And rice vinegar. Makes it a little sweet."

She takes Pete's other egg, pushing it around in his dressing first. She cups her free hand under it as she brings it across the table. The egg disappears.

"And white pepper."

"You were telling me about a contest with Rita Grasso?"

"You devil," she says. "We measured 'em. That's all I'm saying."

"You're a heartless person."

"We'll have to live with that."

She breaks off several chunks of bread and lays them on her bread plate.

"Are you going to eat that olive?"

"Bea, take the plate," he says, passing it over. "I'm finished."

"Thanks. You know how compulsive Stu is about germs? Ever notice how when we have family meals he always manages to get at the bread before anyone else? That's because he thinks other people leave germs on it. If he can't get at the bread first, Alexa does and passes it right to him, even if someone else is next."

"Who won?"

Bea rubs the pad of her thumb over the tips of her acrylic fingernails. "Rita and I decided not to tell."

"Bea, after that buildup, you're not going to tell me how it turned out?"

"Pete, it wouldn't be fair to Rita."

"Bea, I'm not one of the neighborhood girls. Who would I tell?"

"That's not the point. Antny's your brother-in-law. Are you going to tell me how big you are so I can tell him?"

"Anthony doesn't give a shit how big I am."

"And I'm to understand that you care how big *he* is?"

"Of course! I'm interested in things like that."

She extracts another long, skinny cigarette from the lavender box beside her bread plate and taps its filter on the crystal of her wristwatch.

"What are you, Peter? Some sort of size queen?"

"No. But I've been impressed."

"My lips are sealed," she says, flicking her shiny black lighter.

André crosses the dining room carrying their two lunches in one hand.

He replaces the two salad plates with Bea's pasta dish. She stubs out her cigarette.

"Enjoy, please," he tells her.

"Crabs," he says to Pete, raising an eyebrow as he sets the plate. He glides to another table.

Bea twirls pasta strands on her fork and rubs them in the gold caviar mounded at one side of her dish. She pulls it off the fork and chews slowly, breaking some of the eggs with her front teeth.

"God," she says. "It's perfect. It's a ten."

Expertly, she rolls more angel hair on the fork and dips it into the black caviar.

"Oh," she almost moans.

"It must be good."

She dips her fork into the red caviar. "How are the soft-shells?"

"Fine."

She mooshes a bit of black and yellow caviar together and pushes some pasta in it. "I'm going to switch to wine," she says. "Do you want another wine?"

"No."

"Maybe I won't. Yes, I will. I'm walking, anyway."

She catches André's eye. She points at Pete's wineglass and holds up one finger.

She mixes a forkful of all three caviars together. She makes a large ball of pasta and swirls it in the caviars.

"Do you trust Max, Pete?"

"I think so. He's just being protective of Mom, is all. I hear he's good."

She puts her lips around caviar-stained pasta. She chews. She holds up her forefinger. She chews more and swallows.

"You know who is really beginning to piss me off?"

"In addition to Stu, Alexa, and Mary Alice?"

"Yes. Daddy. He just goes over to the hospital when it's convenient for him."

"So do I. We have businesses to run," he says, again feeling oddly protective of his father.

" 'Businesses to run,' " she says, nodding her head. She stabs her fork into the diminishing mound of pasta on her plate. "You think it's easy for me?" she asks. She does not bother to dip her strands into the small piles of red and black caviar remaining; she takes a forkful, bites it off, and tucks it into her right cheek. "In addition to picking up after two increasingly sloppy little girls . . . Hey," she says, holding up the palm of her hand and chewing, "*I* raised them. *I* taught them. Or I didn't teach them. They're *my* problem." She pauses to chew in earnest and swallows. "And *I'll* handle them. But unlike the rest of you, *I* don't have a maid or a cleaning lady. *I'm* the one picking it up and washing it and folding it and answering the goddamn phone for Antny's business and depositing checks and typing up invoices and calling around for replacements on a job when Paul or Tommy or Jed or Mickey played too much the night before and have hangovers or call in sick. Do *I* have time for the flu? Not on your fucking life. I have two businesses, and *I* have time to get to the hospital twice a day."

"Bea."

She holds up her hand again. "Daddy shows up when he feels like it, Mary Alice breezes in *before* her society luncheons or dinners so she always has the perfect reason why she has to fly off again. 'Oh,' Mary Alice says, looking at her smart little Piaget watch as if she didn't know what time it was, 'it's six o'clock and I'm supposed to meet Hal at the Scotts' in fifteen minutes!' and it's 'Goodbye, Mother dear, watch my makeup' and she's out that door so fast you get taffeta abrasions on your calves if you're close enough." She pauses. "Stuart's got it all figured out. He sends Alexa in to complain to Mom about how his firm is too dependent on him, meanwhile he's got plane reservations to Chicago *and* Denver so he can go to the away games just in case the Flyers make the play-offs. How do I know this? His daughter, the freckled Mata Hari Flowers, tells *all* at my kitchen table."

Pete shifts in his chair, thinking to interrupt, but she is saying nothing that he can imagine to be untrue, and if it were untrue and he called her on it, she would freeze him out at their table with small talk and for an uncomfortable period of days, or a week, find reasons not to speak to him. Her perfect skin is thin. The family's rules of behavior are frozen for her at some time in the sixties, when their being together was the main priority, when they could all still fall together in giggling piles on the grassy lot next to the Pine Street house, Cliffie always on the bottom, clutching the ball to his chest.

He thinks of their brother Cliffie, the middle child, who always found a place in the middle of any table, who mediated the disputes of their games and other family misunderstandings, making it look as if he had caused the problem that caused the problem. Bea begins to rail again about their father's insensitivity to their mother in a hospital bed.

Sad suddenly, Pete sighs. He remembers so clearly standing twenty-how-many years ago in the living room of the Pine Street house alone before the gunmetal-blue casket that held his brother Cliffie. In one of the suits he eschewed, Cliffie lay with too much color in his cheeks for January. Their mother, in an act that may have caused her more pain than any other in her lifetime, had come down in the night to erase the comb lines from his hair with her brush. Draped about his still hands, fingernails filed for the first time in memory, was a black-beaded rosary. Pete watched Cliffie's hands and the blue-suited sleeves of his arms for some minutes, watched the center of his chest and the green striped tie and the very white oxford-cloth shirt, waiting for Cliffie's chest to go up and down, even a little bit, waiting for the so still hands to move.

"Hey!" Bea says. "Are you listening to me?"

"I was thinking about Cliffie."

"Cliffie'd be there for Mom."

"Bea, everyone's there for Mom. They just aren't there necessarily when you want them to be."

"If I thought they were there, I wouldn't be complaining, would I?"

She soaks the sauce and caviar remaining on her plate with a bread piece and pops it, delicately, into her mouth. "And I'm going to tell every one of them what I think," she says, chewing. "And I'm going to talk to Mom, too. How can we make decisions if we can't have any information?"

"I think Mom thinks these are her decisions."

"To hear you talk, she's not capable of making decisions. Losing cars. People in her bedroom with signs. God, I'm stuffed," she says, checking out his plate. "Don't you eat the legs? Those are soft-shells. You can eat the legs."

"I don't like the way they look," he says, pushing with his fork at the neat pile of them he has made at the side of his plate.

"What did it say?" she says.

"What?"

"The sign you were carrying in Mom's room."

"It said, 'TELL PETE.'"

" 'Tell Pete' what?"

"I don't know. I didn't write it. She invented it."

"Maybe about her brain tumors."

"I don't think so. She said that she was at her mirror and that she began to turn around and I stopped her with my hand on her shoulder. She said she felt it."

"Do you have any recollection of that?"

"Of course not, Bea. I haven't been in her room since we were kids."

"No, like in a dream. I believe in things like that. You know, out-of-body experiences? Antny's mother says it happens to her all the time. She says she can make it happen."

"Anthony's mother is certifiable, Bea. You're always saying that. At your wedding rehearsal? For the wedding you never went to?"

"God, you pay and pay," she says.

"She kept following me around. Said we knew each other

in a past life. We lived in Ecuador. We were Indians."

"She must have been the chief. Did you ever meet the man she said was missing a bone and you'd spend the rest of your life with?"

"Honey, none of my men were missing any of their bones, I can attest to that. What I want to know is how did she know I'm a faggot? Did you tell her?"

"Certainly not!" Bea exclaims. She reaches for another cigarette. "She does ask me how you are all the time. Wants to know how you're feeling. She never asks how anyone else is feeling. You feeling OK, Pete?"

"Sure," he says, resisting an impulse to press the lymph nodes in his armpits.

"You don't look exactly right. Tired, maybe."

"I haven't been sleeping much," he says, wondering suddenly if he has not been sleeping much. "I have a lot of jobs."

"You don't have The Spark."

"The spark."

"You know. Mom was always saying you and Cliffie had it and the rest of us were just normal, God forbid. Some word. Sounded like a fish."

" 'Prana,' " he says.

"Right. 'My little Hindus,' she called you two. I think you've lost some of your prana."

"What do you mean?" he asks. "I'm the same as I always am."

"And you've lost some weight."

"Have I?" he asks, his heart accelerating.

"Maybe a little. And you're quieter. You seem distracted. Even Mary Alice mentioned it after you left Saturday night."

"Well, I'm fine," he says, annoyed.

"I think you should get your prana checked."

"My prana is just fine, thank you very much."

"It wouldn't hurt to have a physical. When did you have a physical last?"

"Bea, I'm really OK," he says, folding his napkin.

"When?"

"Two years ago."

"I bet you don't even have a doctor. Who is your doctor?"

"Bea, I run every other day. I'm in better shape than most of the people I know."

"Doctor who?"

"All right, I don't have one. Mine moved away."

"When, precious?"

He smiles. "In 1986."

"What do you do if you get the flu?"

"I don't get the flu. I don't even get colds."

"Well," she says, tapping her cigarette with her forefinger and missing the ashtray. "*I* shouldn't be the one to lecture you about the importance of taking care of yourself. We've never talked about AIDS, Pete, and I don't mean to pry, but is that something you need to be concerned about?"

"Everybody's concerned about it."

"Including your family. Mary Alice and I were wondering about it."

"You mean, you had a discussion?"

"Well, not a discussion, exactly," she says. She French-inhales a round cloud of smoke and holds it in while she examines the lipstick stain on her cigarette filter. "We were talking on the phone. She had been talking with Stu, actually, and he was asking her if you had been tested." A last draft of gray smoke snakes out between her teeth. "Have you?"

"No," he says.

"Do you want to?"

"I don't know."

"I don't know if *I'd* want to," Bea says.

He says nothing. He folds and refolds his napkin.

"Well," Bea says, retreating. "What are we going to do about Mom?"

"I say we shoot her."

"Very funny."

"What can we do except what we're doing?"

"On the other hand, I might want to," Bea says.

"Shoot her?"

"Get tested. What about you?"

"Bea, I've never liked muddy water. But this is different. When the test first came out, I thought about going for it. I thought it made sense to go and get it done. Nobody would ever know. My friends, you guys, my insurance company. But I put it off, first because it took months to get an appointment, and then because I was busy, and then because I figured what would it change anyway? And then because I guess I didn't want to know, and now most of the time I *don't* want to know. You know?"

"Sure. But if you've been thinking that much about it, you must be worried."

"Some," he says, deciding not to tell her that some of the men he had sex with are dead. He feels a little headache coming on.

"Maybe you should do it."

"I'll give it some more thought."

"If you think about it, you won't do it. How about if we go together? I'll get tested, too."

"Bea, that's very sweet of you, but what's the point except to get me in there? You don't have anything to worry about."

"Maybe Antny's been fooling around," she says, arching one eyebrow.

"How could he? You watch him like a tree snake at a bird nest."

"I don't go on his jobs with him," she says, stubbing out her cigarette.

"I don't think Anthony would fool around."

"I think he would. I think he did, but I can't prove it."

"When?"

"Two years ago. Some of his rubbers were missing."

"How do you know that? Do you run inventory?"

"Sure. I'm the one who buys them."

"I thought you had your tubes tied."

"I was going to, but Antny didn't want me to at the last minute. In case we decide to try for a boy sometime. Five of them were missing. It was when I had that inner ear thing and I had to spend two weeks in a chair or fall over? Well, trust me. We had no sex in that recliner, but when I got over it, five of Antny's Trojans were gone. Foil and all."

"Did you say anything?"

"Of course. He said how could they be missing? That I must have made a mistake. That I didn't know which end was up while I was sick, anyway. I checked the job schedule. In the middle of when I was sick, he worked on a house on Seventeenth Street. Alone. The house of a certain Pat A. Meineke, who turns out to be Patricia Anne Meineke, who turns out to have grapefruit tits and legs like a Rockette and I know because—small world—she lives directly across the street from Winnifred Sheldon, Barbie's piano teacher, in front of whose house I wait in my car for Barbie every fucking Wednesday afternoon of life unless I am sick in a reclining chair with labyrinthitis. I called her once. I couldn't stand it."

"And you said?"

"I said I was Beatrice from the office of Ferraro Plumbing and I was calling to see if the work done on her pipes was satisfactory. She said it was 'perfect. Just perfect.' In fact, she had another little problem in the third-floor bathroom that 'Tony' could work on whenever he had time. I said unfortunately 'Tony' quit and moved to Utah but I'd send Mickey whenever she was going to be around and she said it could wait."

"Maybe . . ."

"Maybe nothing. He fucked her. Five times. And for months all I could think about was Patricia Anne Meineke's legs wrapped around my Antny. I was a crazed woman. But I was very proud of myself. I didn't wail and beat my breasts. I didn't punish him in a thousand tiny ways. I went out and bought every How-To sex book I could find in paperback and I learned some stuff I haven't even got to yet."

"Wasn't he suspicious about where you got all these new tricks?"

"If he was, he couldn't afford to show it. And it worked. Now he calls me from his jobs once a week or so and comes home for lunch. We don't eat. And I'm buying a lot more rubbers than I used to."

She looks at her watch.

"You coming to the hospital?" she asks.

"No. Later. I have to break down the room when they're done."

"They'll be here for hours."

"This is a megabucks wedding. I want to stick around in case something goes haywire."

"Pete, don't you think you should be there when Mom leaves?"

"When Mom leaves what?"

"The hospital, dummy. When she goes home."

"What are you talking about, Bea? She just had her operation Tuesday. She's in for a while."

"Not according to her. She called me this morning and said she's getting out at two."

"Why didn't you tell me?" he says, irritated.

"Well, I assumed you knew."

"Hell, no, I didn't know. Who's letting her out? She's in no shape to go home."

"Look. All I know is that she says she's going home. Could you have that pretty man bring our check so I can get out of here?"

"It's on me. I'm calling Max," he says. "There's something not right here. I want to know how this happened."

"I'm paying," Bea says, reaching for her purse. "I asked you out."

"It's a business expense. I have to be here anyway. No," he says when she opens her mouth to object. "You go ahead. I'll see what I can find out from Max."

"He's probably golfing. Think about that test. OK?"

» » »

From his pay phone across the hall, Pete can see into the room of Molly LaBerge's wedding reception. About half the guests mill about with drinks and magenta napkins. The rest are seated at the thirty tables beneath the suspended spheres of stock blossoms and raspberry ribbons undulating gently in the air-conditioning.

"Not bad, Flowers," he says.

"Still paging Dr. Frommeyer," the bored voice at the hospital tells him. A few seconds later:

"Dr. Frommeyer."

"Max?"

"This is Dr. Frommeyer."

"Max, this is Pete Flowers."

"Yes," Max says and inhales.

"My sister tells me that Mom is being released from the hospital this afternoon."

"Yes."

"Well, I'd like to know why. She just had major surgery."

"Your mother wants to leave."

"Max. Everybody in the hospital wants to leave. You told me she has two brain tumors."

"Her lesions do not require that she be hospitalized."

"I should think that a mastectomy would. She told me she would be in for a few days."

"Your mother is healing quickly."

"When I was with her yesterday, she barely spoke. She slept most of the time."

"That's expected."

"What about the seizures?"

"She had one seizure and is on Dilantin and that ought to prevent subsequent events. Yes, I'll be right there. Now, is there anything else, Peter?" he says with some sarcasm.

"Yes, there's something else. I want to know why you're releasing my mother prematurely."

"I am *not* releasing your mother prematurely. She is leaving AMA."

"What is AMA?"

" 'Against medical advice.' "

"And you're letting her?"

There is a brief, frosty pause. "I shouldn't have to remind you that your mother does exactly as she pleases. She is signing herself out. Goodbye, Peter." The line goes dead.

Furious at Max, he slams the handset into the pay-phone cradle.

"Goddammit and fuck," he says.

"Ah, Pete," says a woman's voice behind him. "Pete, Pete, Pete."

He recognizes the phlegmy voice of Rachel LaBerge. She teeters toward him across the thickly carpeted hallway, her pointy-toed, spike-heeled pink shoes sinking deep; the wide frothy ruffles of her pink mother-of-the-bride cocktail dress flounce with each calculated step. She holds a champagne glass before her like a scabbard.

"The flowers are spectacular!" she rumbles. "Come in. Come in. Join us. Everyone is talking about the flowers. It's a coup. A coup!"

"Well, thank you, Mrs. LaBerge. I was just . . ."

She takes his arm in hers and steers him toward the doorway of the dining room.

"It's Rachel, dear," she growls close to his ear. "Call me Rachel." She leans heavily on him as she negotiates the carpet, the wineglass a beacon extended now before him. "I have to confess," she says, her voice roupy near his jawbone, "when you first suggested balls of white flowers in the air, it sounded like a prom to me, but this . . ." she says, jerking her glass above her in the doorway without losing a drop, "is spectacular!" She pulls him closer. "Do you know what I want to do with them?" she croaks conspiratorially in his ear. "I want to take them all home and put them in my bathtub! Ha!"

VIII.

Carmen leads him down the central hall of the Pine Street house.

"Just look at this," she mutters, waving her hand at a flower arrangement on a side table. "They're all over the place. I have only seen so many flowers in this house once." The backs of her hands wiggle over her head. "And I told your father this morning," she says in a lower voice, black Dacron slapping at her thighs, "I told him there better not be another funeral in this house in *my* lifetime. And her doing everything she can to make sure there is one, coming home not even four days after major surgery. They pulled three sutures out just hauling her upstairs. And wait until you see your sister Bea's bedroom. I had men in here all morning banging into the wallpaper with hospital bed parts and carts and oxygen tanks and I don't know what else and I told your mother I don't care what she says, you can't turn a house into a hospital. Don't look in there," she says, pulling the double dining room doors closed. "I haven't even had time to clear your father's breakfast dishes. Strangers walking around opening doors they've got no business at. I've never seen anything like it." She holds the kitchen door open for him and waves him in.

"You sit down there a minute and I'll open you some wine."

Carmen clacks across the tiles toward her vast refrigerator.

"There's nothing opened you'd put your tongue to, just that sweet German stuff your father drinks. And where is he? Leaves me with the four o'clock nurse, Mrs. Take-Over-the-House up there, calling for tea every five minutes. Any more starch in those whites of hers and she'd damage the furniture. 'Whatever you want,' your father says to her as he flies out the door, 'just tell Carmen.' Well, she's taken him at his word."

She brings a chilled wine bottle, a corkscrew, and two glasses to the wooden work table.

"You're having wine, Carmen?"

She sits across from him at the scarred table and begins to work on the cork.

"I haven't sat down since I got up."

Her knuckles are deeply wrinkled. The skin on the backs of her hands is thin and crepey. It slides across her tendons as she turns the corkscrew. She has penciled-in hairs where her eyebrows were. Her forehead is furrowed with diagonal lines. The roots of her brown hair are gray.

She pours the wine, takes the first corky dollop for herself. She raises her glass.

"Skoal, Pete," she says.

"Skoal."

He has not sat with her at this table since he moved out of the house. When he was a child, she would sit him down and put his occasionally bored hands to work on routine kitchen chores. He still finds soothing the snapping and stringing of green beans. When his parents went on trips, Carmen prepared favorite foods Phil and Liz would not eat, hot Texas chili, shepherd's pie without the peas, greasy short ribs with French fried potato rounds. She let the children vote on these meals and presented them to their invited friends with paper plates and napkins and great flourish at this table in the kitchen. She sat at the head of the table and regaled them with stories of growing up in faraway, exotic The Bronx, a place that he still has not seen except from the tops of very tall buildings. Though she would share delicious details of her own childhood and sometimes of her teenage years, her private life in the present hardly existed for them beyond the walls of this house.

Carmen holds her wineglass in one hand. She traces cleaver marks in the table with the forefinger of the other.

They speak simultaneously.

"How's business?" she says.

"This must be hard . . ." he begins.

"Go ahead," she says.

"I'm sorry. No, you."

"How's business?" she asks again, flushing a little.

"Good. A lot of work. A big wedding today at Saint Mark's and the Barclay. Megaflowers."

They trace gouges for a moment.

She looks up at him and takes a breath.

"I've been in this house for forty-six years," she says. "In the beginning, I was going to help your mother with Mary Alice and the house until your father got out of the service, then I was going to get training so I could find a real job, back in New York. But then Stu came along, and Cliffie came along, and every time I'd get my mind set to leave there'd be another baby on the way and before any of us knew it, there were five of you and I felt pretty comfortable here. Also, I met a friend here in Philadelphia. I forgot about New York."

She drops her eyes. She picks at the rough edges of a deep nick in the wood.

"I thought I would marry my friend. I thought if he asked me I would do it and there'd be time for your mother to find someone else to run the house if she wanted to, then I'd get married and run a house of my own. But gradually that didn't happen, and when it was clear to me that it wasn't going to happen, I had a hard time about it and I asked your mother for a month's leave. She gave me the leave and a round-trip plane ticket to anywhere in the country. And when I came back from being away, when I walked into the house with my bags, it was like coming back to my own home. Your mother cried, your father even hugged me, and you kids hung on to me so I couldn't get my coat off for half an hour."

"I don't remember that."

"You were four, maybe. Later, while I was putting my things away, I knew I was here for good. And I wanted to be. For the first time. That hasn't changed in thirty-six years."

She looks at the ceiling above her. She waves at it. She looks down at the hole she is working.

"Your mother is angry at me. I don't know why. Maybe it's because she's sick and I'm not. I have to think it's her being sick, because I haven't done anything. It's her brain tumor talking. I don't know," she says, nervous now, rubbing the pads of her fingertips against the grain of the tabletop. "I was going to keep it to myself. Then I was going to talk to your father and I decided to keep it to myself, but then I decided I would tell you because they all do and you keep things to yourself and I have to talk to someone about it because there's nowhere to put it.

"It's no secret to anyone in this family that she hasn't been acting like herself," she says, rubbing harder on the wood. "I've kept my peace about a lot of things she's been doing and saying except to tell your father if she does something too strange. And at first it was just little things around the house. She started getting up in the night to eat. She'd leave ice-cream cartons out melting on the counter, or I'd find half-eaten sandwiches pushed in the cupboards. Then she started leaving the house without saying so. Just disappear for hours at a stretch and come back without any packages. I mentioned that to your father and he said she was sixty-four years old and she had his permission to go anywhere she damn well pleased. After they found her car, she stopped driving. I know she's under a terrible strain. I'd act funny, too, if it was me."

Carmen fills her wineglass.

"But something's happened to her. She knows things. She does it with the phone a lot. It'll ring and she'll call down and say to tell so-and-so she'll call them back, and I answer it and it's the person she said. And she knows things about people. Sometimes she even knows what's going to happen."

She crosses herself. She looks at him now.

"My friend Cory—she works for the Hazeltines—was here two weeks ago, learning how to bone a lamb leg, and your mother walked into the kitchen and she said to Cory, 'Cory, take my advice and have the butcher at the Reading Market bone your roast for you and mind your fingers if you don't,' and she walked right out again."

Carmen holds her left hand out flat to him and raps the palm with her forefinger.

"Two days later, Cory stuck a boning knife *right through her hand* and out the other side!"

"That's just coincidence, Carmen."

"Well, you can say that, but there's more. And I wouldn't say this," she says, pulling her fanback chair closer to the table. "I'm not one to air my linens in the dooryard, but what's going on here is beyond pride and privacy. Last Saturday morning we were up in the library, your mother and me, planning the dinner you all were coming to, and we were discussing whether I was going to do duck breasts in port wine sauce, which your father's not real crazy about but you kids like, or pork tenderloins, which he is, and she stopped talking for a good minute and just stared out the window. She lost every shade of color in her face. Her skin went just as white as that wine label there and I said, 'Elizabeth? Elizabeth, are you all right?' And she turned to me and she said just as if we were still talking about duck breasts, 'Carmen, did you know that I slept with your friend Vincent?' "

Her hands begin to tremble. She folds them, one holding down the other. She looks at the backs of her hands.

Pete's heart begins to race. He places his wineglass on the table, rattling its base against the wood as they connect.

"And I was so shocked I don't think I said anything," she says to the tabletop. "And then she said to me, 'When you took your leave in 1954, I went to the Ben Franklin Hotel with him. I paid.' She even smiled. I couldn't say a word. She said, 'He had a scar like a V in the small of his back.' Vincent had a scar like a V on his back. From a car accident. Is that a coincidence?"

"I don't know."

All his adult life, Pete had not been able to imagine his parents having sex with each other, let alone in the arms of strangers. How could this be? Intelligent and clever, loyal to a fault to the people she loves, how could his mother slink off to a hotel within sight of the third-floor bedrooms of her own house with the lover of the woman to whom she entrusted her children? Had she paid with a check?

"Did you ask your friend about it?"

"No. I had written him a letter before I left. I never spoke to him again." Carmen frowns. "She was never with Vincent," she said. "She didn't know what his name was."

"Apparently she did. Maybe he came to the house looking for you when you left," he says, surprised at himself.

"No. She knows things. She just said that because she was angry."

» » »

He sits in Bea's room in an upholstered chair that matches the wallpaper and draperies. His mother is propped and arranged in her rented hospital bed. Her flesh-colored silk pajamas cover her bandages. A spot of blood shows on the bandage near her armpit. Her hair is fluffy. Her eyes sparkle. She seems pleased to have banished her nurse to the kitchen.

"So," she says. "Alone at last. We have fourteen minutes. I've known that nurse for going on three hours. Nothing in her life is not scheduled."

"You signed yourself out."

"I had to. It was that or mass murder. I couldn't stand it. I feel better already."

"What if there's an emergency?"

"I feel safe in this house. I'd rather be in my own room, but your father said he would not sleep in a bed that goes up and down and they couldn't fit both beds in. What did you do today besides have lunch with Bea?"

"I did a wedding. Saint Mark's and the Barclay. LaBerge. Rachel and Horace? They said they know you."

"I guess they do. And what have you planned for tonight?"

"Dinner at the Holmeses'."

"Is that a new restaurant?"

"A couple. Nora and Gary. You met them here at your anniversary party last year. You couldn't get their names right?"

"I couldn't?"

" 'Gora and Nary'? "

"Well, why didn't you say so? They sent me a card. Signed it Gora and Nary. Handsome couple. What do they do? I forget."

"Gora's a model. Nary has a store on South Street."

"Real estate?"

"No," he says. "Handmade glass. Expensive stuff."

"They ought to sell real estate. A name like that."

"I don't get it."

"Holmes? You know, you're becoming much too serious. You don't even smile anymore. Are you bothered to be turning forty?"

"No."

"Bullshit," she says.

"Mom. You never say 'bullshit.' "

"Bullshit. You hate turning forty. You've been thinking about it a long time. It's because you live alone."

"I like living alone. I chose to live alone."

"Bullshit."

"How didn't I?"

"You shouldn't have left Bill Payne."

Shocked, nailed to his chair, he says, "How do you know about Bill Payne?"

"Honestly. I thought I raised no dumb children. Now just think a little. Unlike your sister Mary Alice, who feels she has to represent every cause in town, there is one charity I have spent a fair amount of energy on."

"Juvenile Diabetes."

"Yes. And who was the chairperson for four years running in the mid-eighties?"

"You?"

"No, you jerk! Connie Payne. Bill Payne's *mother*, for God's sake! We met together every week for four *years*! We used to talk about you two. All the time."

"Why didn't you say something?"

"Why didn't *you* say something? We wouldn't say anything. We were raised not to announce or inquire about the sexual proclivities of others."

"So was I."

"Touché. However, such considerations would seem to be overridden by those of love and family."

"It works both ways, Mom."

"Encore touché. However, never at a loss for words, your mother replies that there was yet another overriding factor. In all your growing up, there was one thing you prized above anything else, and that was your privacy. And your father and I bit our tongues, and each other's, a thousand times to ensure that you got it. How could I have invaded it to ask about Billy Payne? But that's history. We have ten minutes. Run down to the library and pour your mother a scotch on the rocks."

"Mom, you can't drink. You haven't even had your stitches out."

"I only stock medicinal scotch. If you ached like I do,

you'd have one, too. Maybe you should. Hurry up, so I can finish it before that creature gets back. Go on. If I die, you'll wish you'd done it for your old mother."

In the library, he pours a miserly scotch for his mother and wonders if he is killing her. Suppose her doctors have prescribed a drug for her that, combined with alcohol, will create a violent reaction, cause another seizure, poison her before his eyes? "Well, she's sixty-four and can do as she damn well pleases," he says to a stack of thick, glossy art books listing toward the ice maker. Why should he have told her about Bill? He thinks that it's none of her damn business and that she is absolutely right. He would never have brought it up. How did they know? Did Bill know they knew? He would have said if they did.

» » »

His mother sips the scotch.

"Oh. Thank you, my precious. Do you know why I worked for Juvenile Diabetes? Did Stu or your sisters tell you?"

"No."

"The things we don't tell. My brother and sister died of it."

"I thought your sister had a stroke."

"She did. Merely one of its many manifestations. Do you know about it? Its ontogeny?"

"No."

"It is flukey. That's why we did what we did, your father and I. It is genetically linked, but not predictably. It can skip generations. It can show up in each generation. Cliffie had it, but we didn't know. They discovered it the day he was killed. The rest of you are OK, but you carry the gene."

"Why didn't you tell me?"

"Had you shown any signs of marrying, we would have. We thrashed it out a hundred times, your father and I. Whether to tell you kids. When to tell you. We believed that if we told you when you were young, it would frighten you. That you'd have worried about it all the time, made decisions that were unnecessarily cautious. We believed it would have put a pall on our family life."

"You should have told me," he says flatly.

"You least of all," she says, shaking her head. "You, the family worrier? You worried about everything and everyone. Hung over all of us if we got head colds as if it were, pardon me, cancer? You'd have had a field day with diabetes."

"It concerned my life. You should have told me."

"Don't waste our time on indignation. I'm an authority on this subject. I have lived with it my entire life. From the time I was two or three, I knew about it. Each day was a potential catastrophe. I spent more time with my parents in hospital corridors than I did in church. When my brother had his second amputation, my sister was convinced she was next. She was just fourteen. She tried to commit suicide—with fudge brownies. I found her on the kitchen floor in a diabetic coma, sitting in a corner with a Feno's Bakery box in her lap, her face and hands smeared with crumbs and chocolate icing. She spent her entire allowance on two dozen brownies and got eleven of them down before she passed out. I vowed my kids wouldn't live that way if I could help it. We told Mary Alice and Stu and Bea at various times when it looked like they were thinking about getting serious with someone. Mary Alice was so serious about so many men. I think I told her before I should have. This is dismal stuff."

She shifts herself on the bed. She winces.

"You OK?"

"Just a little stiff. Are you dating?"

"What do you mean?" he says, taken aback.

"Dating? Seeing any men?"

"Mom."

"Don't 'Mom' me," she says, waving her scotch at him. "Let's not go back to that silly social schizophrenia, son of mine. You know, I have just about had it with bullshit. Wait a minute," she says, reaching for the telephone on the cart beside her bed. She picks up the handset and presses a number. She rolls her eyes. "Carmen, tell what's-her-name I don't want to see her for fifteen more minutes. . . . Well, tell her to sit down again. . . . Well, tell her she's fired if I do see her before fifteen minutes."

She slams the handset back into its cradle.

"Where was I? Bullshit. I love that word. Nothing like a life-threatening disease to get you back on track. I've been lying around thinking about a lot of things. You among them. For years we've pussyfooted around, you and your father and me. Done this polite little dance with each other to protect your feelings, or ours. Mostly ours, I regret to say. But it's time to cut through the bullshit. You're gay. We didn't want you to be, but from what I read and hear, you didn't have a choice in the matter either. I talked to all the others about whom they were seeing. Now I want to talk to you. So. Do you see Bill Payne?"

"We're friends, Mom. Look, I know you're on some kind of roll about this, but you can't expect me to suddenly behave as if we've talked about this all our lives."

"We should have. And we may not have time for a long-term adjustment, darling most."

"Cashing in your chips, are you?"

"Whether I do or I keep playing, the rules have changed for me. I have given up trivial pursuits. I want to hear about Bill Payne."

"Bill Payne is my best friend."

"Who left whom?"

"You're getting very personal."

"We have a personal relationship, you and I."

"I did."

"You met someone else?"

"No. Bill wanted us to buy a house. He wanted us to live together."

"How long had you been together? Apart, so to speak."

"Two years."

"That seems an appropriate courtship. Even in my day.

Your father and I moved in together after three months."

"You lived together? Before you were married?"

"Yes."

"You never told us that."

"It never came up except with Mary Alice, who could never seem to live alone. Actually, I don't think I did tell her. I didn't want to encourage her. It was the stuff of movies. The war was on. Your father was assigned to the Naval Yard. There were quite a few of us who did it. The War Effort permitted certain . . . moral lapses. Did you ever live with anyone?"

"With Ogawa. In California. For three months. Then he met someone else."

"And that soured you?"

"No."

"I know this *is* none of my business, but why didn't you want to buy a house with Bill?"

"It is none of your business."

"A mother finds out nothing if she doesn't ask."

". . . I didn't want to live together."

"As simple as that? You like living alone so much?"

"No. Yes."

She ignores his ambivalence.

"I'm curious," she says. "Was it either-or? Why end the relationship when you could have continued on as you were?"

"I don't know now."

"And how do you like living alone now that you are forty?"

"Thirty-nine."

"Now that you are thirty-nine, how do you like living alone?"

"I like my space. I'm not home that much."

"What do you do about commitment?"

"Do about it?"

"Do about it. God, you're recalcitrant. I'm not asking

you for a graphic rundown of your sex life, Peter. We're talking pacts. Did you and Bill have a commitment to each other, or would the house have been it?"

"Wouldn't you rather talk about bullshit?"

"No. I'm having a good time. Getting to know a side of you I had not considered much. Virgin territory, as it were. I have been thinking a lot about the nature of commitments. Over the past few days my commitments have sent their emissaries to the hospital in the guise of delivery men. Flowers and fruit. I had the nurses remove the cards and attach my own. One of your father's men delivered the tributes of my commitments to the rooms of patients who apparently had none. It amuses me that they are all racking their brains to figure out who Elizabeth Flowers is. Do you know that only one of my raft of dear friends came to visit me? Got her son to drive her in from Chester County. Poor Patsy can hardly see. Cataracts. They're not ripe yet. We got to laughing so hard the nurses made her leave. I'm putting her in my will. Would the house have been the commitment? asked your mother naively."

"Why is that so important to you?"

"Because commitments are."

"I suppose it would have been."

"You weren't ready?"

"I didn't want to live together."

"Why?"

"Look . . ."

"Am I boring you?"

"This is history."

"Everything is history. Our conversation up to this point is history. History is relentless. How come you didn't want to live together?"

He smiles.

"It would have been a commitment," he says.

"So you ended the relationship."

"Yes."

"Any regrets?"

"Not at the time. Later. For a while."

"Do you love him?"

"He's my best friend."

"You said that. You're equivocating."

"You're pushing."

"I can be Old Mom, if you like. How is the flower business, dear? Your sister Bea was here for most of the afternoon. She said Joanie wants to take tap dance lessons." She sips her scotch. She waits.

"It's my problem, Mom."

"I thought it wasn't a problem."

"It's not."

"You just said it was."

"Did you ever have an affair, Mom?"

She raises her eyebrows.

"Changing the subject? Too hot for you, is it? No. Did you?"

"Carmen said you told her you were with her boyfriend years ago."

"I did? I wasn't. I thought about it more than once, I can tell you. Oh, not with her boyfriend. Either one of them. I never met the first one. I know Robert. He drops in. Did I dream that I did and tell her about it?" she muses. "Did you?"

"What?"

"Ever have an affair? I don't mean that. You must have had lots of affairs. While you were with someone else? That's what you meant when you asked me, isn't it?"

"Yes."

"While you were with Bill Payne?"

"No."

"Why not?"

"We were together, Mom."

"It would have been unseemly," she says.

"Yes."

"A sort of violation."

"Right."

"Of your commitment to each other."

"OK. Yes."

"So what did the house mean to you?"

"What is this?"

"Peter, you haven't thought this out yet. And you never answered my question."

"What was the question?"

"Do you love him? Your best friend?"

He sighs. He looks away.

"He's a wonderful, silly man," she says.

"How would you know that?"

She lays her head back on her pillow. She lowers her eyelids. She smiles at him.

"I know everything," she says. "Will you live alone when you are fifty? . . . When you are sixty-four?"

"I doubt it."

"It's interesting to me that I have been all the ages of my children. . . . What do you want?"

"What do I want?"

"Sure."

"I want a lot of things. I want you to get well . . ."

She sits up again, jabbing her pillows with her good elbow. "Have we had this conversation?"

"No."

"I didn't think so. Well, I'll either get well or I won't. Less messy if I do, wouldn't you agree? Do you remember when you were nine and your father decided that we should all see America? He went out and rented that humongous bus, and I got you kids out of school, and off we went. In the dead of winter. God, what an odyssey. It all fell apart after Chicago, I think. Your father was the only one who could handle the bus. I couldn't help him with the driving. He got irritable in Indiana, and by the time we got to the border of Kansas, everyone was cranky except Cliffie."

"I remember Kansas," Pete says. "It was all white. And flat. Cornstalks sticking up through the snow."

"Do you remember the game we played?"

"We played a lot of games."

"By Kansas, the only game anyone would play with any conviction was the one Cliffie invented. 'Dead Animals.' We all sat in the front of the bus and tried to spot dead animals."

"I remember that. You got points for spotting. More if you could identify the species."

"Your father was so bored, he wanted bonuses for running them down. You children were scandalized. It took us days to cross Kansas, I think. Maybe weeks." She sighs.

"I remember looking out the windows for days. Nothing happened. No mountains. No valleys. No nothing but flat."

"I think your life is like that," his mother says. "Like driving through Kansas."

"What about your life?" he snaps back.

"Oh, my." She places her hand on her bandaged chest. "Driving through Kansas? More like the Himalayas for me. Nothing for me but peaks and valleys. I could do with some Kansas."

"I'm sorry," he says, wishing he had not asked the question.

"Please," she says. "No apologies. My life until recently was like driving through Kansas. It has been. For years. I chose that. You let it happen."

"I resent that."

"I accept that."

"I have an interesting life."

"I'm glad for you."

"I do."

She sips her scotch. She makes a small smile. "Where would you like to be when you are fifty?"

"In Philadelphia," he says.

"I did not mean as opposed to Kansas, necessarily," she says. "What would you say makes your life interesting now?"

"You are a real steamroller today."

"We could talk about the ballet costume Mary Alice is

having made for Holly. I could describe every stitch. I have heard the details. *Ad nauseam.*"

Pete squirms in his chair. He wants to look at his watch.

"What makes my life interesting?" Pete says, his eyes wandering to the wallpaper.

She smiles patiently.

"A lot of things, Mom. That's a complicated question."

"Well. We could break it down into categories, if you like. Who is it who says that we have only two important things in our lives, our love and our work? I don't remember." She waits. She rattles her ice cubes.

"I'm thinking, Mom," he says.

"I can see that."

IX.

In her bed in Bea's room she finds no comfortable position. Her chest throbs when she moves and when she is still. It burns and it aches as if, she thinks, the breast which is gone were stuck with cocktail toothpicks. The Percocet she is taking has changed the position of her mind somehow, left it intact and lucid but moved her consciousness twelve or fourteen inches behind her face so that her brain seems now back in the pillows somewhere and she is looking out through the space it had occupied, as if from inside a hole.

For hours the night nurse has been turning the pages of magazines in the hall outside. The light from her reading lamp shines through the half-closed bedroom door. It casts a large flowered parallelogram on the wall Liz faces. She wishes the nurse and the light were not there. She thinks she could sleep if the light were off and she could see the glistening umbrella of magnolia leaves outside her open window. She can hear them rattling and brushing in the wind. She is annoyed by the sound of magazines pages turning. There are few spaces of silence. The woman looks at the pictures. She does not interest herself in the words.

At least she taught her own children to read. And they did read until they were adults and popular culture overcame them. The Age of the Docudrama. They do not keep books in their houses. Except in the children's rooms. She's seen to that. Had those girls cart books home in plastic shopping bags. Had them delivered by UPS to their houses with duplicates delivered here so that they could discuss them. They'll read, those girls, when they are forty. She will pay for their lifetime memberships to the Literary Guild. She will send in a check tomorrow. How much will it cost? How much does it cost for a year? She can't remember. She won't remember in the morning probably. She is forgetting things. Cancer cells munching away. That is the worst part, she thinks, aware of the cold sweat breaking out on her forehead. What will they do? Grow to the size of softballs, those tumors? Eat up slow section by slow section her whole life experience? Worse than Alzheimer's by a million. Worse than having the synapses wink out one by one, taking her memory of the present but leaving her at least the past, her tumors will take it all, memory by memory, leaving her trapped in the Here and Now of this room, or a room across the street painted some non-color, without Schumacher wallcovering to remind her that she once had impeccable taste and created rooms no one wanted to leave.

If the process were selective, she wouldn't mind. Take most of growing up. They could begin with that. She thinks of the two objects she has seen on Dr. Burd's horrible X-ray plates. Hazelnuts with roots. Opaque. Intractable. They could, with her blessing, take everything up to age eighteen, if they wanted. They could feed on those painful years. Grope around until they found where she's stored the memories of her early years: the sounds of her parents weeping in the night; the sight of their bloody fingernails bitten to the quicks. They could feed on those memories, the little bastards. The acid of those memories would dissolve them even as they took their first bites.

She could strike a bargain with her tumors. Give them enough history to eat to feed them for her natural lifetime.

But leave language. What could they care about language? All they do is eat. If they wanted to eat, she could give them her own sense of taste. Nothing tasted right to her anyway except for salt. She could taste salt. She could not get enough of it, and her caretakers allowed her none, only things that taste of chemicals and metals. Powdered copper and steel. Things that corroded. No gold or platinum in her meals. She adored anchovies. Suddenly they seemed more enticing to her than chocolate ever was. And clams and oysters. Raw. Oh. She could taste their liquor, could taste the thick sea-juice that bathed their succulent, salty bodies. When did she last have oysters for dinner? A month with an R in it. No oysters to be had in May. Or June. Or July. And bread? She could no longer taste yeast. Or smell it. But her girls, who came here smelling of their mothers' favorite soaps; she would bury her nose in their sweet necks for as long as was socially acceptable, and then some. She had been known to violate the rules of affection. As had her granddaughters. How would she hug them with a bruised chest and one arm when two good arms had never been enough? Not like their mothers with their niggardly embraces. She thought she had taught her own daughters to hug. She had always given them bear hugs in doorways, going and coming. The boys, too, until they stopped giving them back. Until they would no longer stand for hugs.

And where could the hugging have come from? Her own mother had not been a hugger. A holder, yes, but not a hugger. But she had been both, and read to her children as much to touch them as to teach them the wonder of language, and all five at once for some too short time in their lives, stretched out on somebody's bed, a child under each of her arms and one on her lap and two across her legs. How did that work? How had she been able to hold the books? And what were the titles that held the interest of five children two years apart all at one time? Titles she had chosen with seduction in mind.

The Jungle Book. When her children asked again for Kipling, she thought she had achieved Nirvana and her mind raced to the next possibility. Now they watched Disease-of-the-Week movies. Would they see their mother someday on their screens, lit up in photons, fighting her noble battle with one tit against brain tumors and all odds? Would they remember that they graduated from Kipling to Tolkien and then through their mother's hubris and the grace of her good memory moved on to an oral and exciting recapitulation of *Beowulf*? Cliffie had loved *Beowulf*.

Thinking of Cliffie, her eyes fill with tears.

Let the tumors feed on that dreadful memory. A year's worth of meals. Eat that whole nightmare day away, and the days that followed. Start feeding on the first pound on the front door by the man who delivered the mail, then on his arm that shook and pointed up to the street corner. Dine on the yellow taxi which pinned her child in a spray of red against the brick wall of the hospital gardens and then on the dreadful moment of her recognition that the blue jacket she saw above the hood against the wall was the jacket she had sewed the zipper of the night before and that the shocked face above it was the face of the little boy she had hugged only moments before. Oh, the horror.

And worse, even, her arrival at the corner, Cliffie's upper body convulsing above the yellow hood, against the red-spattered bricks and his eyes flown open for one horrible, understanding moment when he saw her and gurgled "Ma." That was all that would come out; he never called her Ma, only Mom, and she, having sworn and upheld until that moment her sacred oath to the Holy Mother and to Her Father and Her own Son to protect her children always, failed. Found herself in her bathrobe at the corner, pulling at a runaway cab's flung-open door, thinking that she could pull the whole car off her Cliffie. And it would not move. Nor would the cabdriver, who sat in shock in the driver's seat with his hands still on the wheel and his foot still on the gas pedal, in a stupor, while she screamed for him to put it in reverse and finally dragged him out by his shirt neck onto the sidewalk and did it herself, climbed into the driver's seat and rammed the shift lever into R with her child's face there past the windshield, spurting blood through his mouth six feet in front of her. Too late. Oh.

Let the tumors feed on that and take it from her. Take the memory of that child still stuck to the car hood. Feed on that. She had lived with it for thirty years. They could live on it for thirty more. But would their hostess? Kill her, and there would go the free meals. If they struck a bargain and the tumors were convinced to watch their diets, they might all three trundle on together a good long time.

The fibrous magnolia leaves rasp against the house bricks.

What would the three of them trundle on to, she and her hungry guests? To watching her average children lead their average lives over thirty more years? No music created. No change in the skyline of Philadelphia attributable to one of them. No poems. As artistic as each of them had been in childhood, only Pete created as an adult, and in the most perishable of mediums. Never mind. It was art, even if it didn't last. Not much did. And was there ever a time when they were children that she seriously entertained the expectation that she had spawned a budding George Sand or Stravinsky among her little Flowers?

She did expose them. She did that. There was not a museum in the city whose floor plan they had not walked in the process of their growing up. Bimonthly at least, each of their sweet tushes warmed seats at the Academy of Music. There was a time when they could have led architectural walking tours, unerringly, she was pleased to be able to say, pointing out the work of Chandler, Kennedy, and Keen, and with some enthusiasm. Her children had been so quick to learn until sometime in their teens or early adulthoods.

What had happened then? Sex? The culture hadn't changed except for in the sixties. When she worried they would get into marijuana, all they wanted to get into was other people's jeans, except for Bea, who wouldn't even wear them and showed no interest in boys until Anthony whipped her hormones into a froth that had not yet showed a sign of fizzling. She and hot-blooded Mary Alice, not to mention Studious Stu, who sponsored three abortions that she knew of out of his father's pocket before his senior year in college. And Pete, so good-looking that he took the breath away and didn't know it, and sloe-eyed to boot from some flukey gene she had not been able to trace in his lineage. He who had girls throwing themselves before him like so many overripe wheat sheaves though he wanted no parts of them, save their friendship, the last thing they had on their minds. Unlike Phil, she did not blame herself for Pete's proclivity. Did not believe that had Phil spent more time with Pete when he was a child, played ball with him, Pete would have been normal.

Men and their balls. It was no coincidence that all sports were played with them. Phil had played ball with none of the boys. So much for the logic of that circular thinking. A toss of the genetic dice, his and hers. Nothing to do with balls. Up popped the gay gene, if it could be called that, as mysteriously as the state of Delaware had on his neck and those strange sloed eyes, unknown in their families to her knowledge, just slightly slanted. When he went to California with that Japanese man, it had crossed her mind that that attraction was the result of some cosmic racial tide at work: like seeking like in the genetic sea of possibilities. Could there have been a slightly Asian wine merchant who had a passionate liaison with Phil's great-grandmother and left that sloe-eyed gene? Maybe a bisexual. Maybe an Asian wine merchant who had passed through the state of Delaware on his way to Philadelphia. Pete had not gone for an Oriental since, she didn't think, Bill Payne being the one and only example of Pete's contemporary tastes she knew of, a man whom she could very easily get used to for her son-in-law; a man she was surprised to discover she was pleased he had chosen.

And if she were forty years younger, she might have gone for him herself. She loved tall, thin men with buttocks you could get a grip on, ones that fit your hands. Like Phil's did when they were in their twenties and their thirties, doing it in the strangest places, where the children wouldn't see. They had become aficionados of fast sex. There had been no Velcro. She had resewed a thousand buttons. She and Phil would peel each other's clothes off and be on and in and out of each other in seconds. In those days there was no time for the subtleties of foreplay. It had not occurred to them among the overcoats and scarves of the hall closet or on the thin, cold, gritty carpet next to the water heater or, God help them, standing up against the closed garage door, her skirts hiked, his pants around his ankles as he rammed, and she with her palms cupped around those buttocks pulled him deeper into her, careless of the banging that must have echoed up the alley. Had their children always known them flush-faced?

Had that been where they got it, their eager appreciations of lust? From their parents? Was it all genetic, then, their more than healthy interests in becoming wrapped up in other bodies? No doubt Cliffie would have grown up to that, too. Had he grown up. Would have gone for women, surely. But not interested in girls or boys particularly as she thought about it. He seemed to divide his attentions between both almost indiscriminately at eleven and twelve, whereas the others had all boyfriends or all girlfriends at that age. The bisexual Asian again? Pete's interest in men had been clear to her from early childhood, though she chose to ignore it. The collections of sports magazines. His baseball cards. Though like Stu and Cliffie he excelled at baseball, it was not the pleasure of the doing in his case, but the being with that was the motive, and she did not let herself catch on until he was out of high school and into college, not really even then, until the end of college, when it struck her that, unlike Stu and Mary Alice with their succession of girls and boys brought home for family dinners and sometimes for weekends, Pete brought no one home after his early playmates. And then he left home, to the farthest place in the continental United States with a Japanese friend half again his age to become a florist, leaving suddenly amid accolades from one of the finest business schools in the country, tossing luggage into the trunk of a car whose driver she tried to see and could not in the dawn's early light and driving off toward I-95, leaving her standing in the doorway, with Carmen teary behind her, she waving at the exhaust fumes, the plain white business envelope he had left for his father to explain in five perfectly printed sentences his decision to study Ikebana in a state neither of his parents either liked or approved of.

She had been a slow learner.

She told herself it was her lack of experience with these things.

She told herself it was that they ignored him in the wake of Cliffie's death. That it was her over-mothering when he was a child. It was not throwing balls to him. It was genetic. It was the way it was and she had not faced it squarely in its eye when she began to catch on to it.

And she was sixty-four and he was turning forty and they talked about his business and what his siblings and his nieces have been up to, and what, really, was the point? Was the point that he was coming up on forty and had no one at the center of his life? Was the point that she was sixty-four and had a platoon visiting her at her sickbed?

Was it that when he was old, he would have no one there for him?

X.

Stu and Alexa recline on chaises longues on the square stone terrace outside their kitchen. Stu, still dressed in a dark gray summer suit, has removed his shoes. His tie, a favorite dark blue silk stripe, is pulled firmly to the V of his collar. He has moved his chair into the late-afternoon sun. Alexa has moved hers into the shade of the vast copper beech whose canopy extends some fifty feet over to the terrace. They sip gin and tonics with paper-thin slices of lime. The warm afternoon breeze lifts sections of Alexa's curly, peach-colored hair.

"How was the office?" she asks, looking out over the gorge in back of their house.

"Quiet. I was the only one there after the cleaning service left. My phone didn't even ring."

"They don't appreciate it, you know. They don't even know you're there Saturdays."

"They love me, Alexa," he says, watching the legs of the gin of his drink slow-dance at the rim of his glass. "They always know I was there. They check the desk log downstairs. They know who comes in when and who leaves when. I write clearly," he says, following her gaze out to the edge of the gorge. "Sometimes I print. My name and the times."

"Just the same, you don't have to go in every Saturday."

"I do, Alexa," he says lazily. "It shows at bonus time. You love it at bonus time. . . . Where are the girls?"

"At the Fergusons'. They have to be picked up at six."

"Can you do that?"

"We could go together. Have a drink with Millie and Bob."

"Could you? Bob'll want to jaw about his investments. He's called me three times this week. I don't think I can take him today . . . OK?"

"Sure," she says. She stands.

"Tell them I'm still at the office. No. Tell them I'm in Spain."

"I'll be a while if they ask me to stay for a drink," she says, adjusting the shoulder straps of her white eyelet sundress. Her pale skin is freckled at her shoulders.

"No problem," he says, glancing at her and back to the edge of the gorge.

"Maryclare Wallace called me today."

"Maryclare Wallace."

"Burack and Burack? She's got a new listing. In Devon. Dutch colonial, five bedrooms on thirty-one acres. With a barn."

He sighs. He closes his eyes.

"How nice for Maryclare," he says.

"The price is right. I told her we might have a look at it tomorrow."

He looks at her. She is looking at the gorge.

"No," he says quietly.

She turns.

"This is more than a bargain," she says. "The couple who own it are both in bad health. Maryclare said they'd take seven hundred if we offered it. You know what places that size are going for out there. We could get three seventy-five for this one without trying."

He closes his eyes.

"No, Alexa. No. Why are you doing this? I said, and you agreed, that when this house is paid off we would *consider* the possibility of finding something with more land. And you called her?"

"She called me."

"Your name and number appeared to her in a dream?"

She does not reply. She stands in the shade, her left arm around her waist, the elbow of her right propped on it. She holds her drink at lip level and looks out at the gorge.

"I was in to see your mother today," she says.

Stu swirls his drink. The ice cubes rattle. Ah. Now a little guilt, he thinks.

"You haven't been to see her since the operation. She said that twice. I've told her it's because your office needs you so much."

"It's true."

"You should, you know."

"I call her. I will. Monday," he says and takes a long pull from the glass.

"I'll go for the kids. We're having the Perrets for dinner, don't forget."

"Broiled or baked?" he says.

"I'll go for the girls," she says.

He lays his head back on the chaise. He crosses his legs. He holds his drink in both hands at his crotch. Jays call to each other down in the gorge. The sun warms his cheeks.

He hears the clatter of Alexa's diesel station wagon as she starts it and pulls out of the circular drive into the street and down the hill toward town. He does not like the sound of diesel engines.

He settles his shoulders back into the ribs of the chaise. He watches the reddish-pink patterns that pulsate across his closed eyelids.

"How long, O Lord?" he says aloud.

He thinks about his computer at work. He considers again changing the password on the file he has created. He wonders if "TERMINUS" is too close to "TERMINAL," too computerese to be safe from the curious. Change it to what? "SLUSHFUND"? "GETAWAY"? Who would catch the significance, anyway, the file looking like any portfolio among the fifty or so he manages, and the client's name, chosen for its alliteration and the pun. Peter Parker. Stu's British creation, who receives statements of his account at an apartment with no furniture two minutes from Mary Alice's precious Rittenhouse Square.

Why change the name? he thinks. It has worked for three years. Why not for nine more months? A year at the outside, all things and the market being equal and as long as some IRS functionary or the Japanese didn't fuck it up. The timing would be just right, with the last payment on the house in February, and how gracious he would be, how magnanimous. "And Stu gave her practically everything, you know, the house, just signed it over to her and everything in it, all those antiques worth a mint, just took enough furniture for that tiny apartment he's in in town. And not even the best pieces. Have you seen it? Like an efficiency. One bedroom the size of a closet in their Swarthmore house *and* he gave her a cash settlement. She isn't saying how much, but I heard it's six figures. A hell of a lot more than she deserves, if you ask me, boinking that VP from Scott Paper out in Wallingford for God knows how many years and Stu working like a dog six, seven days a week so she could collect Queen Anne up the gazoo. There's not a reproduction in the house, you know."

In his stocking feet, he pours a fresh drink at the wet bar in the den: gin and just a dollop of tonic. He fishes out the old lime slice and drops in a new one, stirring the drink with his forefinger and licking it, making a little smacking sound with his lips. He falls into one of a pair of Queen Anne wingbacks covered in a chintz print too flowery for his taste and puts his feet up on its matching stool.

When the papers are signed, and the ink has dried, and copies are distributed through the most expensive lawyers in three states, and their checks are written and have cleared from his seriously diminished bank account. Then. Then wait a small but discreet number of weeks and begin to convert Peter Parker's considerable assets to cash. Sell them in clumps. In prearranged batches at irregular intervals, all less than ten thousand. Sell off the GenetiCorp if it takes a month, the Symtac, that whore of so many takeovers, so many times. Even he forgets all the name changes. Sell the minerals and the Teshigahara and the Ikenobo and the Mueller preferred, convert it all to cash deposited in Peter Parker's numbered Dutch Antilles account until it is all sold except for the John Singer Sargent portrait maybe, too nice to part with, picked up for nothing, all the money he had at one time, which he sees once a year when he pays the storage charges dressed in suits tailored in England.

He walks back to the terrace and crosses it, avoiding the moist moss between the paving stones, feeling the warm rock through his socks and a gentle buzz from his gin. Stretching out on his chaise again, he thinks about the apartment he will buy when he finds the right one. When he thinks about this space, it is always near the top of a tall building with a view to the south. A duplex.

He likes to walk up to a bedroom. Likes to walk down in the morning to another part of the house; likes the idea of looking down into high-ceilinged rooms, one wall hung with the John Singer Sargent, nothing else on it but the girl with the long ivory dress looking out, looking into the eyes of everyone who passes. But contemporary furniture. Leather and metal. Black. No long-beaked birds with blue feathers. No fabric flowers. No bedroom with flounced this and that and cloth on cloth and parsimonious sex divvied out as if there was a fixed supply and the end of it in sight. No more effortless intakes of breath as she rides him on his back and examines her face in the curled mirror above the headboard, turning her head slightly left and right as she rocks, checking her lip liner. Checking her eyebrows for stray hairs. Pooching her lips now and then when she thinks he's not looking. Imagining he's Danny Oberrecht with his soft middle and a complexion with high blood pressure written all over it? She the only exercise Oberrecht gets and a pisspoor workout it is, except for her riding up when she ought to ride down, when you're about to die trying to get more friction. When you finally do shoot, trying to recall any tight fuck you've ever had, she's off you and in the bathroom, flushing and turning on spigots like there's no tomorrow.

He can do it for another year. With her, on his back, the only way she'll do it. Once, twice a week. And a couple times a week beating his meat soaped up and slippery in the shower is enough until he burns the mortgage.

On weekdays at the office he never goes into the Peter Parker portfolio. He makes notes on changes in its holdings that occur during the week on small pieces of paper, which he tucks into his wallet among his receipts from automatic teller machines. On Saturdays, at the office, he first updates the balance of their joint checking account. He arranges his own ATM receipts and Alexa's chronologically. He places a diagonal pencil line in the upper right corner of each ATM receipt after he has noted it in his checkbook. He staples the receipts together and stores them in his briefcase to reconcile with the bank statement the first or second Saturday of each month. He totals the week's deposits and withdrawals and notes his calculation of the balance in pencil on the last stub of the checkbook, which he leaves for Alexa in the top right corner of the Queen Anne chest of drawers in their bedroom.

When he has finished the banking, he boots up the computer on the console beside his desk, and while it counts off its RAMs of memory, he takes from his briefcase the floppy disk labeled "PP." He accesses the TERMINUS file. He studies the firm's printouts of Friday's close-of-day transactions, making notes of certain items on a legal pad. His printing is not artful, but precise. He forms his numerals in the European way: sharp, inverted V's for ones, slash marks through his 7's. He labels the holdings into columns of categories. The largest is RETAIN. Four smaller ones are called BUY and BUY? and SELL and SELL? He goes into the

PP floppy disk, a summary of his notes taken from financial channels beamed into his dish at home from Japan, Singapore, and Hong Kong. He adds and multiplies on his desk calculator. He makes further notes on the legal pad. He tears off the tape he has made on the calculator, folds it, and places it in his suit jacket pocket. After studying the legal pad for a while, he adds items to the SELL and BUY columns. He tears off the sheet and three of the blank pages under it. He folds them carefully and puts them in his jacket pocket. He removes the PP floppy from his computer, returns to DOS, and turns off the system. He attends to other matters on his desk.

On his chaise longue, in the sun, he puts his cold, damp glass between his thighs. He takes the calculator tape from the breast pocket of his suit jacket. He squints at his bottom line. He smiles and closes his eyes. He puts the tape away.

"Not bad, Peter Parker," he says in a British accent. Fifty thousand borrowed from Daddy repaid in seven months with interest Daddy didn't want now worth one point seven six million, and if he sells the John Singer Sargent, for which he can get another eight hundred thousand, he can get nine and a half percent without thinking, so, Peter, you clever fellow, do you sell the Sargent and try to squeak by on, say, two hundred forty three is it thousand dollars a year, largely tax free, and retire? But the girls have to be put through the most expensive schools their mother can locate plus whatever horses cost a year. Got to have fucking horses.

Maybe keep the Sargent and risk that his luck holds out and he is not busted for insider trading and Ikenobo continues its meteoric rise and the new interstate ramps do go through and maybe he can double the money in a year. Unless Alexa finds out what has been done behind her callused back and demands half.

He thinks she does it on her back for Danny Oberrecht and why shouldn't the two of them continue for another eight or ten months at least and if it isn't Danny Oberrecht, it'll be some other poor asswipe with a few bucks she'll boink on the side and he'll find out because she lies like a wrinkled rug. Thinks she's so subtle not to have affairs with his friends. Does it with his friends' best friends who tell his friends who drop not too subtle hints when they all get ripped after golf or tennis and he, being the nicest guy in Delaware County, anyone will tell you, never lets on he understands what they're saying.

And fucking AIDS out there and you'd think she never watched the evening news and here he was trying to come up with logical reasons to use rubbers, him with a vasectomy and her with her tubes tied, who knows where Danny Oberrecht's dick's been? Or that Le Guin guy she's been flapping her lashes at at the club. Goes by initials that sound like an oil company, BP, or PD, or something, and has love juice dripping down the thighs of half the women in town. He'd fuck a rattlesnake, they say, if somebody held its mouth open.

But not Virtuous Stu. No, sir. Not Stu. Works hard for his family. Not a breath of scandal in years since that story came out about the couple caught screwing on the twelfth tee at 4:00 A.M. by the greenskeeper of the Springfield Golf Club who stole every stitch of their clothes and called the police and watched from the dark in the rough while they were pursued in the beams of flashlights through the Springfield Mall parking lot and across Baltimore Pike, their pale butts lit up by the headlamps of cars, the man at least six foot and dark and well endowed, the lady who drove into the gutter said, and the woman she could have sworn was Dolly Parton except she had short hair, and they ran, laughing and panting, their feet cut from sharp sticks and stones, their legs bleeding from blackberry scratches and welted up from stinging nettles, ran through the dark yards of the proper citizens of Swarthmore with no clothes on, exciting sleeping dogs as they crashed through shrubbery, exposing themselves to poison ivy, two joggers, and one startled teenage paperboy who told the police he didn't recognize either of them two days before he purchased a European ten-speed no paperboy could afford.

So the jeans were his size. So the sneakers were twelves and the washed-out olive-drab polo was the same color as his lucky volleyball shirt. "Hey, Stu. Hear about the guy who got a hole in one up on the twelfth?" "Hey, Stu, wanna go golfing tonight, hee hee hee?"

He lifts his drink to measure it.

Finish this one and maybe two more before the Perrets. Get a little numb? Or stay a little fresh so he doesn't nod out on the dullest conversation he has ever endured from two people in his entire fucking life and maybe in the history of the fucking world, or fit in another one, maybe dull it with a sandwich or something because sure as shit they'll start up on goddamn France again and the two of them will sit there with those pissy, thin, pulled-back lips that you can't figure out how the words get out of, not moving that you can detect, and Old Alexa will start pulling hers back just like theirs and you won't be able to tell which one's talking, they sound exactly alike, and if she serves strawberries for dessert and he has to listen to the three of them snapping seeds behind their little thin lips, he thinks he will lose it. He will cut his throat with his goddamned butter knife right there at the table.

"Goddamn Pete," he says. He closes his eyes. He grins. He hoots.

"Fucking A," he says, remembering the beginning of 1963, the days of unnatural, quiet, strained evening dinners at the Pine Street house when no one looked at the unset place that was Cliffie's and all their non-conversations did not allude to Cliffie or to his famous punch lines or to his things still scattered around the house, but centered on the safe news: what happened at the plant or in the arts or at the siblings' various schools, to fill the now deadened and somehow brittle air with the sounds of things that passed for life moving forward. For days. And days.

Until Carmen, stretching to prepare special meals every time they sat, found, improbably in that era, strawberries. Grown in Egypt, she thought, or did the shopkeeper tell her some other African country? Morocco? She wasn't sure, but look at them, they're actually red-ripe, not a white one in the baskets. On homemade from-scratch shortcake and she whipped the cream herself, she'd wanted everyone to know, and she stayed long enough by the swinging door to the kitchen to receive her accolades and to be sure every spoon had been dipped into this untimely confection before disappearing through the door and leaving them to their chewing and their strained desserts.

And they all made appropriate "mmmmmm" sounds for a moment or two and the room fell quiet again in the loss that lay heavy in it save for the clinks of six silver spoons on six bone-china bowls. The muffled and relentless cracking of seeds between teeth went on for minutes until Pete cleared his throat and put down his spoon.

"I think Cliffie was right," he said. "It's the worst sound on the earth."

They all looked up. Liz smiled a Patient Mother smile. They all looked down at their bowls and continued to spoon and crunch until Mary Alice looked up in the midst of their smothered crepitation.

"God," she said. "It's awful!" And, taking another spoonful of strawberries, she began to chew in rapid, tiny bites, smashing the seeds between her front teeth.

And he began to chew quickly himself, and Bea, catching on, began chewing faster.

"No. Ssshhhh," Pete said. "You have to keep your mouth closed. It's more terrible."

And they all sat chewing, even their father and mother making fast, teeny bites, and listening to hundreds of seeds snapping.

Bea was the first to let go, snorting a long pig sound through her nostrils, and then their mother went, and their father lost it, spewing to their shocked delight chewed strawberry across the lace tablecloth before him. In a second they were all howling and squealing, beyond control, beyond propriety, past the days-long hush that had fallen on their house, past the shocked numbness of their loss and into the giddy release of hysteria, their faces contorting as they tried, absurdly, for self-restraint and fell instead into forbidden and delicious laughter.

When Carmen pushed through the swinging door, uncomprehending, her brown eyes wide, her mouth agape with disbelief at the scene before her, they all pointed and looked at each other and started again, slapping the table, their eyes now running with tears, some of them gasping for breath, making squeaky little noises that sounded nothing like themselves, and finally calming down, quieting down a bit, they said "Oh" and "Ahh" and took deep breaths and Liz picked up her starched and creased linen napkin and instead of touching it to her eyes as they all expected, she blew her nose in it, and it all began again.

"Fucking A," he says, lifting his drink and chortling. Pete the quietest one in the family and he opened his mouth in the worst of all possible times. All that death shit. All those rooms still stinking of flowers and the family pussyfooting around each other like strangers in a New Jersey beach hotel in the winter and Pete spoke up. He will never forget that moment if he lives to be a hundred and ten, all of them laughing around that table till they almost threw up and Pete sitting there with his hand over his mouth and his eyes saying did he do this? Did he have the power to give joy to these joyless people?

"These joyless people," he says quietly to his drink.

He doesn't know if they are or not. Mary Alice seems to be. Well, not joyless. Not exactly joyful. Satisfied maybe? And Bea, besides the bitching and the carping, seems to like her life enough. And Pete. Who can tell what he's thinking, always saying proper things? Asking the right questions. Pressing the right buttons. Getting us to talk. Old Catalytic Pete from the strawberry dinner forward taking over for Old Cliffie, flexing those thin muscles to become the family's verbal gymnast. His only sport except for running, and why running? And always deferring to Stu in all the other sports and games Stu introduced them to because it made him look good.

Pete loves to make the rest look good. And he'd give Stu his last pair of shoes without having to be asked and make it look like going barefoot was the only aspiration he had in life.

And what if Pete gets it? What will they do? Not like Mom dying. Even Dad. You expect parents to die. You grow up terrified they will and somewhere along it begins to become almost natural. Anticipated. But not a brother. Not squashed by a taxi cab on your own fucking street where you've been safe since you were born.

Or wasting away from AIDS in the middle of life.

And he doesn't say shit. Never talks about himself except about work. And whose fault is that? When they go to games, Stu doesn't say shit. He sits and roots for the guys he wants to have the ball and Pete roots along with him. And he knows that, except for baseball, Pete doesn't know diddly why it's important the puck's going one way or the other and if you asked him to define a "down" he couldn't. And does he ever turn from the game to ask Pete how his life is? If he's healthy? Has he whored around like the rest of them do, having sex in bathrooms and in Fairmount Park or in alleys with strangers doing God knows what awful things and getting it? Has he got it now? Has he got it? And knows it? And keeps his silence?

How could he bring it up? At a game? "Hey, Pete. Fuckin' A. Joe Montana doesn't have AIDS. . . . Do you?"

"Do you know of any sports stars that are gay?"

"Um, Pete. Alexa and I were just sort of talking about AIDS the other day at breakfast . . . Um. We were wondering. Have you been tested?"

Better to get Mary Alice to do it. Or Bea. Bea's bold. She'd say anything. He could get her to bring it up.

And what if he said he did? Told her he had it? Stand by him, of course. Make sure he got what he needed. We all would. The whole family. Even Alexa. Visits everyone who's sick. Visits his mom when he can't. That's something he's not good at. Can't stand hospitals. Can't stand the sounds of them. Can't stand the walking down the hall to a room and seeing into the other rooms. People plugged into things. Waiting.

Since Cliffie, he can't do it. Can't be around all that equipment. The sounds of it doing things. Making him breathe. Making that little chest go up and down.

He clenches the arm of his chair with one hand. He takes a long, cool drink with the other.

Pete wouldn't have it. Wouldn't do that stuff. Always a nut about cleanliness. Wouldn't even let his mashed potato gravy run out of the volcano. God forbid it should touch the carrots. Kept that mountain shape with the hole in the middle for the gravy until the last bite. Always came out even. Enough gravy for the last forkful and it never touched anything else on the plate, and if the dam broke accidentally, or Bea reached over when he wasn't looking and poked it, the plate went to the kitchen, where he couldn't see it, and that was that. Wouldn't make another one. Sat there and scowled until he was excused. Wouldn't even talk.

And neat? The only kid's room in the house with everything lined up like in the army, and the Lord be with anyone who touched something.

Maybe he never even had sex. Maybe he found it too messy. Too sticky, or something. Too nasty.

Pete couldn't have it. Not old Pete. He'd probably do it in a rubber diving suit, if he did it at all. He was too health conscious. Always running. Always trim. He should stay so trim himself.

But if he had it, what would they do? Make sure he was taken care of, of course. They'd make sure he didn't lack for anything. The best care. They'd make sure of that. The public thing would have to be handled. There'd be a field day at the office. The other partners. The junior partners. A real buzz. Could even trigger looking into certain things. Making certain inquiries about transactions. What the fuck. They all do it. They just don't call it insider trading. Who hasn't acted on a tip in our business? You can't walk around with blinders and earmuffs on. They pay people to know things.

But they don't pay enough. They've never paid him what he's worth. And that asshole Suttcliff acting like Mr. Sacrosanct and thinking no one knows he's got more in Teshigahara in his brother-in-law's name than Peter Parker does.

Fucking hypocrites.

He drains his glass. He shakes the cubes.

He'd fix a drink. Take a shower. Get dressed for their dear friends, Carter and Polly Perret, or whatever the fuck her name was, and if she said "Fronce" just once through those skinny lips, he'd throw her right out the fucking Anderson Window Wall into the goddamned gorge.

XI.

Phil stands at the head of the boardroom table after his officers and managers have left. The room, decorated in shades of salmon, acoustically engineered for audio-video presentations, "psychologically" lit, does not please him. He finds its colors too soft, its chairs—curved mahogany with caned backs and pale tangerine fabric seats—too fragile for the tough and difficult decisions that must be made in them. It is not a room you can easily roll up your sleeves in, not a room amenable to coffee marks and confrontation, to hiring and laying off. He wishes he had not paid the bill.

He drums the fingernails of one hand on the long, oval mahogany table. Its yellow and rust and brown grain looks three-dimensional. He likes the table. You can see down in it. It is rock solid. It takes eight men to move it.

He sits again in his chair at the head of the table. He looks out through the gauzy apricot fabric which covers the six windows of one wall, out to the Delaware River, on which his factory sits. His view is distorted by the fabric. He presses a button on the console to his left. Six motors whir quietly; six curtains part simultaneously, allowing in the reflected light of the river below.

He sits in his chair, the only one with arms, at the head

of the board table. He lifts his calves onto its edge. He crosses his legs. His knees ache. Absently, he rubs the knuckles of his right hand where the bone is enlarged and two of the fingers have begun to curve outward. He holds his hands up. The skin of his hands has no smooth places. The third knuckle of his forefinger on the hand that he writes with, achy now for months, is beginning to grow, he thinks. He turns his hands in the light from the windows and wonders what they will look like in five years or ten. He wonders if the day will come when someone will have to button his dress shirts for him. Pull on his undershorts for him in the morning. Will he have to hire a male nurse in white whose job description it'll be to unzip his pants and hold it for him when he needs to take a leak? Will his nurse, his Prick Holder, follow him like a spaniel as he walks through the factory?

"I hate this."

He thought that since his grandfather died at forty-nine and his father at forty-eight, he would not live to see fifty. At forty-five, he increased his company life insurance policy and his personal life insurance payable to Liz. He updated his will. He made discreet inquiries in the industry as to potential buyers of his business and attached the list with contact names and telephone numbers to his will. He put his ducks in a row.

But he did not die.

He keeps the list up-to-date, noting which companies have made offers over the years, the amounts of their offers, the amounts he estimates they would pay. His secretary makes annual clandestine calls to these companies to verify the contact person.

His ducks are still in a row.

Only his joints degenerate. He keeps on living.

"Use it or lose it. Walk in a pool, the doctors say. Who has time to walk in a frigging pool?"

He flexes his kneecaps. The ache flares.

When the new line came out, he'd walk in a pool. Find

an hour a day to walk through water. When the line came out, he'd have to do something. If it spread to the hips he'd end up on wheels, and he would not end up on wheels. Not on his frigging life.

When he looks back on his life, he does not understand how it all happened so quickly, how long days of hard work have added up to so short a period of time that he could have gone from youth and agility to wrinkled, spotted hands and pitted, spurred bone in what seems to him a snap of fingers. Only yesterday he was the age of the son he had lunch with only days ago.

His hand moves toward the phone, back to the tabletop. He resists his impulse to call Pete and tell him—to warn him that it all happens so very quickly. That the wrinkles he saw at the corners of Pete's eyes will spread across his face. That the forehead now just beginning to grow will expand to the crown of his head. That the slim waist will thicken in what seems like a day.

Of all his children, Pete is the most and the least like him. They look alike. The jawline. The nose bump. The cleft in his chin. But not the eyes. Strange and slanted some. Women love it. Mary Alice's friends couldn't take their eyes off him. Girls in his classes. He was so independent. Independent and intractable as a child, unyielding when he thought he was right to the point that it drove his father to raving, still does that he'll have nothing to do with the company, that he pisses all that good business sense, smarter than Stu even, into a frigging flower shop when he could run a corporation that'll gross $280 million this year unless people stop eating. Won't even try it because he is so goddamned mule stubborn. All right if he inherited stubbornness like the nose bump and the chin cleft, but he wasn't born queer, and that, Phil thinks, is the biggest mystery of his entire life. Pete was raised just like the others, just like his brothers, and he was just like his brothers until he was a teenager and sex came along and the whole thing got frigged up.

He could have had any woman he wanted and there were none that he wanted.

He thinks he has become almost used to the queer part. If you think about the whole thing. It killed him in the beginning, but not now so much except for thinking about him doing it with men. The actual doing it, and thinking about it makes Phil almost sick to his stomach.

He flexes his hands into fists and stretches the fingers out; flexes again.

But the rest of him is not much different than being normal if you thought about the whole thing. He had turned into a nice man, a little too nice sometimes, but not really soft in the middle. It seemed so sometimes, but not really when you thought about it. He never asked his father or his mother for a dime beyond an education, and the rest of them wanting down payments on houses and for things that came up and he started a business on God knows what and did damned well according to the accountant, when he thought Pete would fall flat on his ass. In fact, he was sure that he would.

He thinks he should have said something at lunch. He doesn't know why he does that, why he gets his back up when it's sugar that attracts the flies, not vinegar, but every goddamn time Pete pushes, he shoves, and they get into a pissing match and one of them walks away or they both do, and no matter how many times he tells himself he won't, he does. It's fucking automatic. And when Pete made that crack about deciding who he hangs around with and where, and fuck public relations, did he butt in saying that Pete could hang around with any pansy he goddamn well pleased so long as it wasn't at work? Did he say that Pete could live his private life any way he frigging chose? When he thought about it, Pete had never done anything he could remember to embarrass him or his mother except quitting Wharton right when he was a star there and the two of them out telling everybody he'd be getting his master's degree soon and he took off with a Chinaman to fucking California, leaving them to make excuses. It still fried him.

He stands. He walks to the windows, his hands on his hips. A tow drags a disabled trawler up the river.

He knows she's right. It was none of their business, meaning it was none of his business. And in the last analysis, all parents can do is raise them up in the best way they can figure out. And it wasn't easy. It wasn't easy because there's a drunk or a druggie in the cab around the corner and you don't know when he's going to run a light, and no, he would not play that one out again. Things happen. Shit happens and you make the best of it, and they were lucky that the other four grew up not being drug addicts or alcoholics, and that, in this day and age, seemed like a miracle.

And none of them were perfect. Maybe Cliffie would have been. Who knew?

Oddest child he ever met. Said whatever came into his head if he felt like talking, whether he thought you'd like to hear it or not, and Pete got just like him by degrees. Maybe Cliffie would have turned out queer, too, and then what? You thought you knew your kids and you didn't until they started acting on their own; making decisions without you, decisions they knew would make you crazy. Mary Alice slutting her way from one coast to the other, some new guy answering the phone no matter what time of day or night you called her until she met Hal, the only one of hers he and Liz had ever met that they liked and not her type at all—a genuine grown-up. A shock to her mother and to him. A family-type man in a responsible position and no beard and them having to pretend he was just OK so she wouldn't dump him. They had learned that the hard way with Bea. "You're too young. Anthony doesn't care about college. He's not even a plumber; he's a plumber's assistant." And suddenly they were at a wedding, announcing to three hundred and fifty people that the bride and groom weren't even coming. "We don't like big parties. Bye-bye. Thanks for everything."

But Anthony took good care of her and the kids. And he had never had to replace a bit of work that Anthony had done. An artist, even.

And how did he live with her? She'd got as big as a house. Changed her mind every four minutes. Always bitching about something or someone. Good to her kids and to Anthony and to her mother, and Pete was right. She'd drive off a bridge if he asked her to. If he told her which highway.

They all did exactly what they wanted to. No matter what you told them. He had told Stu. Oh, he'd waited until he was asked. And couldn't wait to be asked what did he think of Alexa, and he'd taken his sweet time answering. He had waltzed around that one at the club for round after round of drinks, which he noticed Stu insisted on buying.

"What do you think of her, Dad?"

"She's a beautiful girl, Stu. A beautiful girl." And she was, except for that hair the color of those dumb drapes. And another drink later Stu was back again.

"What do you think of her, Dad?"

"She's a smart cookie, Stu. Went to Holyoke, didn't you say? Has to be pretty damned smart to graduate from Holyoke. Your mother went there for two years, did you know that? Of course you did." And then some talk about colleges or business, or something, and he started up again.

"Do you like her, Dad?"

"It's what you like that's important, Stu."

"But do you?"

"I hardly know her, son."

"Dad."

"No," he had finally said. "No . . . I think she cares more about money than she does about people," knowing as he said it that he did, too, a lot of the time.

"I don't have any money, Dad."

"I think she'll sell you down the river when you do."

He leans toward the window with his hands on the sill.

His kids were always leaving him at tables. When they

were still at home, he didn't wait to be asked for his opinions. He gave them and they left the table. Now he waited until they asked him. When offered, they got up and left.

But it didn't last for the rest of them. At the next sitting down at a table it was as if they had not got up and left. But with Pete, his stomach spitted acid for a long time after. He could not keep his mind on his business. He did not sleep. He'd wake up thinking. It was the same old "Why doesn't he . . . and If I . . ." around and around to no conclusion. Ever.

He walks back to his chair at the head of the table. He stands with his hands on its curved back.

"Because it never hits the mark," he says aloud. Ever, he thinks. Too much waltzing around. He waltzes. Pete waltzes. They never sit one out and talk about the issue.

Which was that the kid was a faggot.

He taps his fingernails on the wood.

He accepted the fact of that. He couldn't be accused of not being pragmatic. What galled him was that Pete would never come out and say that he was. Never came to him to have it out.

Daily he made decisions involving the lives of hundreds of people. Decisions involving millions, megamillions of dollars. His men come to him with their problems, with their own tough decisions. Personal decisions, even. He was often surprised at the things that they would tell him. Not that they were queer, because none of them was, but important things that they came to him with. Problems they were having with their marriages, with their own kids. Life and death things sometimes. His door was always open. To all of them. It was like family here.

He thinks Pete ought to bring it up himself, but that he is too frigging secretive. Even about his business. Didn't bring his business up unless his father did, unless Phil asked. He was always like that. Never discussed anything with him or with his mother ahead of time, just up and did it. He could have had a summer job at the plant any summer he wanted. And making decent money. And what did he do? He announced he had a job standing all day repotting orchids in a greenhouse hotter than hades. Or he up and went to Cape Cod in May without so much as a by-your-leave and called to say he'd be back in September.

His son the balloon vendor.

If he asked, Pete would answer. He would answer if it were brought up.

It was Pete's responsibility to bring it up.

What was he waiting for? His father to be stuck in a wheelchair with arthritic hips? To stand out of range and announce, "By the way, Dad, I'm a faggot"? What did Pete think he would do? Throttle him? If Pete had just said what he meant in the restaurant instead of mincing words. What was he thinking? That his father would turn over the table? That he would throw food?

He did get excited, but he was not an unreasonable man. It was that he did not like surprises. Did not like things thrust upon him.

And where was the surprise in this? This was not exactly what you could call a revelation. Not exactly a bolt out of the blue. The kid hadn't had a date with a woman in twenty years that he knew of. Had not shown up with one to a family dinner since he left home. Did he expect him to stroke out from the shock? Not very goddamned likely, all things considered.

And what would he say if Pete said that?

"Hey, Pete. Not to worry. You're a responsible adult. You pay your bills. You pay your taxes."

"Hey, no problem. I was mortified when you quit school for that flower arranger. I got over it. Many years later."

"Never mind. If I don't hold it against you, will you work at Grand-mère's? We're an Equal Opportunity Employer. I have three people downstairs who fill out forms all day to prove it. One of them's black. We hire the handicapped. I was presented a bronze plaque by the mayor's office. It says right on it."

There would be certain rules. In 1968 he fired his director of quality assurance because of rumors he was queer. It took him months to replace the man with someone as good.

On the management level they had a policy of not interviewing male applicants who were not married by age thirty-two. An exception could be made.

Grand-mère's represented traditional family values. A family was depicted in every TV commercial. White, black, Hispanic. A salad was always seen on the table. A serving suggestion. All of the TV parents were in their thirties. They all had three children. A well-balanced meal for a well-balanced family. And that could not change. No scenes of two fluffs sitting at a table for a meal of meat pies, one of them getting up to flit back and forth to the kitchen with hot pads, the table alive with wrists and fluttering fingers. Fruits of the Sea taking on new meaning? No thank you very much.

Pete would not push for that. He looked like a man's man. Like an athlete. In a suit, he looked very professional. So what if he had no wife and no children? There were normal men who chose not to marry.

Name two, Phil.

Name one, Phil.

But who would dare to even comment? Who on his team would breathe a word about it in his hearing? Or even out of it? Who would risk his extremely generous bonus or his kids' orthodontic care paid for by the Grand-mère health insurance plan?

The faggot jokes would have to stop. He would put a stop to that. Without making a scene, either. One word from him.

"Gordy, we do not bite the hand that feeds us. Didn't you tell me yourself that one in ten of our pies is consumed by a homosexual?"

That's all it would take. Except for attending social events. He'd need a woman to be seen with. He would have one brought in from outside. A woman with a body-by-God and brains—a smooth talker. One who was aware of the program and would be tight-lipped. She'd be told up front. Given a title. Pete wouldn't mind that. It would be Business. He knew what had to be done in this world to make a buck.

"Maybe you can't afford me."

He chuckles.

He loved it. The kid had balls. Whatever he offered him, he'd up it. He'd up it if he offered him more than he frigging makes himself. None of his business. There was more than one way to skin a cat.

He sits in his chair. He picks up the handset and dials his secretary.

"I'm in the boardroom. Get me Ted Gunn."

He returns the handset to its cradle. With his elbows on the table, he worries a thumbnail.

It's for his own good, he thinks, feeling guilty. He wins in the end. What's the difference? Never go blind into a deal. He couldn't insult the kid. Couldn't offer him something that was a joke. Make an ass of himself in his opening shot?

The phone rings.

"Mr. Gunn on eight."

He punches the button.

"Ted. I need something. You do my son Pete's taxes."

"Yes."

"I need to know what he netted last year."

"Why?"

"What do you mean, 'why'? I need to know it."

"Why don't you ask him?"

"It's personal."

"That's why I can't tell you, Phil."

Irritated, he says, "You're his accountant. I pay you to give me information."

"About your business."

"This is about my business."

"It's about his business."

"Ted, I didn't call you for a ration of shit. I'm asking you a simple question. It will go no further than the two of us."

"I'd have to ask him."

"You can't ask him, for Christ's sake. If I thought he'd tell me, I'd frigging ask him myself." He drums his fingernails on the tabletop.

"He's my client."

"Hey, I'm your client." He pauses. "I'm also the biggest client you've got."

"Yes. You are."

There is silence.

"So tell me what I need to know."

"Phil, if Pete called me and asked me what your net was last year, would you want me to tell him?"

"That isn't the same thing. I pay you a great deal of money to give me financial advice."

"And I do that."

"So answer the question."

"You're asking me to tell you how much your son made last year. How is that 'financial advice'? Are you looking to get into the flower business?"

"Fuck no! I'm trying to get him out of it. I want to hire him."

"So make him an offer."

Phil takes a deep breath.

"I called you to find out what kind of offer to make."

"What's the job worth?"

"Jesus Christ, I don't even know what the job *is*."

"Well, do some thinking about that, Phil, and I'll help you come up with a number."

"I want him to take over the company someday."

"Well? What's that worth to you? You have to think that over. I can tell you this. The kid's smart. He's taught me a couple of tricks in the last few years. And I'll tell you something else. I don't think he cares about business."

"What do you mean, he doesn't care about business?"

"I don't know. It's just a means to an end with him."

"What's the end?"

"I don't know. The process bores him. He doesn't need me. He could do all the numbers himself. As good as me. Maybe better. He drops off a box of stuff every February. It's all in perfect order. He tells me what he wants done. I do it. His bottom line is better every year, but it's just sort of the way it's s'posed to be. It's just something he happens to be good at. He doesn't do it because it gives him any particular pleasure, I don't think. I don't know."

"Then why does he do it?"

"I don't know, Phil."

"That's crazy."

"I don't know . . . I don't know why I do what I do sometimes."

"Well, I like what I do. That's why I do it. Maybe you need one thing to concentrate on. The offer's still open. Close that office and move over here. You're doing our work mostly, anyway."

"I like my own office."

"You can have your own frigging office. I'll build you one just like it. Same carpet; same frigging colors. You tell me."

"I don't want to move."

Phil grunts. "Have it your own way. Talk to you."

He stretches out in his chair, crosses his ankles under the table.

He'd give him a hundred to start. A hundred and twenty. On a trial basis. They'd try each other out. A VP of something or other. Let him decide. Would that be enough? A car. A nice car. He could pick it. Something sensible. Something high mid-range.

What if he made more than that now? He'd sit there with that neutral look on his face. He couldn't make that much now.

The kid was not easy.

He should buy his business.

He would, goddammit. Pay more than it's worth. Sweeten

the pot. Have somebody make him an offer he'd be a fool to turn down. He'd have money to salt away. Pete could never find out. He would be furious and quit in a snit. He could find an outside lawyer to handle the offer. All very discreet. All very aboveboard.

He shifts his weight to one side of the curved-back chair. He cannot get comfortable.

"Goddammit!" he says. He dials his secretary.

"Irene, get rid of these frigging chairs."

"What frigging chairs, Mr. Flowers?"

"The frigging chairs in the frigging boardroom! I hate the goddamned things and I want them out. I want chairs I can frigging sit on!"

"I'll call Maintenance."

"No. You'll call that wimp decorator, whoever he was, and you'll tell him to have them out of here by five. By five to*day*, Irene. And the frigging drapes, too. *And* the goddamned motors that run 'em! And I'm painting these walls. I hate this pale shit. Makes me frigging queasy."

XII.

"You're a dear," his mother says, accepting a medicinal scotch. "The others won't do this. They're afraid they'll kill me."

"So am I," Pete says, taking a seat across from her.

She sits in a chair by the window. She wears ice-blue satin pajamas and silver jewelry: a double-strand chain and two thin bracelets; a brooch with her initials, EMF, intertwined is pinned to her pajama top over the breast which was removed. Her hair has been washed and set; her makeup is in place. Her legs are propped on a hassock in the afternoon sun.

"This feels more or less normal," she says. "Next time, I'll entertain you in the library and wear a dress. It looks strange, doesn't it?"

"What?"

"You've been looking at my breast. Or, I should say, at my chest. At the place where it was."

He looks up. "Excuse me."

"No apology necessary. I've made a little game of it. I watch everyone's reaction. I haven't caught Bea looking there yet. We'll spend an hour together and even talk about it, and she won't look. The same with Mary Alice. They look me in the eye, or at the breast that's left. You and your father and the grandchildren can't take your eyes off the one that's gone. I suspect it's because you don't have breasts to begin with. Or you all have greater appreciations for asymmetry. What do you think?"

"I don't know," he says, careful now not to look back at the brooch where her breast was.

"I think I look rather well, don't you?"

"You do, Mom. You look wonderful."

"Is that my book in the bag?"

"Yes. Sorry. I forgot about it."

He hands it to her.

"Thank you very much. I'll give you a check."

"It's a gift, Mom."

"No. Indeed not. I'll tell you what I'll let you give me, though. Send me over some jasmine. Can you get jasmine this time of year? I forget if it has a season."

"I can get it. A live plant."

"I need to smell it," she says. "Fresh. It cannot have escaped your attention that I have been acting a little strangely. Max recommended this book. It deals anecdotally with cases of frontal lobe tumors. He thought this might demystify my experiences."

"Which experiences?"

"Are you sure you want to hear? I brought them up to Bea the other day and she got so alarmed that I decided to change the subject. That fit I took when you were visiting me at the hospital was the worst of them, but the Dilantin they give me now has taken away the really nasty parts. I don't flop around anymore; I just have these recurrent episodes of smelling things that set off . . . well, they're hallucinations, is what they are. Your mother hallucinates, dear."

"Like my coming into your room with a sign."

"What do you mean?"

"You told me the night of the dinner that I had come into your room. With a sign."

"Did I?" she says matter-of-factly. "I've forgotten that one. It's not a regular one. There are two or three basic ones and they all occur to music. My favorite, I think, happens when I open that bottle of hand lotion on the bed table. When I first put that particular lotion on my hands and spread it over them and the scent is strong, the music begins. It is as if I were there again. Not just remembering it, but actually being there, experiencing her singing in that room."

"Who?"

"Mabel Mercer."

"What's she singing?"

"Cole Porter. 'Just One of Those Things.' "

"You hear this?"

"Oh, yes. I don't just hear it. I am there. Or it's here. Physically. That room at the old Cobblestone. On Sixth Street. It's quite wonderful. It's amazing. I am seated at a very small table for four, facing Mabel Mercer. She's only a few steps away. She sits on a peacock chair. Next to her is the piano, the bass player, the guitarist, and just behind him, a man playing snares. Your father is next to me. I know it's your father because I remember the night we went there, of course, but I can't see his face, just his ring on his hand on the table. I can see Patsy Parker's left hand beating time with a cigarette, and George's hands cupped around one knee. But the really curious thing, what makes it bizarre, as if it weren't bizarre enough to have all this happening in this very room and in that very room at the same time, is that the music, the whole event, actually, begins into the second verse of the song. It all starts abruptly with the word 'nights.' The piano drops to a flat and the snare goes che che, the bass thumps twice, and they all continue [she sings], '. . . Just one of those fabulous flights,' and a waitress's arm comes over my shoulder and places a scotch and water in a fat glass on the table in front of me and her hand removes my old one and she stops for a few seconds to listen behind me, smelling of jasmine perfume, and she leaves and the scent of the perfume lingers strong just until 'we started painting the town,' and by 'we'd have *bean* aware'—Mabel Mercer always sang 'bean' for 'been'—'that our love affair,' it all breaks up. It dissolves, becoming more this room than that room, with a few notes and words sort of hanging and going off into the air."

"You seem to like this."

"Oh, I do! I must have been really happy the night we went to see her. I *feel* so nice when it happens, just a little annoyed at the waitress's arm, is all. I'm curious to see what real jasmine would do. I have a theory that the smell of live jasmine would re-create the whole song. Maybe the whole evening. If jasmine-scented hand lotion makes part of the song come, real jasmine might bring the whole thing back."

"Sort of like 'Smell-A-Vision'?"

"More real."

"Wouldn't you get tired of it? I mean, hearing the same thing over and over?"

"I haven't got tired of hearing just part of it. And look how soft my hands are," she says, holding them up. "I've used up most of that bottle since yesterday. Besides, if I got tired of it, I'll have them take the flowers down the hall."

"What does Max think of this?"

"He doesn't seem to think much of anything about it. He says it's not an uncommon phenomenon for people with lesions where mine are. He does seem impressed that my experiences are so vivid. He says some people just hear a tune, or see a part of something, or feel a certain mood. I get the whole thing. What did the sign say?"

"The sign?"

"The one you were carrying when you came into my room."

He feels uncomfortable talking with his mother about her hallucinations.

"I don't know," he says. "It was just some sort of sign."

She sips her scotch and waits.

"Well," she says patronizingly, "was it a wooden sign or a neon sign?"

"You told me it was a paper sign. Hand-lettered."

"And what did it say?"

"You said it said, 'TELL PETE.' "

" 'Tell Pete' what?"

"Mom, I don't know."

"Well, it was your sign, dear."

"It was your sign. How would I know what it meant?"

"You were the one who was carrying it. You must have written it before you came into my bedroom."

He squirms in his seat.

She is smiling. "You have the silliest expression on your face. Are we having a good time yet?"

"Apparently you are."

"Albeit at your expense."

Her eyes twinkle. She looks impish, he thinks.

"I don't mean to make light of it," she says. "Well, I guess I do, actually. I've discovered since I got out of the hospital that you can get away with almost anything if people think you're a little dotty. . . . That sign you were carrying. What does it mean?"

"Mom," he says impatiently. "I'm not going to play this game with you."

"No. I'm serious. I should have said, 'What does it mean, do you suppose?' "

"I don't know, Mom. What do you think it means?"

"I have been thinking about this while we've been talking. At first I didn't know what you were talking about, and then it came back like a dream I had had, and now it doesn't seem like a dream. I remember your hand on my shoulder. I remember the sign. It was written on laundry shirt cardboard. You used to use the cardboard from your father's shirts to make bas-relief maps for geography class. You made a paste out of flour and water and salt, I think. Do you remember that?"

"Yes. There was salt in it."

"I don't know what the salt did. Maybe it made the mountains stand up. When the map was dry, you would paint in the rivers in blue and even the elevations in shades of brown and green. Your maps were always impressive. What was I supposed to tell you? What was so important that you had to print a sign and hold it up? I thought it was about my having cancer, but the day you came into my room was the day of the dinner when I was going to tell all of you anyway.

"I guess there are a lot of things I would like to tell you. There are a lot of things I would like you to tell me. Maybe I should have come into your room holding a sign. Mine made of petit point? Or written across the cover of a book? 'Tell Mom'? What would you like to tell Mom, dear? . . . That you hate turning forty in less than a month?"

"I thought this was about you telling me something."

"Well, when I turned forty, I had a crisis of faith. I don't know that it had anything to do with turning forty. I'm not even sure anymore what it did have to do with. Your father blamed it all on Mary Alice and Stu, of course. Your father has always gone for the obvious. She was going from room to room sighing and long-facing over some jerk much older than she was, and Stu had just gone away to school. It had nothing to do with them. It was simply a crisis of faith.

"I have never expected God to solve my problems. A lot of people do. I hear them at mass or when I just drop by the church to sit awhile. They're muttering there with their rosaries, making the most outlandish promises in return for the most outlandish things. All I ever asked God for was to just hover around, or if He was too busy, to send somebody else to hover around, like the Holy Mother if she wasn't pressured, though I never really expected her to be sent, She not having a minute to Herself, let alone for me, with half the world on Her all day long. And I was always OK. Always had the strength to handle things, never wavered from what I had always believed, even when Cliffie died, even then in the worst days of my life . . .

"Until the day before my fortieth birthday. It was a Wednesday. I always went to morning mass early on Wednesday because it gave me a midweek lift, and there I sat in the pew where I always sat in the church I had always gone to, listening to Monsignor DiDomenico, who had baptized me when I was three weeks old and confirmed me when I was thirteen, going on about the glory of the Holy Trinity and suddenly I knew, suddenly I was struck with the cold-sweat realization that neither in my very heart of hearts nor in the swift workings of my very logical brain did I either understand the Trinity or believe in it! I found that comprehension, rather the lack of it, so shocking, so upsetting, that I got up and walked out of the church. Oh, I *smiled* at Monsignor DiDomenico as I walked out, as if I had just glanced at my watch and realized I was late for a bridge game. I even turned and waved at the man as I left the pew, and while I walked up the center aisle and he went on about the Miracle of God in Three Persons, I thought to myself, with my armpits drenched and my forehead dripping, Woman, you are going to burn in Hell. You are going to fry. God in Three Persons just kissed you off."

"I didn't know you believed in Hell."

"I do not. I did. Then. Until sometime after my fortieth birthday. Until months after it. I stopped going to church. I felt desperately empty. Monsignor DiDomenico called me. He came by the house. I did not tell him that I was having a crisis of faith. I told him that I needed to do some thinking was all, and each time that he dropped by, I would pour him a rye and we would chat as we always did and he never pushed me. How could I tell that sweet man that I had ceased to believe in the Trinity?

"And after he would leave, I would sit and puzzle over it. It was as if *The Three Faces of Eve* had come to the ultimate roost. God plagued with multiple personalities? It made no sense to me at all. I dug out a copy of the catechism. I studied the whole thing, hoping to find some reassurance in it. I was not reassured at all. In fact, I wished I had not read it. It is full of implied threats. It made me feel worse. All those questions and clear-cut answers. And the drawings were the worst part. They made me feel like I was that frightened child again in Sister Inviolata's class. If there was ever a hate-filled woman in God's Church, it was she. A certifiable sadist. She used to sneak up behind our desks and slam books on our tiny hands. I am surprised I learned to love to read.

"I found no answers among the answers of the catechism except that I came to realize that it was the Holy Spirit part of the Trinity that I had the most trouble with. I had some personal knowledge of God and of Jesus, but none at all of the Holy Spirit. There was nothing there I could relate to, and I was especially bothered that I could find no logical explanation of how that kind of thinking came about in the first place. It had to have been a committee and they must all have been very high on something when they decided to approve it."

"So how did you resolve it?"

"Oh, I guess in the end I just missed my church too much to stay away from it, so I started going back. I felt like a terrible hypocrite at first. I didn't take communion, and I never went near a confession booth. God forbid I should tell a priest I no longer believed in a basic dictum of the Church. But by and by I began to feel more comfortable. It wasn't, after all, that I didn't believe in God, it's just that I don't see him as a schizophrenic."

"Do you take communion now?"

"I have not taken communion since. That would be hypocritical. Until I meet this Holy Spirit and He explains this to me in some acceptable way, I am not doing any communions. I do my communing directly."

"Mom, have you considered that maybe you're not a

Catholic anymore? According to the edicts of the Church?"

"Of course I'm a Catholic. I've been a Catholic for sixty-four years."

"But if you don't believe in the Holy Spirit, which is the element of faith that allows you to believe in the Trinity, then you don't believe in the Trinity, and you have to in order to be a Catholic."

"Bullshit."

"Hey, I didn't make up the rules."

"It is bullshit," she says, agitated. "And 'making up the rules' is precisely why. This *Spiritus Sanctus* stuff is all after the fact. There was God, and then he had a son, Jesus Christ, and if that were not enough of a miracle by itself, then a bunch of people, men probably—this sounds just like something a bunch of men would figure out—get together and decide that the club was not exclusive enough and that all the members also have to believe in something extra. 'I got an idea,' one of them says. 'Let's make it a spirit!' After all, everyone back then was afraid of spirits. 'Yeah,' the head one says, 'but we'll call this one the *Holy* Spirit.' And that's how it happened. I'm convinced. And as far as my being a Catholic goes, I have more than paid my dues to the Church. I am not going to have a little technicality like the Trinity get in the way of my love for my church. My faith in the Duality will just have to do.

"It was Freud, by the way," she says.

"What about Freud?"

"When you were here last, we were talking about your life. We only have our love and our work? It was Freud who said that. I remembered in the middle of the night."

"Ah," he says.

"How is the quality of your love and your work? At forty."

He sighs.

"Would you like to talk about something less significant?" she says.

"My work is fine, Mom. I'm very busy."

He would like to shift his mother's gears, have her talk about herself and just listen.

"I know that you are busy. You keep saying that. Does it make you happy, is what I'm asking."

"Sure," he says.

"I mean, does it satisfy you?"

"It does and it doesn't. It's like anything you do, Mom. Nothing is ever satisfying all the time."

"I know that. I mean, on balance?"

"I don't know. I don't think about it much."

"What's to think about? It's either satisfying most of the time, or it isn't."

He crosses his legs. Uncrosses them.

"It's not so cut-and-dry."

"Maybe it is. Maybe if you don't know if it's satisfying, it isn't."

"I don't think anything is that simple, Mom."

"Oh, bullshit. How about the love part? Is that satisfying?"

He looks at his mother with some wonder.

"What is this inquisition? What has got you going on this?"

"Is there something new here?" she asks. "Since all of you were born, I have wanted you to be happy. Now I am simply asking you if you are. It seems to me that after forty-how-many years of being a parent, I do have a right to a couple of straightforward answers. You have all been my work and my love. Look at it as what? . . . A self-evaluation. It helps me to gauge if I am happy or not, though I grant you that my happiness does not necessarily depend on yours. Who is going to ask you if your life is satisfying? Your friends? Do they?"

"People are supposed to ask themselves."

"Do you?"

"Well. I think I do."

"I think you do not. I think that if you did, you would

be able to answer quite quickly or tell me right out that it is none of my 'frigging' business, as your father says. It is, in a way, none of my business. In another way, it is my business to ask you, because I love you. I think you are driving through Kansas and not enjoying the trip. I think your work does not interest you much beyond being a means of making a living and I think that you have no one you love in the center of your life because if you did I would know it because you are quite a different man when you do. You are flat, Pete. Like this trip you are on. I can see that I am offending you. I'll stop this, if you want."

He sighs. He looks around Bea's room, at the wallcovering, the draperies, so quintessentially his mother's taste, elaborate patterns on plain fields. How strange the accoutrements of her illness look, tanks and dials and wires around the mechanized bed made up with paisley, 200-thread sheets from Bloomingdale's.

"No," he says.

"I'll tell you something. I think I am not going to come out of this intact," she says. She puts her hand over her brooch. "Heaven knows that I am not exactly intact at the moment. I have spent a lifetime learning to trust my intuitions. They are telling me now that I have a good chance to survive. I begin radiation the day after tomorrow. Did I tell you? I was supposed to begin right after the operation, but of course I went AWOL. Two hundred rads each treatment. They're saying ten to fifteen treatments."

"On your chest?"

"In my brain. I am going to lose something in the process. I don't know what it will be, but I do know that it will be something vital, and that conversations like we are having right now will not be possible."

"You don't know that, Mom."

"Yes. I do. These tumors that I have are living in the place where I care, and I think that if they kill them, they are also going to kill the part of me that cares and that I will be spending the better part of my time, if not all of it, doing something like what you are doing, coasting along on some Möbius strip through someplace like Kansas. But it will not matter to me, or I will have no control over it, and you do, and that is why I am poking at you so to take a good look at the landscape of your life and to make your work and your love mean important things to you. Freud was right, Pete. What else is there when you think about it?" She heaves a breath. "It's five-twenty, isn't it?"

He looks at his watch. She is not wearing one. Her digital clock is out of her sight.

"It is. How did you know?"

"It's the tumors. If I start out knowing what time it is in the morning, I know what time it is all day. I am going to do you a favor. Your dear sister-in-law, Alexa, and your nieces Flicka and Black Beauty are due here at five-thirty. If you want to stay, you may, but I am sure we will be talking about horses and little else."

"I'll pass. Thanks for the warning."

"Well. Lay a wet kiss on your pushy mother's old cheek before you go. You'll give Freud some thought?"

"Yes, Mom. I'll give Freud some thought."

XIII.

In his den, Bill Payne sits cross-legged on the floor by his bookcase, sorting through magazines. He has piled hundreds of issues on the carpet, pulling them down from the shelves above him. They date back for years.

It is perverted, he thinks. What did he think he would do with them all? What's in them to save them? *Smithsonian*, December 1988. A model train on the cover. He has never cared about model trains. Ever.

He pages through the magazine, shaking his head.

Ah. Man Ray. Well, of course, Man Ray. He loved Man Ray. He'd gone out of his way to see Man Ray. Went out of his way to see this exhibit. Trained and taxied to Washington, D.C. Played hooky on the coldest day of January to stand in awe before the photograph of Kiki of Montparnasse's bare back with violin sound holes on it. Could not get a single pedestrian friend to play hooky with him. "Man Ray. Is that a rock group?" "Man Ray who?" Fucking philistines. Why didn't he have any intellectual friends?

"Because you didn't choose any, you silly twit," he says, putting the magazine in the "save" pile and picking up another.

Except Pete. Who had a mind like greased lightning and used it now about as often as lightning comes to town.

When they were together, Pete would play hooky now

and then. When things were slow enough that he thought Doris could handle it and he thought he could handle the guilt, they'd take off. Go to New York. Grab the first Metroliner that came along when they were ready for it and sit with a thermos of Bloody Mary mix and another of ice and lemons and zip through New Jersey at a hundred and twenty miles an hour, talking about life and art and music and about their friends, and later, at the Museum of Modern Art, drag each other away from favorite things to make the other look at something he didn't like, but tried to, because the other did, with only a few artists where the lines crossed. The big Monets. They would stand before them like hayseeds. Little smiles on their faces.

And why did the lines cross there, of all places? Pete's tastes running to the rudeness of Rouault and his own to the whimsical. Duchamp. Ray. The better Dadas. Why were they both drawn to those huge, delicious blurs? Pete for the flowers, he supposed, and he for what? For the dreamy blues? The rarest color in nature in spite of the sky? How nice to stand there and be of the same mind when their tastes and interests in just about everything else in the world, except maybe for Thai food and sex, could not have been more divergent.

When Pete was very bad and feeling good about it, Bill could talk him into staying over in New York. They'd check into the Plaza or the Grand Hyatt with one bought toothbrush and their shoulder bag of empty thermoses and eat Oriental food in the Village and sing at the piano at Marie's Crisis and be ogled at and hit on by sleek New York men, and back to the hotel for more of their favorite things. Who cared that they felt like shit at work the next day? Who gave a shit in the face of adventure?

» » »

In his kitchen, he prepares a salad. He prefers his greens bitter, his dressings tart. He removes cooled escarole leaves from a rolled-up towel. He tears them into bite-sized pieces. He includes the chewy ribs.

Suppose he asked Pete out. Not for a regular dinner. They always did that. He always did that. He called Pete. Casually. Buddy-buddy. "How about dinner Saturday night?" It had become a routine, a fait accompli. The two of them or the four of them or the six of them if Geo and Paul had dates. Suppose he called Pete and said right out that he'd made a reservation for Saturday the nineteenth. For the two of them. At Susannah Foo's. For dinner. Was he free? Pete would rather eat there than anywhere. And if he was not free, he could say, "Would June second be good?" And if not June the second, he could say, "No problem, I'm free on the ninth. Would the ninth be OK for you?" And when Pete said yes, then what would he do? What would he say then to make it clear that this was not just a Saturday night dinner? That it was a date. An officially sanctioned date. As if they had just met in a bar or at a cocktail party and talked for a while and had more than a flicker of interest in each other? That they had shared phone numbers and didn't know whether to call the other first. Was it politic to be casual? Wait for the other to call? Pete being a waiter and he a caller. He'd never been good at waiting. For anything.

When he first met Pete, he didn't wait. Got his number in the soup aisle of the Great Scot Market. Had nothing to write with. Memorized it. Called him that night: "This is Bill Payne. We met at the Great Scot today. Would you like to have dinner?"

He could do that. Call him and say, "This is Bill Payne. We met at the Great Scot Market five years ago. Would you like to have dinner Saturday the nineteenth?"

He peels radicchio leaves from a small head and tears them into his bowl. The leaves are nearly the color of Pete's birthmark. Port wine.

He could not believe his luck five years ago. Meeting a grown-up man. A responsible person who expected to pay his share. And never seemed to care if Bill had a lot of money. Never talked about money. A man with conversation and hot to boot. Oooweee. A meeting that ruined his life forever. Made it impossible for him to settle again for less. Made it impossible to find as much since.

Oh, not perfect, God knows. The most stubborn man he ever met. Makes up his mind on the spot and starts driving nails into his shoes and that, baby, is it.

And eats awful. Loves fat. Bacon with anything and thinks running makes it right. Would probably drink lard if you warmed it up.

And bored and boring living on his own. Hadn't been to a concert that Bill knew of since they broke up; he a man who knew more about classical music than Bill and Dad-dums put together. And getting him to go to a serious play since then? You might as well try to convince the Queen of England to give up her corgis.

And Pete was the one who taught Bill to like Brecht, except for the plays that go on for three days, the ones you have to carry a sleeping bag to, and, frankly, Bill even liked those when he and Pete used to go together. God forbid Pete should enter the Annenberg Center. Pumps up his brain now on *Cats*, which has played this town two zillion times. He cannot recall the last time Pete mentioned a book, good or bad, that he'd read. It was as if he had decided to turn off his brain. Like Geo and Paul. Charge the cells up every week or two as they did. With their Macy's and their Bloomingdale's cards.

A kick in the ass now and then is what Pete needed. Needed someone around to fucking stimulate him. Some-one to say, "Girl, brush those cobwebs away. We are going to the theatah." "Fuck the Bronsteins' bar mitzvah. Screw the Gotrockses' wedding. Tonight we're gettin' high on Yo-Yo Ma."

He seals the remaining radicchio into a plastic container. He removes his stainless-steel kitchen shears from his neatly arranged utensil drawer and begins to snip curly en-dive.

Needs a husband, is what he needs. And he was not

talking one of those chunks of meat Pete usually picks, with pecs out to here and minds like egg cartons. He was talking balance. He was talking Renaissance man. Six foot five, a hundred and ninety-five pounds of pure, unmitigated sex with a mind like Aristotle's and wit like Oscar Wilde's, and what was he anyway? Chopped liver? And why the hell did it happen? How had it fallen apart? He was a fucking dream walking. If there was ever a great catch in the United States of entire America, this, honey lamb, was it.

He puts his scissors in the sink. He rests his hands on the counter edge and leans his forehead against the cool steel cabinet.

You moved too fast, Grace-Anne Marge Lucille, he thinks. You wanted the vine-covered cottage and you pushed it too hard and you should have used your noggin like your mother taught you and waited until it was his idea, because as sure as God made little green apples he'd have wanted to live together eventually anyway because he hates it when he can't find something and it was always in the other place, and did you really give a good flying fuck if it ended up being his house or yours so long as it was ours? And the only vines you have ended up with now are intertwined on that magnificent, cost-a-mint, drop-dead Sarouk Farahan out there in the living room that you walk on. Dumb.

"Dumb. Dumb. Dumb."

» » »

He sits in a flexible iron chair on his terrace at the top of Academy House. His salad bowl rests in his legs, akimbo. From behind him, through the open sliding glass doors, he listens to the music of Elgar.

A good salad. Maybe a perfect salad, having that *certaine piquante je ne sais quoi*, except he knows what it is. The judicious use of champagne vinegar and lime juice, the just-right combination of acid and oil augmenting the bite of the greens.

He wishes he knew more about music. What is so enigmatic about the *Enigma Variations*? The same theme recognizable throughout. Stated in the first. There still in the last. What did he not hear? Take a course, Bill. Fill your evenings with some noble pursuit. Call the universities and find out who is teaching a course. The Enigma Revealed: Hidden Music Found; Liaison With Helen Weaver Hinted.

He forks an escarole leaf, combines it with a piece of sun-dried tomato, chews the two looking out to the sunset reflected in the windows of the Hershey Hotel.

How to make lovers of friends who have been lovers? How do you go from being best friends to touching pee pees again? Did one state of intimacy preclude the other?

"The story of my life," he says, rocking.

His enviable life. Two apartments combined into one at the top of the city, lord of a lot of what he surveys. Three buildings within his line of sight that he owns; more to the north and to the west. Enough money in the bank to last several lifetimes. A body that is, although a little long of leg, a knockout. Thoughtful. Considerate. . . . Giving.

But apparently not very subtle. Or maybe too subtle. But where did subtlety ever get him with Pete anyway? All the stupid angst he went through after suggesting that they be "fuck buddies"? And that wasn't even what he wanted. He had no interest anymore in sex for its own sake. And being fuck buddies implied it was just until something better came along. He should have kept his mouth shut.

"No," he says, swirling his salad around with the fork.

Foolish person.

What he should have said that night is, "Come on. Bring your drink. I'm ordering pizza. Let's go out on the terrace and talk." And then, while they were waiting for pizza, sitting out here in these chairs with their drinks, he should have said . . . What should he have said? "Pete . . ." A terrific beginning. "Pete . . . Do you ever think about getting together again?" Right. Bring it up like do you need a little salt on that? Or just flat out said: "It makes me crazy when you want to be with someone else you want some fresh oregano on that?"

But Pete said he hadn't been with someone else. For a year and a half. And he had been assuming all that time that every time Pete looked at someone else they ended up in bed. Biting his tongue and the insides of his cheeks. Being gracious. And he hadn't been doing it anyway. With anyone.

"Strike while the iron is hot, Bill."

But was the iron hot?

He leans his head back on the cushion. The chair rocks. His fork waves in his hand.

Where had there been the first clue that Pete even thought about getting back together? He hadn't seen the first sign that he wanted anything more than what they had. Being best friends. Talking about things. Being around for each other when they needed it.

That was not nearly intimate enough. Not by a long shot. He was not good at loving from a distance. He was definitely a hands-on lover. He needed daily interaction. Needed to wake up to someone who cared if he was there or not. Needed someone to come home to.

Or come home together with, maybe, if he took the job. If Pete came to work for The Empire. One thing to work together. Another to come home together and spend the night, having spent the day.

Maybe it wasn't such a good idea. Considering such a blatant ulterior motive. Considering that what he really wanted, more than the working together, which he did think would be good for them both, was more the coming home to each other. Sharing things, more than sharing work. And would Pete find the combination burdensome? And would he? In the long run? If so, ipso facto, he saw a logical shift over time. Once Pete learned the business, learned how to deal with the problems of buildings, once he had his feet in the water, so to speak, knew the program and could "impact on the variables" as Daddums was so fond of saying, Bill might slowly slip himself out of it, turn The Empire over to him and instead of their coming home together, he could be home already when Pete came home.

"Hi, sweetheart. How was it at the office today? I have your cocktail ready. I have prime rib roasting in the oven, just oozing fat the way you like it, or would you like to run first, honey lamb of mine?"

". . . How grotesque."

He stirs his salad. Leaves the fork in the bowl.

He thinks he might be biting off more than he can chew. Difficult enough to lure an old lover back, without the complications inherent in the rest of his scenario.

He rocks the chair on its curved steel legs.

Fuck buddies. He should have had his lips sewn shut.

"You ball-less wonder," he says, rocking.

He who had never been afraid to take a risk. He who came out to his parents at sixteen. At the dinner table. Right there in the middle of passing the peas he had said to his stuffy, football-freak father, "Daddums, enough already about Marcia Hopwood. I am in love with Richard Egan." And while his father picked peas off his lap, Mums, he could have kissed her, said, as if it were a passing comment on the weather, "Richard Egan the movie star? Isn't he adorable?" And Sister Woman, the family toady, who leaped up, "Daddy, I'll get the ones on the floor. He's too old, Billy. I love Russ Tamblyn."

He has stood up to two mayors of this city and once to the entire city council. He has defended the poor and the disenfranchised. He has never allowed a person to put down AIDS people in his presence. But he cannot for some reason tell the man he has loved for years and years that he still does. That he would like to get together again more than anything he can think of.

So what if Pete said no? Would that be the end of the relationship? The end of Western civilization as we know it?

And if he said yes? Or maybe?

And does he remember the legs touching? Does he not remember the attenuated conversations as they fell asleep in one of their beds? Does he remember the times they were so full of each other that they could go on for maybe days with no sleep at all?

XIV.

In her kitchen, Bea folds the plaid pleats of one of her daughters' school uniform skirts on her heavy, squeaky ironing board. The room, warm from the veal knuckles which braise in her oven and from a stockpot of simmering red gravy, is cluttered with the projects of her day: Her black Ferraro Plumbing appointment book, a stack of Antny's completed work orders and her Ferraro Plumbing invoice pad and checkbook, the checkbook to their joint account bulging with household bills to be paid, an accordion file of bills payable by Ferraro Plumbing arranged by due date, a book, *Accipiters, Harriers, and Buteos of the Eastern Shore,* and tape, purple paper, and green ribbon to wrap it to take to her mother, cover the tabletop in loose, overlapping piles. Bunches of lettuce and greens repose in the sink, half-filled with water. Eggplants and onions lie in the drying rack on the drainboard. Ten starched, pressed white blouses hang in the kitchen doorway, their wire hooks bent back to catch the lip of the doorsill.

She irons the skirt four pleats at a time. Having pulled them flat by tugging at the waist and hem, she holds her iron flat just above them to steam them. She presses them in one slow, steamy drag from the waist down. She turns the skirt and pulls the next four flat. Perspiration forms at her temples. She swipes at it occasionally with the loose sleeves of her cotton shirt, splotched now with moisture between her shoulders and elbows.

She irons uniforms on Fridays, ten blouses, six pleated skirts, because she needs to know over the weekend that she will begin the week with a clean slate.

She stands her iron at the heel of the board. She walks to the stove, and with a wooden spatula she turns the gravy from the bottom up, making sure that the flat edge of her spatula scrapes each square inch of the bottom of her pot. As she turns it, she examines the sauce for signs of the alterations she has made to her mother-in-law's sacred recipe, changes which have made it her own over the years: the addition of pureed red bell peppers, of two mashed anchovy fillets, of marinated artichoke hearts minced so fine that they appear to be garlic. Her mother-in-law has asked her twice in three months to make an extra batch "so I can freeze it. I'm so busy, you know."

Bea revels in the deceit.

"And what am I, a lady of fucking leisure?" she says to the simmering stockpot, smacking the spatula smartly on the pot rim, annoyed that being asked to make an extra batch of her gravy is as close to a compliment as she is likely to receive from LidaJean Ferraro. "Well, Mrs. Too-Busy-to-Make-Gravy, you're not too busy to sit in your mules and your housecoat and your beehive hair in spoolies watching 'The Young and the Restless,' that's for shittin' sure."

She smacks the spatula onto the stovetop, checks the time on the clock on the stove, resumes the steaming of her pleats.

She loves and hates her mother-in-law. When she was first married and moved with Antny to a rented row house on Antny's parents' block, she found herself politely outcast by her neighbors, only tolerated by her husband's friends, who spent no time with her unless Antny was present. Having been all her life without presumption and self-approbation, she learned that she was seen as a "rich girl" by her new community, as if she had brought with her to South

Philadelphia her parents' considerable affluence, as if moving from a house of seventeen rooms to one with five, all in dire need of plastering, was somehow an act, rather than a commitment. She had even left most of her expensive clothes in her closets on Pine Street. Replacing them with discreet purchases at DiBello's and Bianchini's Dress Shoppee, she traded her tailored wools and watermarked silks for cotton blends and even polyester. She accessorized with objects found and bargained for in flea markets. But she could not leave a lifetime of taste and knowledge of what worked for her and what did not in her closets. She always looked too good in inexpensive clothing. Her imitation jewels were taken for real stones. She might have worn what she had left at home for all the good it did her.

It was LidaJean who'd taken the bull by its horns, she who campaigned for her son's wife behind her back at canasta tables and at firehouse spaghetti dinners where her red gravy received its largest and most appreciative audiences, told anyone who would listen, and who would not listen to LidaJean Ferraro, who at once denied and played to the hilt rumors of her distant Italian gypsy lineage, whose thunders of the Vatican, said to be inspired by the Blessed Mother Herself, were believed in and feared by all her enemies. She told the community that her new daughter-in-law had surprised even her, that the girl was in fact common as dirt, that she mixed her own plaster and troweled it on her new walls in her cut-off jeans, that she had planted a fig tree and a "Chicago Peace" rose, both of which had bloomed in her dooryard, where crabgrass had not grown before, told them that the girl had earned so much of her respect that she had even shared with her the recipe for her own red gravy, "and you know that I do not give that out." The neighbor women began to call on Bea, catching her with her chestnut hair gray with plaster dust and moist specks of her mix stuck to her long eyelashes and her cheeks, and no matter that her most recent batch of plaster dried in its plastic pail in a bedroom or the kitchen, and she asked them to sit and served them sun-cured iced tea with her own mint in tall glasses marked with her plaster fingerprints and chatted with them about the high cost of living. The girlfriends and wives of her husband's high school buddies began to ask her over for coffee, began to ask her where did she get that beautiful pin, that blouse, is it silk? those slacks, are they garbardine? At DiBello's. At Second Chance. At the flea market on Snyder Street. Seven dollars! Fifteen-fifty.

The price for her acceptance has been the mortgage of her privacy, paid in daily and twice-daily installments. Having bought the house they had rented, she bought into her mother-in-law's proximity. LidaJean is a persistent collector of debts. She visits whenever she receives inspiration. She has learned to subvert all the tricks. When there is no answer at the front door, she walks around the half block to the dooryard pass-through behind the houses to surprise Bea sitting with a cigarette on her back steps. She barters baby-sitting, her most valuable family asset, in exchange for impromptu coffee klatches at Bea's cluttered kitchen table, and Bea, too grateful for LidaJean's role in her new community's acceptance to ask her even to call first, accepts the visits as she accepts the arrival of mumps, chicken pox, and head colds. She deals with the afflictions. Cleans up the vomit. Pours the coffee and sits, nodding, commenting when necessary, for the half hour or forty minutes that they take. The visits have become as much a part of her life as fixing breakfast is.

It is not the intrusions on her time she resents, so much as the intrusions on her space. LidaJean does not approve of her daughter-in-law's choices in home furnishings, finds them "too plain" and "boring." While Bea is drawn to simple lines and to fabrics which make statements in color and texture rather than in pattern, LidaJean is attracted to the highly wrought and to things that shine and move, particularly in the forms of lamps: lamps dripping with crystal prisms; table lamps with umbrellaed tassel shades and tessellated mirror bases on which stand brass antelope and fawns in relaxed attitudes; floor lamps featuring chains of cut glass beads hanging within glass cylinders with scalloped shades made of gold-colored metals. Sconces mounted on reflective wall plates and draped in rope glass beads hung with brass tassels stand guard at either side of all her doorways, stairwells, and framed "original paintings." Her generosity is unbounded. On anniversaries she has delivered to Bea and Antny similar creations, packed in tri-wall boxes or in crates. Their dazzling contents grace the basement rec room and LidaJean grouses over coffee that they ought to be in windows, "where the neighbors can see them. You're too modest, Bea."

She turns the skirt. Wipes her brow.

As Mother says, LidaJean is her cross to bear. But let the kids be sick and she is here in an instant. And her own mother would be, if she asked her. Would drive here in her nightie under a trench coat, with some bleary-eyed pediatric specialist in tow if she thought he was necessary. Would go to the ends of the earth for any of them if they asked her. And close mouthed? Won't even talk about her own problems to anyone, let alone theirs. She can't get over that, still. Can't believe that woman spent a year living with something wrong with her breast. Can't believe she dragged her daughter off to the dermatologist if she got a zit, and Mary Alice, God knows, all but lived with the gynecologist until she moved away from home. "Irregular," her ass. The only thing irregular about Mary Alice was she'd get in a snit if she wasn't getting any regularly. And blood tests. She swears they all had a thousand of them and here she was mother-henning her own, getting them jabbed every six months in spite of assurances from every blood man on the East Coast that there was not the first sign that either of them was diabetic. Better safe than sorry, but her mother made her so mad she could shake her, knowing a year ago that something was wrong and closing her eyes to it, she who stood by while nurses taught her and Mary Alice self-examination practically before they had anything to examine, practically before self-examination was invented, for crying out loud. Why did she do that? What possessed her? How hypocritical. How inconsistent can you be?

Her doorbell rings. She wipes her brow with her shirt sleeve, exhales deeply.

She will never get her bookwork done. The veal knuckles will burn. The gravy will be ruined, and just fuck the ironing. For*get* it. No. She will keep ironing. Get that done, at least. Fuck the bookwork.

She checks the level of the coffeepot. The doorbell sounds again, two short, impatient rings.

"*Yes*, Ogress. I'm *coming*!"

» » »

LidaJean Ferraro has cleared a space among the papers at the kitchen table. She stirs her coffee, heavily diluted with milk, for a long time. Her right leg rests on the chair seat across from her.

She is a small woman. Her hair is covered with a wildly colored scarf. Curlers stick out of its edges and make round mounds on her head under the fabric. There are large, dark circles under her eyes which she covers with makeup after noon and at night. Her spoon clinks from side to side in the cup.

"So. How is your mother? Have you talked today, yet?"

"No," Bea says, straightening another four rows of pleats. "She's moving around more now. Stayed out of bed all day yesterday."

"That's good. She can't sit around, you know. Use it or lose it, they say. Is she downstairs yet? I should go visit huh, but I can't take those stairs at your house, you know. Don't get old, Bea. It's a bitch."

She continues to stir her coffee, finally putting the spoon down to light one of her long, thin, mentholated cigarettes.

"You know," she says, exhaling smoke, "she's one fine lady, your mother. I always said that. Always. And I'll tell you, Bea, I didn't expect huh to be. I don't think I told you that when you and my Antny got engaged and she called me to invite us to huh house for drinks, I told Paul I didn't want to go." She shakes her head. "Wanted no parts of it. She sounds very snooty on the phone, you know."

LidaJean brushes ashes from the front of her sundress.

"Sounds grand, if you know what I mean, but let me tell you that when you meet huh, she is one fine lady. I mean, no airs about huh. Salt of the earth. And first I thought, this is going to be the longest couple of hours I ever spent, and I'm thinking can we have one drink and get the hell out of here, sitting up there in that library room with about a million books, and she's read every damned one of them, and me saying to myself, Blessed Mother get me through this, and the next thing I know Paul and your father are jawing about machines and your mother and I are going on about South Philadelphia and churches we both went to and you kids and all and the next thing I know, I'm saying sure we can stay for dinner, we've got nothing planned, and before you know it, it's one o'clock in the morning and we never got up from the table making wedding plans and I'm thinking, no offense, Bea, but maybe my Antny hasn't made the biggest mistake in his entire life. And, you know," she says, shaking her cigarette in the air, "your mother did a very clever thing. You know what she did? . . . When she found out Paul and I like to dance, she asked *me* if I'd take huh around to listen to some bands for the wedding. . . . That about blew me over. *Then* she asked me could I help huh and Carmen plan the food and you could have knocked me over with a feather, and I didn't even know I was being had, that's the kind of person your mother is. That was very, very clever."

She takes a swallow of her coffee. She stands. She goes to the stove. She stirs the red gravy. With her back to Bea she says, "I had a dream about your mother. Two nights ago." She waves her free hand at her shoulder, warding off objection. "I know you don't like to hear this stuff, but I've been right before. You know I have. This one's a puzzler. I didn't mention it yesterday because I was still thinking about it. Your mother and I are in a car. I'm driving. It's a convertible. We're out in the country somewhere and it's warm, like now, and we're talking. I don't know, just talking, or something, and she tells me to pull over. And I'm saying, 'Liz, what for? We got to get where we're going.' And she's real pushy, telling me to pull over, and she's pointing to the side of a road and she's saying, 'There. By the tree. LidaJean, pull over!' And I stop the car and suddenly, we're sitting under the tree on blankets or sheets, or something, and we're having a picnic. A real fancy picnic. Baskets and real wineglasses, and pretty little sandwiches with the crust cut off and your brother Pete is there and now I see your mother is wearing like a sash across her chest with some sort of seal on it like ambassadors wear and she's holding out huh hands, and in huh hands are two birds, I don't know what kind, she would know, but one bird is white and the other is black, and while I'm thinking what's she doing with these birds at a picnic, she releases the white bird and she hands the black bird to your brother."

LidaJean blows on the spatula and tastes the sauce.

"Mmmm. I got this recipe from my mother, who got it from huh mother, and so on."

"Yes. You told me. How does it taste?" Bea says, fishing for a compliment.

"Salt, I think." She stirs some in and returns to her chair.

"So my mother's going to be an ambassador and give my brother the bird."

"Bea. Dreams are symbolical. The sash and the seal are the symbols of huh disease. So are the birds. The white bird is a symbol of huh being cured. She released it and it flew away to live a normal life. It's the black bird that I worry about. The black bird is a symbol of illness. She gave that bird to your brother, and he did not release the bird. He held it in his hand."

"LidaJean, my mother would not give Pete a disease," Bea says, making a pass on her pleats.

"Well, of course she wouldn't. You can't take these things word for word. Everything has meaning." She takes a cigarette from her pack and taps the filter on the tabletop.

"So life's a picnic, LidaJean?"

"The picnic is a symbol of normal life, of things going on regular. Things will go on regular for a while, but the black birds rests in his hand.

"Let's call a spade a spade, Bea. Your brother Pete likes men. That doesn't bother me. I like men, too. And there is a reason he goes for men. In a past life he may have been hateful to queer guys. Mistreated them, or something. Made their lives miserable. So in this life he is one so he'll learn a little charity."

"So I hated plumbers in my past life, and now I'm married to one."

"You don't have to be sarcastic just because you think this is bullshit, Bea. Everything is connected. Everything. What's important is you should keep an open mind and tell Pete about my dream. This AIDS is everywhere. Watch television, if you don't believe me. They're telling people to use condoms on television. On *tel*evision!" She waves her cigarette at Bea. "And don't think that hasn't got Monsignor Imperatore bent, as our Joanie says. He spoke to the Holy Name Society last Wednesday. He hasn't spoken to the Holy Name Society since they made him monsignor, but that's another story, and was he hopping. He jumped all over television stations for preaching immorality and encouraging everyone to sleep with everyone else with condoms and I'm sitting next to Flora Aquilino. Ha! And she's about as old as God and shouts because she's hard of hearing and she leans over to me and she screams, 'What's "condoms"?' Oh, I about died. And Monsignor says, 'An excuse for iniquity, Mrs. Aquilino. And they're to be condemned for putting a lady such as yourself in the position of having to ask.' "

"What do you think about that, LidaJean?"

"Which?"

"Oh, addressing the Holy Name Society, and condoms on television."

"Live and let live, I say." She lights the cigarette she has been holding. "They can say whatever they want on television, and at the Holy Name Society, too, for that matter. We're all going to do what we want to, anyway, don't you think?"

"Yes."

"You'll tell your brother about the bird dream?"

"I don't know," Bea says, clipping the skirt to a hanger. "He thinks you're a little quirky, LidaJean. All that stuff you told him about being Indians together?"

"Well, I can't be sure about the Indian part. It feels like we were maybe Indians. But the bone part I *am* sure of. There's an important man in his life he knows, or a man he's going to meet with a bone missing. That is a true fact. There are things I know about your brother, Bea. When I met him, I knew I knew him. Don't try to pin me down about particulars. We're not allowed to remember. Probably it would be confusing. But there are certain people I meet I can tell things about. I met . . . maybe four in my entire life."

"How do you know you've known them before?"

"I don't know. I just know. How do you think I knew right away your brother goes for men? I knew that like in a flash. As soon as he walked into the wedding rehearsal. And looking at him you can't tell that. I mean, your brother's not a swish. No more than my Antny is. Looks like a ladies' man, the way he walks. Real confident. But I knew. Something in my head told me. It's a gift of God, you know. Some people think it's a curse. They're afraid of it. It's not a curse."

"My mother's getting it."

"What do you mean, your mother's getting it?"

"She knows when I'm coming. She knows when I'm calling on the phone. Yesterday I called before I went over and she picked up the phone on the second ring and said,

'Hello, Bea, dear.' It was the middle of the day. I could have been a repairman. A wrong number."

"Coincidence. It's something you're born with. You don't just get it."

"Well, Mother did. Here's one for you. While Mother was in the hospital, she left a message on Pete's answering machine telling him to check his tires. He didn't bother because he thought she was drugged up, or something. Monday his delivery man blew his right front tire on Academy Road. There wasn't a bit of tread left on it. The man could have been killed."

"Did she dream that?"

"I don't know if she dreamed it. She hears music, too. Where there isn't any music. She says she can make it happen. With hand lotion."

"It's huh disease doing it. Predicting the future always comes through dreams. She hasn't got the same as what I have. I was born with mine."

"Well, it's more than coincidence."

"When I was a very little girl, my mother's friends wouldn't come over to visit huh if I was in the house. They said I had the Evil Eye. I never had that. That's something different."

"Mother's mind just goes off somewhere every now and then. She says she listens to Mabel Mercer."

"The Evil Eye *is* a curse. It comes from Satan. What I have is a gift of God."

"She puts hand lotion on to get it going."

"A lot of people don't know the difference. My mother's friends thought I could cast spells. I could never do that. Wouldn't if I could. Everything comes to me in dreams or from something like auras from people. But it isn't auras. And it isn't what they call vibrations."

"What gets me is that Mother thinks it's normal."

"I never once used what I knew for an evil purpose."

"I guess if she didn't act strangely sometimes, it wouldn't bother me."

"No. I can rest easy with God about that." She sighs. "Well, there's no maid coming to do the dusting." She stands. She holds her dress at the sides of her waist and wiggles a little inside it. She picks up her cigarettes, puts the lighted one in her mouth.

"Send one of the girls over after school with the sauce," she says. "Thanks for the coffee. What's that, veal?" she says, indicating the stove with her nose. "You making it my way? With the roasted garlic cloves? Antny loves my roasted garlic cloves spread on bread. You got good bread? Want me to send some over?"

"I made bread last night."

"You want I should call Conconi's? I can have huh save you a couple loaves of bruschetta? She'll do it if I ask huh. Antny loves huh bruschetta with roast garlic."

"I made bread. Thanks."

LidaJean waves her hand in the air. "It's no trouble. I'll have Paul drop off a couple loaves. He can pick up the sauce at the same time. Nice bracelet. Where'd you get that?"

"Second Chance. Nine and a quarter."

"Nice."

XV.

Distracted by the shop chatter of Doris and her daughters, Pete put his bookkeeping in a box and carried it up to his apartment. He sits at his desk, the bills laid out neatly to one side, completed work orders and invoice forms to be typed on the other, his large company checkbook in the center. He begins with the flower wholesalers, paying their bills on long, yellow checks with his logo in the upper left, a gold tulip drawn by Bill in art deco style. He fills in the checks in rapid, straight up-and-down print, the upper and lower case letters all in perfect proportion without flourish. His signature, except for the P and the F, is illegible, a series of mounds and ridges.

As he writes the checks and puts them in envelopes, he glances now and then at the yellow pages directory, which lies by the phone at the corner of the desk.

If he called for an appointment, would they tell him to come right down? "We have an immediate opening, Mr. Flowers. Aren't you lucky?"

He could say that he travels a lot. That he'll be in town again in a month. Time to think about it. Time to get his brain together. Time to adjust to the idea or to decide that he doesn't like the idea at all—that he made a mistake, an error of judgment. That that wasn't he who called in the first place. That another Pete Flowers made an appointment, must have given his number, must have been confused, overwhelmed at making the decision to call in the first place.

He could give them Bill's name. Go in himself. Give them the blood. Have Bill go back in a week for the results with instructions that he could call and tell him if the results were negative and keep quiet if they were not. And if he didn't call? Assume he forgot? That Bill was waiting to surprise him? That Bill had picked a date of some significance in the future that required a special gift? A nifty surprise?

If they told him he was positive, what then? Sell the shop? Write his will and wear haircloth? Pace his days off like Petranek upstairs? Lie in his bed at night in a cold sweat, waiting for the first morning he wakes up drenched, his sheets soaked through into the mattress; begin examining his mouth every day for thrush; wait at his window in his haircloth shirt for the first series of exotic diseases to blow in? Toxoplasmosis?

Move in with his mother; spend their days together concertizing? She making Mabel Mercer and he, who? Bernadette Peters? "Pass me the hand lotion, Mom. It's too quiet in here"?

He stands. He stretches.

Maybe he should run. He hasn't run in two days. Take a run first. Up to the Falls Bridge and back. Nice, even pace. Sweat through a tank top and shorts, and watch some legs and asses, and shower and feel good and call then, if there's time, then call someone for dinner. Bill or Paul or Geo. Get dressed up, even. Try the Two Quails, or Two Chimneys. Or see if Bill's in the mood for Chinese.

"Definitely take a run," he says, unbuttoning his shirt. "Work, work, work. All work and no play makes Pete a dull boy."

At his dresser, he pulls out sets of running clothes, lays them out on the bed.

Is Pete a dull boy? Is this driving through Kansas? When the only decisions he finds remotely exciting are whether and when to run and in what colors. Does he wear the blue shorts because the slit at the side shows off the sinews in his thighs? Or the red rayon ones that show off the bulge? Does he make the phone call to make the appointment to find out if his drive through the heartland is nearly over? If it isn't, keep on driving?

» » »

He jogs down the wide, cracked sidewalk in front of Boathouse Row, a mile from home. He has run the same course hundreds of times, in all seasons, in all weather. He has driven it in his van, clocked the distances, set off the miles and half miles by landmarks along Kelly Drive. He follows the flow and ebb of greenery along the drive, the planting of new sycamores and the mowing down of them by cars run amuck in the night, the appearance of new geese families and the goslings' motley moults to maturity. He has jogged on the paved path. He has jogged on the grass at the Schuylkill River's edge. He has misstepped and slid on his back down the river's muddy bank, rear end first, into its shocking February water and crawled out, mortified, to attempt to jog three miles home in his water-and-ice-crystal-heavy sweatpants and sweatshirt, only to flag down a police car after a quarter of a mile, fearful that he would die of hypothermia, ignominiously, in a stand of non-deciduous azaleas.

The mid-May air is warm and humid. The black, folded bandana tied around his forehead has soaked through. Drops of sweat drip on his back from the knot. The river surface is placid. The reflections of trees on the west bank are only slightly skewed in the current.

Because he has a well-organized life doesn't mean he's not happy. He is able to avoid the problems, the pitfalls. He has been in this business long enough to know what he can plan on and what he can't. He deflects Eva Lovesey's high hopes of banks of acacia in October. Annually he allows Cal Penner's crepey hand to rest on his knee and sometimes on his thigh for much too long as they drink his houseman's sweet manhattans in his terrible, frilly den while Pete convinces him to abandon his plans for jillions of fuji mums dyed to match his fucking dining room drapes.

Oh, he is subtle. He is so diplomatic. He can charm the most single-minded of them into choosing what's right for their occasions. He is very good at what he does. They don't even know what hit them.

He is alert for stones in his path, for gravel cast onto smooth, paved places.

Driving through Kansas . . . Where does she get these ideas? It isn't the same. Not the same at all. No analogy. It isn't that he's bored. He is busy from the time he gets up until he goes to bed. He has as much work as he can handle.

He increases his pace slightly, changes his breathing. He thinks he feels something like sand under his right kneecap, feels a grating that was not there before, or is it vibration caused by the pebblestones leached up from the soil he now runs on?

A hundred yards ahead, a shirtless man rounds a bend, jogging toward him. His skin glistens. He is muscled, thin-hipped. His pecs bounce with each footfall.

A true vision coming and he is so bad at this. Doesn't ever know what to say. Does he wait till the man is closer and drop off to the side and collapse in the grass with a charley horse? Does he let his left arm drop as the two of them pass and pat the guy's tiny heinie? Inadvertent. An accident of proximity. Does he begin a conversation now, a hundred feet apart? "Terrific day for a jog in the park, huh? Great shorts you're almost not wearing? Memorize this number: 555-9300. It takes incoming calls?"

The man is smiling. Perfect teeth. "Hiya," he says as he passes.

Should have gone for the charley horse. The old charley horse routine.

He turns in stride and looks back at the man, who jogs on, looking back at him. He waves at the man. Turn around,

Flowers. Fall in the grass, Flowers. Hold one knee to your chest. Assume an expression of agony.

"You are such a jerk."

He keeps running. He does not look back again.

He should have gone for the heinie. In one graceful, natural gesture let his arm swing down and back, his hand cupped just so to match the curve of the guy's right buttock and a gracious, hurried jogger's apology: "Sorry." "Pardon." " 'Scuse."

How was it that he was ever able to meet anyone in his lifetime? How did he manage to get close enough to any of those men to sleep with them? He has never walked up to anyone in his life. Never said the first word. Never smiled first across a crowded room. They did. Even Bill. Especially Bill. Most especially Bill, who turned a corner with a cart in the Great Scot Market, coming from the light bulb section to soups as Pete was choosing bouillon crystals. He will never forget that moment, never forget turning with the red-and-white jar in his hand to put it in his cart. There was Bill, rolling his own cart down the aisle toward him, smiling as if he were the cat's meow, and as he stood with the bouillon in his hand, his entire body went whacko. His runner's legs turned to jelly and his hands shook. He had never seen a man as wonderful. Before or since. "That's just full of sodium," Bill said, and then he said, "You are the handsomest man I have ever seen." "Yes," Pete said, meaning the sodium, and Bill said, "Well, I've never been modest myself. I've been humbled, however. May I call you?"

May I call you? May I call you? "You may call me anything you want," he said all the way home with his handlebags of groceries.

Bill memorized Pete's number. Swept him off his fucking feet. . . . And the rest, as they say, is history.

His knee is definitely grating inside. There is no question. He is running on concrete again, smooth except for the cracks between the blocks.

"Step on a crack, break your mother's back." What sadistic little creep invented that?

He begins to avoid the sidewalk cracks. Catches himself. Begins to pace himself to hit them, feels guilty. He stretches his arms out. He shakes the sweat off.

His love and his work. As if it all came down to a simplistic equation. There were other elements. What about music? What about art? Weren't they also our love or our work? If we're not artists? And if we are, is our work our love?

And he goes home after his work and just watches the news. All those compact disks stored in their built-in, carpentered cubbies. A hundred and fifty? Two hundred? The best of the best of the world's music gathering dust for Mrs. Wayne's ostrich feathers on a stick. So much for art. And his work? He was the best in his market. He gets calls for work he cannot do justice to. He turns down work which he cannot give his attention to. Routinely.

Does it give him satisfaction? A kind of satisfaction. CDs building up at Continental Bank. The choicest blooms set aside for him for the fabrication of too-elegant-for-words arrangements for his well-heeled clientele. A process that is beginning to smack of routine, beginning to be, what? Tiresome? Does he hear himself sigh when the shop phone rings? Does he reach for a work order with a little less enthusiasm than he used to? Well, it amounts to a kind of satisfaction. A pale color of satisfaction, still holds the interest, like the peachy tan at the edge of a marchioness peony, but verging on tired, Mom, if the truth be told. Like forty feels today. The end of an era, in spite of the cruise from the man back there without a shirt.

And love?

"I get by with a little love from my friends," he sings as he runs.

And from his family, whom he loves and doesn't think much about until their concerns impinge on his own. Until they get breast cancer and it spreads to their brains and the concern becomes worry that if one cancer doesn't get her, another might, when the time was not long ago that they could assume that they would all of them be healthy and always around for the obligatory seasonal dinners.

His knee has begun to pain him each time his right heel hits the ground. He alters his pace; slows just a bit.

Was there a special gene? he wonders. A gene in their makeups that kicked in at some certain age or incident, fired by the passing of precisely forty years, that sent out the sudden message to the system in general that a disease avoided could no longer be warded off? A Fatal Flowers Flaw? Breast cancer for the women? Arthritis for the men? Would he have his father's joints? Would they all become sand-filled and creaky? Would his fingers swell and bend to the right or to the left so he would no longer be able to place the stems or sketch the designs? So much for his work.

And love? The part of the equation he likes to leave out. For years something that he thought would fall into place when its time came again like the shopping cart turning the corner from light bulbs to find him at soups. The sudden compounding of chemicals. The race of the heart he now got from running at that magical point when endorphins kick in, but in the years since the day he met Bill, no cart had rounded a corner. No man had stepped out of a taxi into his startled path. No key rings had fallen onto a hotel lobby floor for him to pick up out of politeness and hand to a man whose physical presence and smile stopped him flushed in his tracks. Oh, there had been small rushes of blood to the groin. There had been nights passed with the sources of those rushes. There had been more than a few mornings of waking up to Dicks of Death without the gift of conversation. And had another gift been passed during one or more of those embraces? Did another Fatal Flaw insert itself into one of his leukocytes? Latch onto the first appealing one that floated by as he had latched onto its donor? Did his bloodstream teem now with its progeny? So much for his love.

He had put love on the back burner. Put it there so long ago that it had stopped mattering. Learned to be a single person and to like it. Learned not to look for love. Not to think about it much. Except in recollection. Except for memories that dropped in for no reason. Of the long, long torso he had lain against. Of listening to the midnight ramblings through one ear and, through the other, against the side of his chest, to the body sounds and the vibrations and rumbles of that voice that went on and on telling stories, making observations from a mind from which there was no respite.

"Like my mother's," he says aloud, surprised, as his feet pound the pavement.

The same sort of mind, darting from idea to idea, picking ideas up, examining and commenting, holding on to some and discarding the rejects like a shell picker at a beach. And just as discriminating. "Why" their favorite word.

He had never considered that. Had never seen the similarities before, how much their minds worked alike. Neither of them able to sit for longer than a minute without picking up something to read, some new idea to absorb them, something new to integrate into their rococo minds already embellished to the hilt. How they abhor an empty space. How they rush to fill a too-long pause in conversation. While he cannot seem to get enough of space and silence.

Not enough to have had a mother all his growing up who pushed and prodded and poked relentlessly to make him consider the moment and its meaning, he had to choose a lover as rabid as she. Had he been shopping for one? And, thinking that Bill had been an impulse purchase all this time, did he find that he had been on a list all along? How very curious. How bizarre to see that connection after all these years.

He leaves the path and lopes to his left across the grass toward the river, its surface undisturbed by sculls or water birds or stone-throwing boys. Though the ground is uneven, the deep grass cushions his footfalls, comforts his knee.

What had it been? Had he grown weary of having no space and silence with Billy? And what had been the difference after he left? An increase in his gross receipts. Instead of spending time with Bill, he walked through clients' houses and corporate halls after hours with his notepad and his Polaroid. Instead of spending the allotted time facing his demons, sitting by himself and reading his road maps to the encouragement of Mahler's Songs of Youth, searching for routes that would lead him out of Kansas, toward Colorado, where, as he passed through the Rockies, he could have given deep consideration to his work and to love, one of which he had too much of, and of the other not enough, he worked.

When he should have been driving on the downside of the Rockies, passing through Pueblo and Trinidad, avoiding turns to the left toward the unbroken horizons of Hutchinson and Wichita, when he should have been asking himself on the road if he really wanted to know if love had placed his leukocytes at risk, he worked.

» » »

He stands in the rare-mammal house of the Philadelphia Zoo. His running clothes have soaked through. Drops fall from the knot of his black bandana. His wet socks cool his ankles.

A troop of ruffed lemurs watch him from their tree limb. Their long, black tails hang like limp rope. Their hands rest on the shoulders of their neighbors. They watch him watching them. He stands motionless before them for ten minutes. They watch him shift his weight. They watch him walk slowly back and forth at the edge of their enclosure. He stops. He waits for them to sing.

"Hello?" he says. "Do you do requests?"

The lemurs watch him. They follow him with their round, impassive eyes as he begins to pace again before the bars of their cage. Only their wondering, orange eyes move. They do not sing for him.

XVI.

In his shower, his eyes closed to protect them from shampoo, Pete thinks about the visit to his shop by the agent from Century 21, who, polite and discreet, offered him much more for his business than he knows it is worth.

» » »

Climbing the front stairs of the Pine Street house, he wonders if his mother will just chat, or confront him on some issue or other. Probably confront, he thinks, a hop onto one of her bandwagons and away they'll go, she prodding his unexamined life and he shifting left and right, trying to anticipate and to avoid.

She sits asleep in an armchair, a book in her lap, her hands collapsed upon it. She wakes when he steps off the hall carpet onto the dark, hardwood floor of the library. She lifts her head, seems confused for a moment, and pulls herself together.

"My precious," she says, holding her arms out for a hug.

"Star of my firmament," he says, bending over to give her one.

"Oh, that's a good one," she says. "A bit vaunted, but I like it. Sit. Right there. Carmen put wine in that bucket behind you and there's a glass somewhere. I will have a tiny bit of that Chivas. You are so considerate to plan your visits at cocktail time."

"Where's the jasmine I sent over? You're not in the mood for music?"

"In Bea's room. My theory did not hold water. The plant smells heavenly, but it did nothing for Mabel Mercer. You'll have to tell Carmen how to feed it. I'd murder it."

He hands her a drink, pours his own, and sits across from her on a flowered sofa.

She closes the book in her lap. She handles all books with consideration. When she buys a new one, she prepares it to be read, opening the book in the manner in which she was taught at Our Lady of Eternal Sorrow grade school, breaking in the binding by measured degrees, ten or twenty pages at a time, front then back then front, her spread-out hands pressing against the open pages and down, evenly, against the spine, ending near the book's middle.

"Bea brought me this," she says. "She knows I'm partial to hawks and to the Eastern Shore. Isn't that thoughtful? I wonder, though, if there is some implied meaning. Does she see me as a predatory mother?"

"So," he says. "How are we feeling today?"

"We are feeling lackadaisical. They have added a new drug to my pharmacological pantheon. I am not sure that those words go together, but there's some reassurance in being able to say them. Decadron. It's a steroid. It reduces swelling. And don't get all disjointed like your brother. I may gain some weight, but I won't get hairy and muscle-bound and any more ill-tempered than I am. I've been on it for three days. I haven't had a bowel movement since I started it and all I want to do is eat.

"Stu was here. He came for lunch. Yes, isn't *that* shocking? Carmen made those crab cakes he could never get enough of. He picked at his food and fidgeted all the time he was here. Couldn't wait to leave. It was the first time I've seen him since the day of my operation. He was starting to make *me* fidgety, so I said, 'Well, I know you have to get back to your office,' and he was out of here like a rabbit. Carmen is in a state; did she say anything to you when she let you in?"

"No. Just that you were up here."

"She's in a high snit. We ate here at the coffee table. She came in to clear for coffee and I said never mind the coffee, he left, and you never heard such a clatter of Limoges in your life, and 'Look at these. He didn't even eat them, just put holes in them, and me picking through crab meat so he wouldn't find a single shell. Well, he's had the last of Carmen's crab cakes, I'm here to tell you, Elizabeth, and not even saying goodbye.' She was down there banging around for at least an hour. . . . Have you talked to him lately?"

"We don't call each other much. I don't call because Alexa usually answers, and he doesn't call unless it's time for our annual Phillies game."

"When he called and said he'd like to drop by for lunch, I thought he wanted to make plans for Memorial Day, but he didn't even mention it. Well, you will all have to come here this year. I don't think I'm up to being carried to Paoli or Swarthmore on a litter."

"Maybe we should put it off this year. Do something on the Fourth."

She looks peevish.

"Your sister said the same thing. *And* your father. We are not going to treat me like a sick person. I won't have it," she says, cranky now. "There are certain things I can do and certain things I can't do, and since I can't make it to the suburbs, we will have Memorial Day right here. Those granddaughters of mine are going to grow up with a sense of family, and holidays are the only time we all come together. And we are going to come together. Right here. I've decided that. I don't want to hear any more about it. Carmen and I will plan a late-afternoon dinner. It will be a picnic. A traditional Memorial Day picnic. A covered dish.

You will all bring your specialties. I'll have Bea make that cannelloni thing you all go on about. Mary Alice can do her potato salad, the one with the bacon. Alexa is going to want to bring her tired old macaroni salad, but we'll come up with something else for her. God, I hate her macaroni salad. Hellmann's and boiled macaroni. I hope that child has more imagination in the bedroom than she does in the kitchen. . . . Well, what are you looking at? It's true, isn't it? Do you remember that dinner she made for Megan's confirmation last year? She knows how to boil, and that, my dear, is it. She'd boil a Thanksgiving turkey if she had a pot big enough. Thank the Lord, I made sure my children learned how to put a meal together. What do you want to bring?"

"I don't know. What would you like?"

"Does Bill cook?"

Do I hear a bandwagon pulling up? he thinks. "He's a vegetarian."

"A fish-and-chicken vegetarian?"

"A green-things-and-nuts vegetarian."

"He doesn't cook?"

"He can. He's pretty good. He'd cook anything I wanted. He used to make two meals when we were together. What I liked and what he liked."

"What dedication. We need a green salad, I think. Bring him."

"What?" he says, shifting on the couch.

"Bring him. To Memorial Day."

"Mom," he says, crossing his legs.

"You think I'm joking? I'm quite serious."

He looks at the Audubon prints which, when they were children, occupied a small section of paneled wall since given over to book shelving. Their frames are propped now on the floor against bookshelves. Storm petrels. Shearwaters. Arctic terns. All seabirds, he notices for the first time in nearly forty years. All white, or gray and white.

"Except for Rachel Bohigan, since you moved out of

here you have never brought a guest to a family event. Do you know that?"

"That's not true."

"Name one."

"I can name three. Nora and Gary to your anniversary party. My date was Nora's sister, Kathleen."

"That was not a family event. That was social cacophony. We had more than three hundred people. If ten percent were family, I'd be surprised. Trust your mother. You have not brought a guest to a family event since you moved out. When you were twenty-two. That was eighteen years ago, the way I figure it.

"Tell me. What do you think would happen if you brought Bill here to our Memorial Day? Or someone else, for the sake of argument. Maybe you'd rather bring someone else. Don't let me choose for you. You choose. What would happen?"

His mother looks at him expectantly. Her arms rest on the arms of her chair. She holds her scotch in her stronger hand, out in the air. The liquid quivers in the glass, shaking with the slight palsy she has exhibited since her hospital stay. She smiles very slightly at the left side of her mouth as she did when she caught him at fibs when he was a child.

His many fantasies of bringing a male friend to a family event have all ended badly. His family and in-laws behave civilly enough toward his guest in the beginning. He is, himself, uncomfortable, anxious that an awkward subject, like sex, will be brought up, that the presence of his guest, an outsider, Bill more often than not, will drape a pall over the lighthearted banter of these gatherings. That his brother, loose-lipped from gin and tonic, will ask a pointed question and bring silence to the room. That his father will let go an aimless faggot joke. That uneasy and unnegotiated truces signed and honored since Alexa joined the family will become too demanding and complex to rewrite. That war will suddenly break out among their nations. That shit will hit the fan. That he will finally, after forty years, in the simple act of walking with a friend through the doors of his parents' house, be admitting to all of them what they have all known or suspected about him for most of his adult life, that he is the family freak and pariah; that he, their dear, amusing, dependable, reasonable and intelligent, objective and stalwart sibling, brother-in-law, friend, and, since Cliffie died, Prodigal Son, fucks men and might be fucking the one he walked through the door with. The End of the World as he knows it. Apocalypse. Armageddon.

"That gives you pause? The question?"

"What was the question?"

" 'What would happen if?' "

"I don't know."

She rolls her eyes, rattles her cubes. "That I should raise such fainthearted children," she says. "Let me conjure up a scenario: Carmen greets you at the door. You walk into the house with . . . Bill, let's say. Carmen scowls when she sees him, and becomes sullen. She leads you both to the butler's pantry and tells you to stand there in the dark and disappears muttering nasty things about you under her breath. Finally, she comes back and calls through the door for you to go out in the yard where the others are assembled. Your father, who has been turning steaks on the grill, sees you with a man, drops his tongs, and grabs his chest in agony, shrieking 'Queers!' Mary Alice, Bea, and Alexa cover the children's eyes and push them all into the house; Stu, Hal, and Anthony turn from their conversation about ice hockey, look at the two of you walking toward them, and all throw up, squeezing their rear ends for protection. I, who had been resting comfortably on my lounge chair in the sun, absorbing my badly needed vitamin D, clutch my rosary, heave once, and die on the spot. General chaos. The men, seeing that I am dead, fall upon you and dismember you. You're right. Don't bring anyone. It's just too dangerous."

"Well," he says, "our scenarios have similar themes."

"Think about it. I am going ahead with a party. I've

decided. I'll tell you what to bring after I talk with Carmen.

"You'll do the graves?" she asks.

"They're done."

"Already?"

"I bought some nice stuff and sent Doris and her girls over last week."

"I thought you did them yourself."

"I did them once. I hired people after that. I can't," he says, thinking of the stone etched with Cliffie's name and the dates of his life. A frog shifts its weight in his throat.

"I can't either," she says. "Well, I can, but it puts me in a state for days. I used to do it myself, before you got in the flower business and I dumped it on you. I'd get Bea to go with me. Pack her and some garden tools into the car and we'd drive to Gaudio's and buy all the wrong plants, things ill-suited to the rigors of cemetery living. We were both partial to exotica, stuff from the greenhouse. One year while you were in California we did all the plots in gardenias. We bought a couple hundred dollars' worth. The car reeked of them. We picked blossoms off the plants and put them in our hair and in the buttonholes of our blouses as we worked and cracked jokes and it wasn't so bad with her there. . . . She was a howl in her early teens. You were, too. Before you got so serious about life."

"I'm not that serious about life, Mom."

"Don't be silly. Of course you are. You had an outrageous sense of humor when you lived here. And for a while after, until you became an adult. Whenever we had a family crisis—Stu getting expelled for the umpteenth time from Bishop Neumann or Mary Alice getting sent home again for mouthing off to Sister—it was always you who got us all laughing again. Even your father. Someone had to be disciplinarian, but at night, in our room, he would lie there guffawing at things you had said. Hilarious things. We would giggle together in the night. Why did you stop that?"

"I didn't know I had."

"Well, you did. It was as if someone told you that you

were grown up as of a certain date and to put away your silliness. I think your father and I did that to you. I think we took away your joy."

"That's nonsense, Mom. You've been great parents. Both of you."

"Great parents also make dreadful mistakes. When it finally became clear to us that you were somehow not interested in girls, it took us a while to realize that you were interested in boys, and after we figured that out, we began to accuse each other of being the cause of your abnormality."

"I am not abnormal."

"Now, don't get huffy. I can see that you are working up to a huff. And don't get crazy about semantics. For this family norm, you *are* abnormal. You know, your father accused me of being overly protective. I accused him of caring more about his meat pies than about his children. It was an argument that went on a long time. It came up whenever the evidence became too clear to be ignored, and we, of course, missed the point entirely. If I have been protective, I was equally protective of all of you. After Cliffie was killed, I made you all miserable with my clinging. I know that I did. And you can thank your father and Carmen for making me untie the strings. But you all got the same obsessive mother-henning, and your father ignored you all equally, running off to his plant when there was a crisis and even when there wasn't, and you were the only one out of the four of you who turned out to have a sexual problem."

"I don't have a sexual problem, goddammit, and I am not abnormal!" His face is flushed. He wants to leave the room.

"If you don't think you have a problem, son of mine, you are pissing in the wind," she says, clearly pleased with her slide into vernacular. "The sexual problem is that you are living a double life. You have one face you wear for your family and another you wear for your friends. *That's* abnormal, and it's a sexual problem because it arises, in a manner of speaking, from your refusal to let us share any part of your homosexual life. Does Stu know you're gay, for example?"

"Yes. He must."

" 'He must.' You haven't told him."

"Not right out."

"And Bea?"

"I told her. Before I went to California."

"And Mary Alice?"

"We've never talked about it, but she knows."

"You never even talked with Mary Alice about it? Well, that astounds me. If there is a card-carrying, certifiable sexual libertarian in this family, it's got to be Mary Alice. Did you think you'd offend her? Stu would be chancy, I can see that. He probably wears Brooks Brothers pajamas. But Mary Alice? I bet she's done it with goats."

"Mom."

"I could tell you stories that would curl your toes. Whatever you've done, you've got nothing on her," she says, casting off doubt with a wave of her hand. "And I'm not telling tales out of school. Her life before Hal was an open book. I'm putting him in my will, by the way. The man is a saint." She crosses herself, looks at the ceiling. "And thank you, Blessed Mother, if you finessed that meeting. You're doing this to yourself, you know," she says, waving her drink at him.

"You're damned right," he says. "Out of self-preservation. Do you know what it was like to sit around our dinner table all those years? Do you know what it was like to make dates with girls so I'd have something to share at the table? Girls with big boobs so I could get teased about them? Girls I just wanted to be friends of? If I had announced after Carmen placed dessert that I was thinking of asking Mark Lauffner to the prom, can you imagine the unholy hush that would have fallen on that table? Can you imagine the speed with which I would have been driven to the Adolescent Unit at Forty-ninth and Market? No time for history.

This boy needs electroshock therapy. Jesus, Mom. You and Dad would have maimed each other fighting for the pen to sign the permission slip. Our son the faggot? Not in this house."

His mother gives him a painful smile.

"Well," she says.

"Well nothing." He sips his wine. Looks away from her.

"That must have been terrible for you. Living among aliens. And we did not make it easy. If I had it to do over, I'd have had one of these conversations with you when you were sixteen. But we didn't do philosophical conversations then, do you remember? Oh, I talked a lot with you children, but I guess the object was always to teach you something, or to expose you to some idea I thought you needed to consider. Did we ever have a heart to heart while you were growing up, you and I?"

"Sure we did," he says.

"About what?"

"I don't remember, Mom, but I'm sure we did. It seems like we did, so we must have."

"I don't think so," she says, looking sad and regretful, shifting her right shoulder against the back of her chair. "I missed too many of the important issues in your lives. I think I was a better governess than a mother. I went for a specific lesson each time and ignored the overview. Sex, for example. And look at you. I say 'sex,' and you begin squirming in your seat. You are proving the point I was about to make, which is that I did it by the books. I decided that my children were going to be informed about sex. I read everything that was in print about teaching children about sex, which, back in the forties and fifties, took all of about an hour and a half, and when Stu and Mary Alice began to ask questions, I gave them answers, and the same with the rest of you. I cringed from nothing. I wanted none of you to cringe from sex as my parents' generation had. I even practiced drawing the mechanical aspects. Do you remember my drawings?"

"They were very professional."

"Thank you. They were. I drew new ones for each of you. I was especially proud of my uteruses. By the time Bea was ready, I could freehand the entire reproductive system, male and female, in minutes. Your father, who has never been shy about sex, invented business meetings and critical phone calls. He was useless. We couldn't both run. Well, in spite of the beautiful drawings and the vocabulary lessons and my best-laid plans, Stu and Mary Alice and you were left wanting. I somehow left out the part about commitment in the scheme of things. I think they saw it as theater. Mary Alice played Earth Mother coast to coast, while Stu did Johnny Appleseed on the college circuit.

"And you I failed the most, dear heart. Did you know then that my perfect sketches of uteruses and fallopian tubes were pretty much a waste of our time? Apparently vasa deferentia and Cowper's glands attracted all your attentions even then, and I missed the fascination."

"Yes. But I needed to know where babies came from, and you did a good job on that part."

"But it was all academic."

"Yes."

"When did you know?"

". . . I don't know, Mom. I knew, and I didn't know. When I was a little kid, I always liked women. Some of the women who came around here were very beautiful. Some of them were very clever. And some of them were both. When you had your literary club meetings up here when I was, what? Five or six? I used to hide in the dark behind the high chest in the hall and wait for the women to come up the stairs so I could see their stockinged legs when they passed. I would sit out there on the floor and listen. I liked the way some of them smelled. Their perfume would hang out there in the air a long time after they walked up the stairs. But before Carmen served coffee, I left and went downstairs to wait in the living room. I'd wait for Carl Shroder to come to pick up Mrs. Shroder. I'd wait for the doorknocker to clank, and I would always be there to let him in before Carmen even got through the pantry door. I couldn't take my eyes off him. I'd show him my baseball cards and I'd watch him while he looked at my new ones, waiting for Mrs. Shroder to come down, and I'd lean as close to him as I dared to show him special ones so I could smell his cologne that was so faint you had to get close to catch it and I knew and I didn't know that women would never do what that leaning-to-smell-Mr.-Shroder's-cologne did. That has never changed."

She nods. "I wish I had known."

"You couldn't have known. I didn't know."

"When did you know for sure?"

"I don't know. Sometime in high school. After track practice, maybe. Probably in a locker room. Probably then when all the guys went on about knockers and bazooms and I had to pretend. Or before the next big dance you had to show up at and I would begin this calculated search for a date with whom sex would be the remotest possibility."

"When you and Rachel Bohigan were seeing each other, your father and I began to relax."

"She's the first person I came out to. We were perfect for each other. She's a lesbian. We covered for each other. People thought we were an item. We could go to dances and parties and have a good time. She was drop-dead beautiful. All the guys wanted her. She killed them in little, black cocktail dresses. All the girls wanted me. We were both safe. We'd neck, if we had to, to make it look good. Rachel Bohigan and I got each other through senior high school."

". . . I think you and your father should talk."

"About sex?" he says, smiling.

"Well, I guess. I mean about your being gay."

"Why?"

"He would like you to. To clear the air."

"To clear the air."

"Yes."

"I don't remember his ever sitting down with me to tell me he's straight."

"It's not the same thing, Peter."

"How is it different?"

"You know he's straight. He's proven that all his life."

"So I have to prove to my father that I'm gay?"

"Maybe that was a poor choice of words."

"I never had to prove to you I was gay. Why should I have to prove it to him?"

"We're having this conversation. It clears the air for me. You should clear the air with your father, too. I know he wants you to."

"How do you know that?"

"He told me he would like you to."

"Why doesn't he just ask?"

"Why don't you just tell him?"

"Why should I?"

"Why not?"

"It's not incumbent on me to explain my life. I have nothing to apologize for. I don't ask him to explain his life."

His mother is pressing the palm of her hand at the edge of her forehead. She is squinting.

"You don't have to *explain* your life. You don't have to a*pol*ogize for anything," she says. She looks down to the end of the room to the window. She stops moving. She does not speak.

He waits a few beats. She sits in the same position in her chair. Her face is relaxed except for the slight squint. Her gaze is beyond the window glass.

"Mom?

"Mom, are you all right?

"Hey!"

He stands. He walks around the cocktail table to his mother. He cups his hand on her shoulder and shakes her gently.

"Mom."

She does not move or speak.

"Jesus."

He goes to the intercom and presses the Kitchen button.

The intercom crackles. "Yes?"

"Carmen, is there a nurse here?"

"She's down here. What's wrong?"

"Send her up."

He walks back to his mother. She has stopped squinting. Her palm still rests on her forehead. She stares at the window.

"Hello?" he says.

His heart pounds. His palms are sweaty.

There are sounds of footsteps on the back stairs, then in the hall, and the sound of fabric slapping. A nurse hurries into the room, followed by Carmen, pale with anxiety.

The nurse puts one hand on his mother's cheek and the other on her wrist.

"Mrs. Flowers?"

She peels back one of his mother's eyelids and looks in. She stands.

"Did she just stop midstream, or did something happen?"

"She just stopped."

The nurse counts pulse beats. "She's OK. She just went away for a while. She'll be back."

"Why?" Pete says

"It's OK," Carmen says. She folds her arms over the bib front of her apron.

"Her synapses just sort of close down," the nurse says. "Like a computer that's overworked, or that's in a hot room. She'll turn on when she's ready."

Pete looks at the nurse looking at his mother. She is about his age. She looks very calm. Just curious, smiling slightly. He wants her to do something. Does not like her comparison of his mother to a machine.

"How long?" he says.

"Sometimes a few seconds. Ten minutes is the longest I've seen."

"Can't you give her something?"

"No."

Carmen turns and sighs. She leaves the room.

The nurse sits next to his mother.

"You want to sit for a while? Or you can leave if you want. After this long, she usually wants to just vegetate for a while when she comes back. Sort of go through a RAM check, you know? Monitor the circuits?"

"How often does this happen?"

"Some days never. Some days a couple times. Sometimes you don't notice it. After this long, she usually blocks out an hour or two of what happened before the incident." She watches his mother, looking her up and down, smiling at her. She removes the scotch glass and holds his mother's hand. "Till she catches up with herself, you know? Then she remembers it. But she always knows what time it is. Eerie, huh?"

XVII.

"Hello?"

"Hi," Bill says.

"Hi."

"It's not too late to call, I hope? Am I waking you?"

"No."

"How was your day?"

"It was OK," Pete says. "I'm unbuttoning button-down shirts. I was waiting for the news to come on."

"What did you do?"

"Do?"

"With your day."

"Umm, seven funeral pieces for a viewing in Bala, couple of knockoffs for a bridal shower, two restaurants, a church altar. . . . You?"

"I think we bought a pier."

"Like a ship pier?"

"Yeah."

"What will you do with a pier?"

"We need a pier," Bill says. "We didn't have any. It's nice. Great view of Camden."

"Get out."

"Yeah . . . So. Why are you unbuttoning shirts?"

"To take them to the laundry."

"Ah . . . A couple of things. Do you remember how you made carrots and vermouth?"

"Yeah."

"I need it."

"It's easy. Carrots and vermouth."

"You bake 'em in vermouth, or what?"

"No. You sauté them."

"And that's all?"

"No, you peel them first, then you slice them into rounds, like thin? And you heat some butter in a frying pan, and you throw in some chopped-up garlic for a minute, then the carrots, and when the carrots are a little brown, you throw in the vermouth."

"How much?"

"I don't know. A half a cup?"

"And that's it?"

"No. Salt and pepper, and some sugar, if you want."

"How much?"

"I don't know. A teaspoon?"

"And that's it?"

"No. A lot of chopped parsley."

"With the vermouth? I'm writing this down."

"No. At the end."

"And that's it?"

"That's it."

"Sounds easy."

"Piece of cake."

"Also, you want to have dinner Saturday night?"

"Why not?"

"I mean dinner."

"Right."

"I mean, us."

"Sure."

"I was thinking Susannah Foo's."

"I love Susannah Foo's."

"Maybe just us."

"OK. You want me to call?"

"No. I already called."

"OK . . . This isn't a setup, is it?"

"What do you mean?"

"Like a surprise party, or something?"

"Pete, I wouldn't do that. You don't like surprises. It's just dinner."

"Fine. What time?"

"Eight-thirty."

"OK. So, how was your day?" he asks Bill, sitting on the bed with a shirt in his lap, unbuttoning buttons.

"Fine. I bought a pier."

"Right. You said that . . . View of Camden."

"Right . . . Well. I won't keep you from the news."

"Probably nothing happened today."

"I don't know."

"Mmm. Well, I'll let you know if something happened."

"Did Levee call you?" Bill asks.

"No."

"He decided to go to Saudi Arabia."

"Get out."

"Really. He called a while ago. Says he's tired of being poor. They told him he'd have to change his name while he's over there. They'll arrange for him to get a passport under another name."

"What's the name?"

"He's thinking about it. Says he likes Abubakkar. He's thinking maybe he won't tell his parents. Maybe call them from Jidda. Collect."

Bill's voice goes nasal: "I have a collect call for anyone from Abdul Abubakkar in Saudi Arabia. Will you accept the charges?"

"No shit. They'll disown him."

"He's an only child."

"It won't matter. Can't you hear Rose? 'Our son is dead. His name does not exist.'

"I didn't think he'd do it. When would he go?"

"He said they want him over there in three weeks."

"Jesus. Three weeks. We should invite him to dinner to celebrate."

"OK. Next week. I'll see if Geo's free."

"No, I mean this week. Saturday. Levee loves Susannah Foo's, and Geo's going to the shore the next weekend."

"He's going this week, I think," Bill says.

"No. It's next week."

"Levee's busy Saturday, I think."

"Bill, he's never busy Saturday night."

"He's probably got a lot to do."

"I'll call him."

"*I*'ll call him," Bill says. "And I'll call Geo. Anyone else you want me to call?" He sighs.

"How about Nora and Gary?"

"How about your brother and sisters?"

"Huh?"

"I said, 'Maybe she's at her brother's or sister's.' "

"Bill, they live in Oregon."

"All right. I'll call Nora and Gary. And I'll call Levee. And Geo. And Susannah Foo's."

"OK. Eight-thirty?"

"Unless I can't get a table for twenty until nine."

"We're talking six people. Billy, if you'd rather not invite Nora and Gary, it's OK with me, you know."

"No," Bill says. "I love Nora and Gary. How could we have a celebration without Nora and Gary?"

"Right. Me, too. That's what I was thinking. Well, if we can't get a table there, we'll eat somewhere else. Lickety Split. Everyone likes Lickety."

"Right . . . I love Lickety."

"Is something wrong?"

"Oh, no," Bill says. ". . . Nothing's wrong. Nothing at all. It'll be a party. All of us there."

"Old Levee finally deciding something . . ."

"Old Abubakkar."

"Right."

» » »

Bill moves the phone from his lap to the couch cushion.

"How romantic," he says, walking to his tall living room windows. "How fucking romantic." An intimate, candlelit dinner with four of their dearest friends elbow to elbow. Just the six of them.

"Bill, just say 'no.' Practice it. It's very easy. A little word. A simple sound. 'No.' Again. 'No . . . No. No no.' Get used to forming the sound. Tip of the tongue on the roof of the mouth, then a circle of the lips: 'NO!' "

Such a powerful word. A magical word. A word that gets you what you want. No, Pete. Not this time. "No. I'd rather be with you." No.

He had planned this in his mind so long. It took such courage just to place the call and ask him out to dinner, just the two of them. He *knew* how to cook goddamned carrots and vermouth; it was the only contrivance he could think of when Pete's phone started ringing. He had taught Pete how to make it. With*out* the fucking butter.

No.

He loved Levee. He loved Geo, too. He loved Nora. He loved Gary. But No; not Saturday night.

Was this an omen? Maybe it was an omen. Maybe he'd been paying too little attention to the signs of the universe. He should go to Reading Terminal Market and buy entrails. Carry his plastic bag of offal home and spread it out on the slate floor of the foyer. Draw a few pentagrams, maybe.

Maybe the timing of the cosmos was off. Maybe he was always parsecs ahead of Pete. Maybe Pete wouldn't catch up until they were old. When all the young men Pete wanted and didn't have a shot at were out boogying in the clubs and chasing each other and the two of them were sitting in this room or some other room after they'd washed off their plates of soft, old-people food and were resettled in their recliners, trying to choose between cable TV and pun-filled conversation. Maybe then.

Maybe never. Maybe he should pack up all his could-be's and his might-be's and roll them up with the entrails into yesterday's newspaper, tie them up with biodegradable cord and toss them through the stainless-steel door of his trash chute. And should he stand there a moment as his package of pipe dreams and shoddy plummets twenty-three floors? Should he wait to hear the thunk? Should he drop it and turn, with no regrets, to his future, salted with optimism and peppered with the knowledge that there would be no other men out there who could even tempt him?

"No," he says, scowling at the Hershey. "No, you self-indulgent, sorry son of a bitch.

"What did your Mums always tell you? 'William, my dear, when life gives you a bag of lemons, whip up a batch of sorbet.' "

XVIII.

They sit at their table in Lickety Split at the corner of Fourth and South streets. Pete, Bill, and Geo wait for Nora, Gary, and Paul. They are lined up on a banquette under a vast French poster for *Lolita* and a ceiling lit with thousands of tiny white Christmas lights.

"Paul will never find a place to park," Geo says nervously.

"Park what?"

"My car," Geo says. "I gave him my car."

"Where'd he go?"

"To Rose and Lennie's."

"Jesus."

"He's telling Rose and Lennie?" says Bill, incredulously.

"First he was going to call them. Then he decided he had to do it face-to-face. He was a mess."

"The Holmeses are here," Pete says.

In the foyer, Nora and Gary exchange hugs and kisses with Mickey, the owner, who points the way to their table. Nora waves and moves toward them down the aisle in a sleek, short tan suit and tan stiletto heels. A model for a name-brand shampoo, she is often seen on TV, her shining hair, a recent burnt umber, in slow motion. Gary strides behind her in baggy work khakis, sneakers, and a black silk shirt. Most of the diners in the room turn to watch them. Their gaits are fluid and elegant. They move like cheetahs.

The three men stand to greet them. Nora hugs and kisses each of them, then Gary does, and they take places at the table, Nora sliding into the banquette seat between Pete and Geo, Gary and Bill taking chairs across from them. Heads still turn in the direction of their table.

"Where's our Paul?" Gary asks, pointing to the empty chair at the corner of the table.

"New Jersey," Geo says. "Rose and Lennie's."

"He's not coming?" Nora says. She rakes her delicious hair back with her fingers, preening for those diners who keep looking over.

"Oh, he'll be here."

"He's telling them?" Gary asks.

"He's telling them."

"Maybe they won't let him leave. Lock him up. Keep him there," she says. "To protect him?"

"More likely they'll kill the little fuck to protect him," Geo says. "It took them three years to adjust when he got his own apartment. Can you imagine how they're going to take Saudi Arabia?"

"Why's he doing it?" Nora says.

"Money," Pete and Bill say together.

"Only money," Geo says.

"Well, why doesn't he just get another job? Or tell his company he wants more money? Or maybe he wants to go to Saudi Arabia."

"He doesn't want to go to Saudi Arabia," Pete says, and drops it, remembering he was told in confidence about Paul's fear of flying.

"Hey," Geo says. "He could be making more with any other firm. He should have left Barnaby a long time ago. I mean, the guy is a goddamned cement *ex*pert. But no matter how much money he makes, he'll piss it away. If he saves fifty grand working over there, it'll be gone the first month he's back. Money burns holes in Levee's jeans. He *has* to spend it. He'll blow it on a fucking *Corvette,* or something. Live with him!" Geo says, agitated now. "Hey, this is no secret. Remember years ago when he asked me to teach him about money? I put him on a budget? He'd sign his paycheck? I'd take it and deposit it and give him an allowance and we'd sit down twice a month and pay his bills? We sat down four times. Four times. Count 'em. He lived on his allowance just fine. Never asked for an advance. In the first two months, he ran up nine hundred in cash advances on his credit cards. I said, 'Give me the cards.' He said, 'All of 'em?' I said everything made of plastic. Even the one from your health insurance plan that has your group number on it. Gimmee. He wouldn't do it. Said he couldn't live without his cards. Said he'd rather handle his own money. Fine, I said," Geo says, tossing his hands in the air. His black eyes flash. He plucks at the creases in his tailored slacks.

"And I love the guy," he says. "Absolutely fucking love him."

"Is that why you broke up?" Nora asks.

"No," Geo says. "Ah. He arrives."

Mickey is grinning and shaking Paul's hand. He waves back toward their table.

"Paul," Nora says. "You look like you've already been to the desert. So you told them?"

"Oh, God!" Levee says, pressing his large hands into his face. He looks haggard. His shirt is wrinkled. The armpits are damp. "It was a nightmare," he says. "It was worse than a nightmare. It was real!"

"What happened?" three of them ask at once.

"Thanks for the car, Geo. I mean, really. You don't know. Really. It was my getaway car. I parked it in Abbott's Dairy."

"Paul, there *is* no Abbott's Dairy anymore," Geo says dryly.

"You know where I mean. The parking garage they built over the ruins."

"Screw Geo's car," Pete says. "What happened?"

"Hey!" Geo says. "I got three thousand miles on that car. Cost me thirty-four grand."

"Geo, it's time for a new one," Bill says. "What happened, Levee?"

"Oh. What a night. What a *night*!"

"So what *hap*pened?" Pete asks, poking his forefinger into Paul's thick hand.

"I drove there about five o'clock . . ."

"Was it a warm day?" Geo asks.

"Yeah. Pretty warm," Paul says. "I got there maybe five forty-five."

"No clouds?" Geo asks.

"No. I don't think so," Paul says, looking puzzled. "Maybe some."

"Geo! Stop that!" Nora says.

"Lennie was mowing the grass," Paul says.

"Lennie retired so he could mow grass," Geo says.

"Rose was cooking dinner."

"Rose was born in a casserole dish."

"Geo! Let him talk!"

"So she pours me some tea and we chit and chat while she peels potatoes and she tells me about this byoo-tee-ful Jewish widow just moved into the neighborhood, one kid, but a *nice* kid, and her husband who was killed in a train wreck, 'you can't be too careful these days, Pauly,' but left her with jillions, and she's had her over twice already, comes from a nice family even, and can I come over next Saturday night for dinner to meet her? I got plans, Mom. 'What could be more important, Pauly? It's all right your hanging around with shiksas, but forget marrying one. It would kill your father, Pauly, the same as actual murder, and you're thirty-four do I have to remind you, and we're not getting any younger, your father and me, and there is a built-in grandson already, a little boy I could fall in love with, *you* could fall in love with, he even looks a little like you around the eyes. You'd be ahead one before you even started your own and Sondra wants more children she told me, how's eight o'clock?'

"And I hear the lawn mower stop and I'm thinking I got

to get the barometric pressure before Lennie comes in and I tell her no, I'm busy, but I have this offer from my company, like a promotion. 'A pro*mo*tion! A pro*mo*tion! Leonard!' she yells. And I hear the garage door close. But I have to go to another country, I tell her. And she grabs the edge of the sink, 'Another *coun*try! *Per*manent? What other country?' Just a few months, I say, the Middle East. 'Israel,' she says, and she lets go of the sink and her eyes light up and she says, 'You've been transferred to Israel! Leonard!' No, Mom, I tell her. Saudi Arabia. I'm going to Saudi Arabia. And she puts her fingers under the front of her dress and moves them like her heart's beating, and she says, 'Saudi A*ra*bia.' And her one leg begins to dance and she grabs the sink again and when I'm reaching for the car keys, Lennie walks in, and he looks at her and he says, 'Rose?' And she's pointing at me with the vegetable peeler, and she says, 'Your son has decided to *kill* himself, Leonard.' And Dad says, 'My God! Pauly, you in trouble? You need money? You're in the prime of your *life*!' Now Rose has got both hands on the sink and she's doing this Irish jig with both legs and she says, '*You* tell him, Pauly. *Tell* your father. He's going to Saudi A*ra*bia, Leonard!'

" 'He's not going to any Saudi Arabia,' he says. And she says, 'Lennie. Sit, Lennie. You want some water? I'll get you some water. Here. Drink, Lennie. Your pressure. You look like your face is going to explode. Do you want to have a heart attack? Look, your father's having a heart attack!'

"So I explain about the terrific opportunity my company is offering me and what an honor and about all the money I'm going to make and they like that part a little and they quiet down and Dad finally says, 'Jews can't *go* to Saudi Arabia,' and I'm trying to think of a way around telling them, but I'm thinking, how would I get their letters over there and Rose's boxes of food if I don't? So I just blurted it out. I said I was changing my name to Peterson and I'll be perfectly safe once I take off all the labels Rose has sewed on my underwear that say 'Paul Levee,' and the only compromise they have to make is to put Peterson instead of Levee on the return address of their envelopes when they write to me."

He looks around the table. He takes a couple swallows of Geo's scotch.

Geo rolls his eyes.

"And that was it?" Pete asks.

"No. My father said, 'You'd give up your name? Your heritage? For money? I'll *give* you the money. How much? Name a figure. Rose, get me the checkbook.'

"I said, it's just for a few months. I'd be borrowing a name for safety's sake.

"Then he got up from the table, and he said, 'Well, Mr. Peterson, you'll excuse us? Mrs. Levee and I must make arrangements for the death of our son.' And Mom began to wail and they left the room and went upstairs. . . ."

"What did you do?" Nora says. "Did you call them back? Go after them?"

"No. I left."

"I don't believe it," Nora says. "Oh, Paul. How awful. What will happen?"

He sighs.

"They'll both have fatal heart attacks in the night. They'll try to have strokes. If that doesn't work, they'll go out in the garage and drink dandelion killer and die in each other's arms beside the lawn mower. Sondra Bronfeld will find their bodies. She'll call me. Rose probably gave her my number."

He smiles. "They'll get over it. They'll take a hard line while they think about it. They won't call for a long time. Maybe until Monday. Then Rose'll call and leave moaning messages on the answering machine and Lennie'll begin to drop to his friends about how his son the concrete engineer has been given a plum foreign assignment. In Egypt, he'll probably say. And Rose'll tell her canasta cronies how her son was the only one selected to supervise such a complicated job. And when they write to me or send me carrot cakes, they'll use the leftover labels from Lennie's business. I'll get mail to Paul Peterson from Consolidated Electrical Supply. He couldn't give up the post office box when he sold the business."

"So you're going," Pete says.

"I'm going. I'm gonna do it. I'm taking the job. Goodbye, Philly. Hello, Jidda."

"Good for you," Gary says. He pats Levee on the back.

All the friends congratulate him with hand pats and toasts.

Pete smiles at his beaming friend, envies his daring and his audacity. Thinks that he didn't believe that Levee would really do it. Thinks he is glad that he will. He looks at Bill, who is looking at him. Bill is looking at him in a thoughtful, wistful way. A bottom-lipped, enigmatic smile. Bill looks down at his glass of mineral water. He turns the glass slowly between his fingers. The curious smile lingers.

» » »

Throughout the dinner conversation about calories and fat, about filming a shampoo commercial in San Diego, about crime on the streets and drugs and the homeless, Geo and Gary inflaming the rest with arch-conservatist rhetoric, through a rift about the false inflation of the price of coffee, Pete enters a few times when he feels a stab of passion, but more often retreats from the table talk. He finds his eyes settling on Bill, finds his attention focusing on Bill's observations and Bill's objections, and, when he returns to himself after arguing hotly with Gary for a moment or two over a statement made by the mayor, finds that his legs are crossed between Bill's under the table, becomes aware that the toes of Bill's stockinged feet are moving ever so slowly up and down on his calves while Bill, leaning back in his chair with his arms crossed, calmly tells Geo that the city council's abdication of responsibility, as much as the mayor's, will sell the city into poverty. When Bill finishes speaking, he doodles with a finger on the *faux marbre* tabletop, his toes still moving slowly up and down on Pete's calves.

Pete settles back on the cushioned banquette, looking at Bill, who lifts his gaze to him and smiles the same wistful, curious smile. Bill lifts his chin a few centimeters. The rubbing continues, slow and rhythmic. Pete feels warmth between his legs and, despite himself, he smiles, and then, embarrassed, he looks down the table toward the conversation at the other end. He leaves his legs exactly the way they are.

"Paul, what about Freddy?" Nora asks.

"Yeah, what about your son?"

"We dropped the lawyers. We're doing a trade."

"Jesus," Geo says.

"If I give him my Sony VCR and his choice of any five of my porn tapes, he'll keep Freddy while I'm away and give him to me when I get back."

"Talk about sleazy sex deals," Bill says to Pete. "Better get that one in writing, Levee. Who pays Freddy's vet bills?"

"He pays."

"Just remember," Geo says. "The Greg Conrad tape's mine. You got it on loan."

"*Private Workout?*" Paul says.

"Who's Greg Conrad?" Nora asks. She and Gary look at each other.

"Hung like a bull moose," Bill tells them.

"How unattractive," Nora says.

"Hey," Gary says. "You guys ever see *Raging Pussy*?"

"The sequel to *Born Free*?" Bill asks.

» » »

At one in the morning, turning down an invitation to walk to Gary and Nora's for a nightcap, Pete and Bill hail a taxi to share uptown.

"Broad and Locust first," Pete tells the driver.

"Sixteenth and Locust," Bill corrects.

"Sisteen Locoost," says the driver.

They ride in silence for some blocks.

"You OK? You were quiet tonight," Bill says.

"Sure. I didn't think I was."

"Maybe not . . . That was fun."

"It was," Pete says. "I had a good time."

"Me, too."

They ride up Lombard Street. The cab has bad shocks. The driver slouches in his seat and steers with a forefinger. He turns right at Broad.

"My . . ."

"I . . ."

"Go ahead," Pete says.

"No, you."

"It's OK . . ."

"No. Please . . ." Bill says.

"My parents are . . . um, having a party. A picnic on Memorial Day . . . You want to come?"

"You said your parents are?"

"Right."

"When's Memorial Day?"

"I don't know. It's always on Monday. I think a week from Monday. I'll find out," Pete says, looking out the window.

"Sure. Let me know."

"OK. . . . You?"

"What?"

"You were going to say?" Pete says.

"I don't remember."

The cab stands at a red light at Pine Street. The driver hums reggae with the radio.

". . . Who's coming?"

"Family," Pete says. ". . . Could you make a tossed salad?"

"To bring?"

"Yes."

"For how many?"

". . . There'll be seventeen, unless the nieces bring friends, but you don't have to make for that many. The kids mostly don't like salad, and there'll be a lot of food."

The light does not change.

"You making something?"

"Yeah. I don't know what it is yet. Mom hasn't told me. Hey. Buddy. I think the light's busted."

"How do you know she needs a tossed salad?"

"She mentioned it. Hey. You can go," Pete says, tapping the driver's shoulder.

"Red," the driver says. "Is red."

"Broken," Pete says. "The light is *bro*ken. You can *go*!"

The cab does not move. The driver shifts nervously in his seat.

"*Vous pouvez continuer,*" Bill says. "*Le feu est brisé.*"

"*C'est permis?*" the driver asks, edging across Broad Street.

"*Absolument. Vous venez de . . .*"

"*Je viens d'arriver de Guadeloupe.*"

"*Soyez le bienvenu,*" Bill says as the taxi lurches forward.

"What if he had been Vietnamese?"

"They speak French. And now, if you'd like to discuss tax-free municipals with this guy, I'll be happy to translate. The rewards of a liberal education."

"You're too much," Pete says.

» » »

His back against the door he has closed behind him, Bill stands in his slate-covered foyer. The lights of east Philadelphia and New Jersey glow beyond the window walls of his dark living room. He says, "What does this mean?"

He walks to the center of the room and sits down in the dark.

What would he say to Pete's family? What would they say to him? He would recognize them from Pete's photographs. Once, years ago, he shook Mary Alice's hand in the aisle at a concert. "Mary Alice, my friend Bill Payne. Bill, my sister Mary Alice Flemming." "Did you like the Mahler?" "Yes," she said. "But long," she said. "Yes," Bill said.

The extent of his personal knowledge of the family.

What would Pete's parents say? What would he say to them? "Hi, I'm Bill Payne. Your son and I burned sheets till the sun came up. For years."

Why did Pete invite him?

What did they wear to picnics at their house?

» » »

When he steps through his door and bends to pick up fliers stuffed through his mail slot, Pete hears a door close upstairs. He stands and listens. He walks up the steps to the second floor. He stands outside his own door and listens. The house is quiet. He unlocks his door. He opens it cautiously. He snaps on the wall switch. His apartment seems to be as he left it. He walks from room to room, turning on lights. He pulls the shower curtain open in his bathroom. He looks in the closets, moving his suits and jackets aside. Above him, on the third floor, he hears pacing, hears the faint squeaking of floorboards, from one end of the house to the other and back again. He looks at his watch. It is quarter to two.

He is wide awake, wired.

» » »

He sorts clothes from a pile he has placed on the dryer. As he drops dark things into the washer, he thinks about Saudi Arabia. He tries to remember if there are mountains there or if it is flat like Kansas. He sprinkles detergent over the clothes.

He sees the five of them standing in the door of the loading gate at the international terminal. Terror waltzes in Paul's eyes. Clutching Freddy in the crook of his arm and his knuckles white on the handles of his gym bag, Paul hugs each of the friends. Freddy licks their faces. Though Hope and Doom hunker on his shoulders, Paul smiles wanly and turns to walk down the collapsible tunnel to the aircraft.

Pete presses the button marked Start. Water rushes into the tub.

"OK. OK. All right. You'll be forty years old in no time," he says to the gurgling machine. "Get a life, maybe."

XIX.

"Health Alternatives. Tom Evenson."

"I'm calling about testing," Pete says.

"Sure," the man says. "What sort of test were you thinking about?"

"Um, AIDS," he says.

"Would you like to be tested?"

"Yes."

"And when would you like to come in?"

"Isn't there a waiting list?"

"No. You can just walk in and we'll see you pretty quick. When would you like to come?"

"I'll make an appointment."

"No need to do that. Just drop in," he says. "The least busy times are midmorning and midafternoon."

"Maybe I should make an appointment," Pete says.

"No problem. For when?"

His bedroom seems very warm to him. His heart races.

"You have anything open in 1993?"

There is a slight pause.

"I could maybe squeeze you in. Did you have a month in mind? Or a season?"

"How about tomorrow," Pete says.

"Sure," the man says. "Or you could come over right now."

"Now?"

"You know where we are?"

"Yes," Pete says.

"Now's real good. Have you out of here in twenty minutes."

"You mean just come over?"

"Sure. There's no one here. It's a good time. Or would you rather wait till tomorrow?"

"No. I'll come . . . Did you want my name?"

"No. Just come in."

"Is it that anonymous?"

"Absolutely. We'll ask you for a name, but it's just something to tag the test to. You can make one up, if you want. Be creative, though. We get too many Smiths and Does. So, come on down."

"I'll be the one in the cow costume," Pete says. "I'll take Door Number Two."

"Oh," the man says. "I get it. What color cow? I'll watch for you."

"See ya."

It was enough to call, he thinks. He could just stop by one day this week. Some afternoon when there are not a lot of orders. When Doris's girls are in. When it's easy to go out.

He'll take a shower. He'll think about it while he's taking a shower. He strips off his T-shirt.

In the bathroom, he turns on the hot water, and while the water comes up, he stands on his scale. He steps off it and on again. "Best out of three," he says, stepping off and on the scale again.

He has lost two pounds since the day before. He feels his cheeks flush.

He gets into the shower.

"Maybe tomorrow," he says, pulling up the shower tab. The water is hot. "Maybe next week."

He lathers his head with shampoo. He soaps his body. He rinses his hair. His fingers work the soap into his armpits.

Not too hard. Just gently. On the surface of the skin, then more firmly. He presses his fingertips in a circular motion into his armpit, feeling for lumps. He changes hands and moves to the other armpit, working the soap in and pressing his fingertips in a circle. Are those swellings there? Are those lymph nodes? He moves back to the other side. It feels the same.

His hand slides down his side to the V of his groin, his soapy fingers prodding the space where his thigh and his abdomen come together. Are those nodes there? Are they swollen? Are they normal? He puts his fingertips on both sides of his groin. The sides feel the same.

"Flowers," he says, putting his face up to the shower head, "this is insanity." He has to stop doing this. Every shower he takes is becoming a feel fest. And on the street? He has to stop feeling himself all the time through his pants pockets out there. In taxi cabs, in the homes of his clients, walking behind them through their rooms. Has to stop feeling his crotch all the time. Has to keep his hands out of his armpits. He's getting calluses under his jawbone for Christ's sake. And every hot and humid day when sweat breaks out near his hairline, near his receding hair, he thinks it has begun. He has to stop thinking about his leukocytes.

And if they tell him he's positive? What does he do then? Get calluses all over? What does he do if they take him into that room with the fucking tropical fish and the framed dancing kids on the walls and smile at him over the clipboard and tell him that his life is limited?

He sighs. He stands with his back to the water.

He'll cope. He'll deal with it. He'll handle it like he handled being called out of class at Our Lady of Perpetual Solace grade school by the nun with the pinched lips and no blood in her face who told him Father Devlin would be driving him home; "something" had happened to his brother.

The frog comes back to his throat.

"Ahh, what the fuck," he says. He puts his head under

the water and rinses his hair. He'd be Mr. Swann. No. Go the whole nine yards. Be Marcel Proust. Gustave Flaubert. Who the fuck cared?

He'd handle it.

He pushes the shower tab, reaches for a towel.

If they were going to tell him today, he didn't want to do it. Maybe call them back. Maybe ask them if they give the results right away. Maybe ask them, if they did that, to wait in his case. Wait a discreet week and send Billy in. "Mr. Flaubert, how tall you've become."

"My friend could not come today. He has dyspepsia. You will give his results to me."

"Dyspepsia? Heh, heh. Well, that's the good news. Guess what else he has!"

» » »

He sits on a couch in a waiting room. The walls are painted ivory. They are hung with framed abstract art posters. The furniture is small-flowered. Comfortable. He reaches for last week's *Time.* On the magazine table sits a cardboard rack of brochures on many sexually transmissible diseases.

An attractive woman in her thirties enters the room. She has brown, short-cut hair. She walks with assurance.

"Mr. Flaubert?" she says. Her smile is ironic.

"Yes." He stands.

"My name is Judy Masterton. Please call me Judy. Sit, please," she says. She settles herself into an armchair next to the couch. She has a clipboard.

"Gus," he says. The slightest of smiles plays across her mouth.

"If someone else comes in, we'll move," she says. "You've come to be tested for the HIV virus. Are you here because you think you're at risk?"

"Well. I'm gay," he says. He wonders where the man on the phone is.

"Do you have unprotected sex?"

"No. I mean, not for a long time." She writes something down.

"How long?"

"More than two years. Maybe three?"

She raises an eyebrow.

"I haven't had sex with anyone for about two years. And before that, it was very . . . um, ah . . . protected."

"You used condoms?"

"Yes."

She writes something down.

"For how long?"

"The year before that. Maybe longer."

"Are you an intravenous drug user?"

"No."

"You are . . ."

"Male?" he says nervously. He winces.

"I was leaning toward male, Mr. Flaubert," she says, showing her ironic smile. "I was going to guess your age. Thirty-sixish?"

"Fortyish. Thanks."

"Thirty-nine? Forty-one?"

"I'm forty," he says for the first time in his life. It does not feel too terrible.

She makes a note.

"I am going to give you a list of things to check off. You don't have to check anything if you don't want to, but the answers to the questions may help others. It only takes a few minutes. You can take it to Tom through that door and he'll draw some blood. Your results will be back from the lab Tuesday morning. Tom will give you a card. It will have a number on it. Bring it in with you when you come back. You have to come in person to get the results. Do you have any questions?" she asks without moving.

"No. I don't think so."

"I know you're anxious about having the test," she says. "I'm glad you chose to come here. If it turns out you are HIV positive, we'll have a great deal of very useful information for you here. Also, the center works with AIDS specialists here in the city and around the country. If it were necessary, we could get you involved in the very best protocols.

"Before you leave, Tom will give you an envelope containing some printed material. I'd like you to read it all before you come in next time," she says. "OK?" She makes no move.

"Sure."

"Have you thought of any questions you'd like to ask?"

"Do you have any tropical fish here?"

She looks at him a few seconds. "No," she says. She tilts her head. "Why?"

"I just wondered," he says.

She stands. She hands him the clipboard and her ballpoint pen. She smiles.

"I think that *Madame Bovary* still stands among the ten best novels ever written, don't you?"

"Yes," he says, his face a blank. "Thank you." He takes the clipboard and pen.

Her smile is very gentle.

"It's better to be tested than not," she says.

"Right," he says.

"And have a nice weekend."

"The best. Thanks," he says.

He looks at the clipboard. The first part of the form asks his experience with a long list of sex acts. He is relieved to see several he would not dream of performing.

» » »

Intending to return to the shop to work, Pete stands outside it instead, looking in his display window past the Coolbaughs' tall Regency vase, which spills with blossoms in the English style and which his driver will place with exaggerated care on the round table in the center of their marble foyer to the tune of one hundred and fifty dollars every week of life. Inside, at the showroom cooler, Doris bends, extracts, rejects, and accepts spires of delphinium from a pail. She holds her head tipped back as she examines each stem through her bifocals. She is slow and exacting. A perfectionist.

He will not join her and her daughter in the construction of funeral arrangements. He does not want to think of death or of dying.

He turns and walks toward the center of the city.

» » »

At the bar at Woody's, he moistens a cocktail napkin with saliva and wipes away the smear of dried blood from the inside of his elbow. He balls the napkin. His hand pauses over an ashtray. He tucks the blood-stained napkin discreetly into his pants pocket. He hides the needlemark in the bend of his arm. He tilts back on his stool. Beads of water condense on his Bloody Mary glass. He wonders at his choice.

He thinks about Tuesday, when he is to go back to the clinic for the results of his test. He touches the top edge of the card in his shirt pocket, the card with the number written on it, the number which matches the one on the vial which has begun to move through the testing system. His number. He imagines a rubber-gloved hand holding a thin glass pipette over his vial, imagines clear drops of reagent falling into it, sees the color of his blood change in a flash of chemistry to blue, he thinks. Not a neutral, pretty blue, but a sudden, shocking, acidic, evil blue.

And how will she tell him, the woman with the small, ironic smile who admires *Madame Bovary*? How will she manipulate the muscles of her face to show hope when despair may be scrawled across the front of her blue-tabbed file folder?

Sweat breaks out on his scalp and his forehead. He downs a third of his drink.

And what of his mother's calm before confirmed, terrible knowledge? Should he drop by her house and ask her for a dose of her courage? Meet with her in the library over large, medicinal scotches and bird books? Tell her she has nothing on him with her jasmine lotion and Mabel Mercer, that the color blue suddenly conjures for him the Grim Reaper, whose cold fingertips he feels now on the back of his neck?

» » »

He has covered his dining table with layers of newspaper. On a large forest-green-painted rectangle of ¾-inch plywood in the middle of the table, he outlines art deco letters from a stencil. Janet Baker sings German *lieder* from the speakers at the end of the living room. He knows what the songs are about. He understands few of the words.

He leans to his work. He squints at the pencil lines. He wishes he had spent more time sanding the finish.

Occasionally he hums along as he draws letters, occasionally he hums in sync with Janet Baker, following the notes of these familiar songs he has not listened to for years, until a thought takes him from the music, and his humming becomes random and off-key.

He cuts along the outline of a tulip he has drawn on heavy paper, the tulip that is printed on his checks. He smiles as he thinks about cutting traced flowers in grade school with little chrome scissors with safe, rounded tips and dull blades, of each of his classmates cutting identical flowers traced from the same stencil for Sister to paste after school to their classroom windows, their flowers identical to the flowers of the other grades of children who, in identical clothing, traced and snipped up and down the hall in the period called "Art," creating a perfect, symmetrical window garden for the reassurance of parents driving by and of visiting archdiocesan administrators. No chance, he thinks, for a sunflower to have sprung overnight in that paned symmetry of tulips.

"And what after this, foolish boy?" he says, tracing the tulip along one side of his sign. "Are you putting your cart before your horse? Throwing your usual caution to the wind? Leaping before you look?"

» » »

With an overpriced brush made of mink hair, he fills in his penciled letters with gold paint. He frowns over his work. His tongue tip flicks over the ends of his moustache hairs. His brush tip, sure and precise, slides down the length of an L, gilding its leading edge.

» » »

He holds his sign to the light, turning it, examining the lines of the letters he has painted. He is pleased with his work.

He puts newspaper on the floor. He leans the sign against a radiator to dry.

» » »

On his sofa, in the light of the late afternoon, he holds a wineglass by its stem in his lap, watches the sunlight move slowly by millimeters in the skewed shape of a window across his carpet toward the phone on the floor by the fireplace, toward the yellow pages, which lie open on the floor at the A's, toward the pad with flight dates and times double-underlined in ball pen.

The room is silent. The building is silent. No traffic moves on his Saturday street.

He looks at his walls, looks from one framed print to another, remembering where and when he bought them, remembering the history that they comprise over half his life. The paint behind them is gray, painted over taupe, painted over moleskin. He cannot remember the color of the walls the first time he put paint to them. Were they white?

"Nothing here that belongs to someone else. And you are forty."

» » »

He sits hunched forward on the sofa, his forehead pressed to the cool, wet bowl of the wineglass. His sign dries against a radiator.

Too late? he thinks. Too little, too late? "Too Late the Phalarope"? What is that, anyway?

And, remembering the stockinged toes moving lazily up

and down his shin under the table at Lickety Split, and the far-away, years-away gaze of his friend across the coffee cups and saucers, No balls, Flowers? . . . Leave 'em in the Plains states with your humor? . . . You sit around on your CD's, groping your lymph nodes, scared shitless to face a lady Tuesday with a file folder. Love is too dangerous? Work is a bore?

He stands. "OK."

He stalks to the kitchen. He pulls tools from his junk drawer, spreads pliers and screwdrivers and jars of bolts and lock parts over the top of his Formica counter until he finds his hammer and, on the bottom, in the back, stray masonry nails.

» » »

Holding his sign against the front of his building, he pounds masonry nails through the corners of the plyboard and into the bricks beside the front door of his shop. He is fearful that the wood will split. It does not.

When the last nail is driven, he walks out into the street. The gold paint gleams on the green:

FOR SALE
BY OWNER:
BUSINESS,
TWO APARTMENTS
555-9300

"OK," he whispers.

XX.

As he gathers up the debris of his painting, he regrets that he has burned the bridges offered by his friends to leave the city, to inaugurate the beaches of New Jersey or Delaware, to spread in the sun and to blister; to drink too late into the night; to sleep too late into the morning; to eat with others in new and in familiar places. He tries to remember a Saturday night when he chose to stay home. When he chose to be with himself.

He believes he has made a mistake to stay in the empty city on this of all weekends.

He could still drive to Margate. Be there in time for hors d'oeuvres on the patio. Be there in time, certainly, to laugh and joke over dinner with Gary and Nora and Paul.

He could still drive to Rehoboth and join Geo sardined upright in the bar of the Blue Moon, stand with him under the fuchsia-lit, arched ceiling, hold drinks the colors of summer shirts, shout at each other above the too loud music and cruise the lean, tanned young men who seem to own the summer.

He could walk to his parents' house, hang around, endure their wary wonder at his dropping in. Wait for their inevitable invitation to share Carmen's marinated pork roast or her rum-soaked Cornish hens and try not to sound too eager.

Or call Bill at Sister Woman's, or Bea, or Mary Alice, or

Stu, and say he just happened to be driving in the neighborhood. Avoiding a serious talk with himself.

» » »

In his bedroom, in the fading rubescence of dusk, he sorts dirty clothes into piles of lights and darks.

» » »

In his living room, in an armchair, he reads, rereads a newspaper baseball column to the muffled rasp of buttons against the drum of the dryer in the laundry.

» » »

In his kitchen, his elbows resting on the open doors of his refrigerator and freezer, he stares from the bright emptiness of one side to the frosty, jumbled chaos of the other.

He watches wispy, frozen drafts of condensation waft from the shelves. He watches the point at which they disappear.

» » »

At his dining table, with a paper towel spread for a place mat, he eats one of his father's meat pies from its aluminum container. The crust bears the impressions of what could be human fingertips. He imagines metal hands pinching pie dough on a conveyor belt thousands of times a shift, three shifts a day.

As he eats his father's meat pie, he considers sums of money worthy of his skills, tries to extrapolate the price, on balance, of a lifetime of millions upon millions of meat pies. He sees himself in his sixties, tall, gray, and rich, strolling up and down the assembly line of steel alloy hands pinching pie crusts, his father by then a stern portrait in the boardroom, his own starched, white smock spotless, his forehead grown back to the crown and covered by a useless hairnet.

He adds another thirty thousand to the salary.

» » »

In his kitchen, damp-sponging counters scrubbed clean by Mrs. Wayne, he puts himself through the paces of controlling office buildings and apartment houses. He attends meetings. He settles disputes with disgruntled tenants. He instructs accountants in obscure tax advantages. He has his secretary place calls to health food stores, swim clubs, theater matinees, to exercise spas throughout the city in search of Bill. They quarrel about the nature of fiscal and corporate responsibility. They slam doors in each other's faces. They reestablish uneasy alliances. They begin to meet only at meetings.

» » »

In his tub, his face held to the sharp spray of the showerhead, he soaps his armpits, refusing to grope them, and debates with himself whether to go back to the clinic on Tuesday, or to wait. He reviews his schedule for Memorial Day week. He includes tasks he would normally delegate. He justifies procrastination until, remembering his mother beside him at the head of her dining table, cupping the breast she no longer has and chiding herself before her family for her own abuse of knowledge, he rejects hypocrisy with a groan that carries above the sound of water splashing.

» » »

Naked in his bed, in the dark, an arm and a leg draped over the pillows he has arranged at his side, Pete considers the road map of his life, examines the routes that lead out of Kansas, the blue one, even, that stops a short distance into Missouri.

He is forty years old, more than halfway to seventy.

He is forty years old going on forty-one, going on forty-two if he's lucky, on a slow and ineluctable slide down a mud-slick riverbank to oblivion, or to a meeting, long before he planned, with Cliffie.

"Who never took anything lying down," he mutters suddenly, sitting up, groping for the light switch. "And *you*, you stupid ass!" he says, turning on the lamp.

He heaves his legs over the edge of the bed and sits, his hands clutching the mattress.

"Go ahead, Flowers. Just go right ahead. Live in the

future until there isn't one because you haven't got the balls anymore to make one happen, you dumb jerk."

He stands. He runs his hands through his hair several times.

Had he heard the Fat Lady sing yet? Had he? Oh, maybe he heard her humming a little, while she cooked up some breakfast eggs, or while she stood at her closet choosing a dress for her performance, but he had not heard yet the first clear note of the Fat Lady's song. No, sir. Not yet.

"No, sir," he says, sauntering, naked, out of his bedroom and into his living room, turning on lights as he goes, punching the Power button of the stereo, then the KRZ-FM button, and pumping up the volume to 30. "Take *that*, Petranek!" he yells, shaking his fist at the ceiling.

"Time to play *ball*, Flowers!" he cries as he squats at the telephone on the floor, a forefinger running down the A's of the yellow pages. "Yes . . . sir. Motherfucker."

XXI.

Mary Alice pours coffee into her mug. She sits at her place at the round breakfast table. She sips the coffee. She sighs. She looks out to the field of timothy grass that a neighbor will cut for hay. When? she wonders.

The phone rings.

She sighs. "Shit." She reaches behind her to the countertop.

"Hello," she says.

"Mine are gone," Bea says. "Yours?"

"Gone, but not forgotten."

"It's too much," Bea says. "Would boys be less of a production?"

"We'll never know, I hope," Mary Alice says. She sips from her mug. She looks at the edge of the woods.

"Actually, I'm calling about Mom, Mary Alice."

She feels an adrenaline surge. "Is she all right?"

"Well, for the moment. I'm calling about Memorial Day. Did she call you?"

"Yesterday. I'm supposed to bring potato salad."

"Cannelloni."

"Good."

"Mary Alice, I'm sure you agree that this is not a good idea."

"We all love your cannelloni. Just bring something else, if you'd rather. She won't care."

"I'm not talking about cannelloni. I'm talking about having a picnic. It's too soon. It's too much for her."

"I don't think she'd do it if she didn't feel good about it."

"She just had major surgery, Mary Alice."

"Bea. I saw her yesterday. We took a walk. We walked down to Front Street and back. That's what? Sixteen blocks?"

"I'm talking about her mental state, Mary Alice. She has brain tumors. She has frontal lobe metastases. *Two* of them! This party is out of the question, Mary Alice. We have to convince her to put it off."

"I don't agree, Bea."

"How could you *not* agree? This is our mother, Mary Alice," Bea retorts.

"She wants to do it. Stu doesn't want to do it for some reason. I volunteered to have it out here. I told her Hal offered to drive in and pick up her and Daddy and take them back. She wouldn't hear of it. She got angry at me for suggesting it."

"Well, something else is going on with Stu, and I'm going to have a word or two with him, but I can tell you without question that she is in no shape to be throwing a big party."

"Bea, this is not a big party. It's just the family. We're all bringing the food. Carmen will manage things. Mother has a cleaning service. Daddy will cook steaks, or something. She doesn't have to lift a finger. What is the big deal here?" She rolls her eyes. She raps her teaspoon on her place mat. She hears Bea puff on a cigarette, hears her exhale into the mouthpiece of her phone.

"Mary Alice, I cannot believe what I am hearing. I cannot believe you are taking this attitude. Our mother just had her breast removed . . ."

"Two weeks ago."

"She reports to the hospital and endures two hundred rads of radiation to her brain. Her hair has begun to fall out. . . . Did you know that, Mary Alice? Our mother's *hair* is falling out! She dials my number and thinks she's talking to you and you encourage her to throw a field day at her house. Mary Alice, I think you are behaving very selfishly. Very selfishly . . ."

Mary Alice rises from her chair. Her lips purse.

"Stu I would expect, or God knows, Alexa, but *you*, Mary Alice; I cannot countenance your behavior. It's shocking to me. It's beyond the pale, Mary Alice. You are *only* thinking of yourself. The only time you go to see her is when it's con*ven*ient for you. When the Azalea Committee forces you to come into town for a meeting."

"Bea," Mary Alice says. She raps her spoon against her thigh. "I am going to hang up in about thirty seconds because you are being goddamned rude, but before I do that I am going to do something I never do. I am going to give you a little advice. My advice to you is that you run around the block, or take a cold shower, or pop a Valium, or cop a joint, or whatever it takes, and that you decide that you are going to either keep your mouth shut about this, or you are going to encourage Mother, because this picnic pleases her. But whatever, when I see you Monday, I had better see a gracious smile on your face from the minute you get there until the minute you leave, because if you don't get on this program, I will be on you like maggots on spoiled meat. And on second thought, Beatrice, leave out the running around the block part. You are too damned fat! I am hanging up on you now."

She drops the receiver into its cradle. She stands at the counter with her head tilted forward. She breathes deeply.

The phone rings.

"Inez?! Don't you touch that phone! You let it ring!"

XXII.

The elevator opens. Bill steps out carrying two large shopping bags.

"God, Bill," Pete says. "You buy out Reading Terminal Market?"

"This one's a bowl and dressing and stuff. This one's all salad. I put it in a Glad bag. What'd you make?"

"You don't want to know," he says as they walk onto the street. "Banana bourbon pudding. A real artery blocker. Spoonful of this and you go senile. Eight egg yolks. Six cups of milk. Thirty-six vanilla wafers? Mom asked for it. You look terrific."

"You can't see the chafe marks. My bedroom looks like Filene's basement on Washington's Birthday. I've put on everything I own since ten this morning. You look great."

"Thanks."

"New shorts?"

"Yes."

"New shirt?"

"Yes."

"You must be depressed."

"What?"

"You only buy clothes when you're depressed."

They walk down Broad Street. They turn left at Pine. Pete shifts the heavy baking bowl of pudding from arm to arm. He plays and replays family picnic disaster scenarios.

"I think we're the only people left in town," Bill says.

"Looks like."

". . . Nice day for a picnic."

"Beautiful."

"You OK?" Bill asks at Twelfth Street.

"Sure . . . I think."

"You nervous about this?"

"Try terrified."

". . . I could just go back, you know. Do they know I'm coming?"

"No."

"It would be easier probably. You know. If you just went by yourself? Really. I wouldn't mind . . . I have a lot of salad here I could eat . . . till JuVember."

Pete glances at Bill. He grins, embarrassed. He brushes his shoulder against Bill's as they walk.

"Stick to me like glue," he says. "This is my Rite of Passage."

» » »

"We should have gone around back," Pete says as they wait at the front door of his parents' house. "I should have brought my keys."

I should have got the flu, he thinks. Appendicitis.

Sounds of conversation flow over the brick garden wall. A child squeals. The bolt is thrown inside the door.

Pete breathes in. "OK," he says.

"Hello, Pete," Carmen says. "Oh," she adds, seeing Bill. "You brought a friend. Come in. Come in."

"Carmen, you're not dressed," Pete says.

"Well, certainly I am," she says.

Pete flushes and walks in. "I mean, you're dressed dressed. That's very pretty," he says, admiring her pale blue shirtwaist dress.

"Thank you," she says, looking up at Bill.

"Carmen, this is my friend Bill Payne. Bill, Carmen Cesano."

She extends her hand. "You'll be comfortable here," she says. "We have high ceilings."

She bolts the door. She leads them down the hall, waving them on with a hand over her shoulder.

"Well, I'll tell you, this party is the best medicine your mother has taken yet. You two are the last. They're all out in the garden. She's been in and out of my kitchen about a hundred and fifty times. I had about forgot what it's like to cook with Elizabeth and I'm ready to take a *broom* to her! At least the kids haven't been underfoot. Stu's got 'em out there playing something, rolling around in the grass and his missus interrupting every minute or so about they're soiling their clothes as if she didn't know what Tide was for. Here, put those on the sink counter and I'll deal with them. Do they have to go in the refrigerator? I hope not. I don't think you could cram a lemon in there with all this stuff, and did they make you bring something, too, Mr. Payne? What are those bags?"

"Bill," he says. "Salad."

"A green one? We need something green. Go on, now, you two join the others and I'll see to these. There's a bar set up out there. I sent some cold wine out with your father. And if you don't find what you want, Mr. Payne, you'll let me know? God knows we have it somewhere."

"Bill," Bill says.

"Bill," Carmen says. She flashes him a fulsome smile and, turning, rolls her eyes at Pete. "Go on, now."

Pete opens the kitchen screen door for Bill. At the far side of the garden, his father and Hal hunker by the gas grill, turning valves. Mary Alice, Anthony, and Alexa talk in the shade, glasses in hand.

"Unto the breach?" Bill remarks as he passes through the door.

Pete flinches. He follows Bill out onto the terrace.

Stu is the monkey in a raucous game of Monkey in the Middle at the lower end of the garden. He leaps in the air. He dodges a volleyball in a circle of eight screaming little girls. He is red-faced and panting. Mary Alice's jeweled hands sparkle in the flutter of her conversation. Bea stands with a woman in an ivory turban at the edge of the magnolia tree. Bea looks up. Surprise and something like shock flit across her face. She speaks to the woman in the turban without moving her lips and lifts her head slightly in indication. The woman in the turban turns. She wears large sunglasses. He recognizes his mother. "Pete!" she calls, crossing quickly the fifteen feet that separate them. He sees his father stand and squint, hears him say to Hal, "Who's that?"

Liz smiles broadly as she moves. She holds out both her arms.

"Well, hello!" she says, grabbing their nearest hands. She offers Pete her cheek. "And you are Bill. I'm Liz Flowers," she says, three notes descending. "Liz," she repeats, squeezing Bill's hand. His father stands at the garden border with his hands on his hips. He still squints. He looks at Hal and shakes his head.

"I am happy to meet you," Liz says. She flicks Pete a grin. "Finally. Your mother and I knew each other. We had quite a few laughs together, but I'm sure we'll talk about that. Come over here," she says, pulling on Bill's hand. "I want you to meet the rest of the family.

"Bea. Come here, dear. Bea, this is a friend of Pete's, Bill Payne. My daughter Bea Ferraro. I don't know if you remember Bill's mother. Connie and I . . ."

"Well, I'll be dipped," Mary Alice oozes in Pete's ear. "Get me my bifocals. Am I seeing what I'm seeing? You brought a *date* to a family affair?"

His cheeks heat up. "Don't start, Mary Alice. You don't know what this is like."

"I love that man," she says, looking Bill up and down as he shakes hands with Bea. "Now that is a tall drink of water. Would you look at those legs? I've never seen him in shorts. I've never seen anything like that in shorts.

What's the story here? I knew his mother, you know. Oh. Now we're going to have a good time. Alexa's in motion."

"Oh dear," Pete says in a tiny voice.

Alexa has left Anthony standing in the grass. She waves at Pete, but traipses toward Bea and Liz and Bill.

"I want my blankee," Pete whines. "I want to go home."

"Watch her hands. A dime'll get you a dollar she'll run her fingers through her hair when she catches his eye. What did I tell you? Does she know your story?"

"I don't know."

"I don't think so," says Mary Alice. "Stu doesn't tell her much. Hot man. MMM-mmm. You seeing each other again?"

"I don't know," he says, wondering how she knew they saw each other ever.

"Look at those thighs. Chew!"

"Mary Alice."

"Look at Mother holding Alexa's arm. There is no blood going into that hand. And look at Mother. Giving Alexa gangrene and wearing that dear little smile on her face. She looks good, don't you think?"

"I didn't recognize her in the turban."

"Hair's falling out. Radiation. Just in two little places, but she's sensitive about it," Mary Alice says matter-of-factly. "So. Are you seeing each other?"

"I don't know."

A hand grips his shoulder.

"*Hey,* Pete," Anthony says. He hugs Pete with both arms. "Who's your friend? That sucker could play center for the Lakers."

"Bill Payne. He's in real estate."

"He's a builder?" Anthony says, rubbing his palms together.

"No. Just owns a lot of buildings. Commercial stuff. And apartments. Probably a lot of pipes in them, Anthony."

"Music to my ears. And I don't think I have a card on me."

"Hey, Pete!" Stu calls from the circle at the end of the garden. "Get over here! Give an old man some help!"

"Later!"

Stu waves and jumps into the air. The little girls squeal.

"I'll say hi to Dad," Pete says, excusing himself from Mary Alice and Anthony.

He walks through the grass toward the grill. The two men are on their knees, tinkering with connections.

"Hi, Dad. Hey, Hal."

They stand, his father holding on to Hal to right himself.

"One of these days, I won't get up," his father says, extending his hand. "How're you doing?" he asks, a little warily, Pete thinks. His father glances toward Liz and Bea and Bill.

Hal shakes his hand warmly. "How are you, Pete?"

"Out of gas?" Pete asks them.

"No, we're not out of frigging gas!" his father says. "The frigging line's clogged somewhere."

"Let me look," Pete says.

"Look all you want," his father says. "You won't see anything we didn't in the last twenty minutes."

Pete raps the tank with his knuckle.

"Got a screwdriver?"

"There. On the grass," his father says. He rubs his knees through his slacks.

"Who's your friend?" he asks, as if it didn't matter.

"Bill Payne. He and his father do real estate."

"Here?"

"Yeah."

"What kind of real estate?"

"Commercial stuff." He unscrews the bolt which secures the tank to the platform.

"What's his father's name?"

"Art."

"I met him," his father says, looking cranky. "Son of a bitch beat me on a bid once."

"Ah," Pete says. Wonderful news. He lifts the tank free of the grill. "Feels like you're out of gas."

"We're not out of frigging gas! I sent a man over this week to change it out," his father says. "Here, give me that!"

Phil grasps the tank handle and lifts it.

"Well, for Christ's sake, Hal!" his father says. "Frigging thing's frigging empty!"

"Have any more?" Pete asks.

"Two more in the garage. There frigging *better* be two more in the garage, or that bastard'll be pounding the pavement tomorrow."

"I'll get one," Pete says. He walks to the garage to a chorus of "Uncle Pete" from his nieces. He waves at the girls and their friends.

When he returns to the yard with a new tank, his father and Hal stand with Bill some distance from the grill. Hal's and his father's backs are to him. His father's arm waves in agitation at his side. He seems to be shaking his finger in Bill's face.

"Oh, Jesus," Pete says.

Tempted to leave the tank in the grass and go to them, he carries the tank to the grill instead. From the grill he can see that Hal is smiling, that his father and Bill are smiling as his father talks, still wagging his finger about.

"How long, O Lord?" he says, setting the new tank on the platform.

» » »

"Let's eat over there," his father says, indicating the edge of the magnolia with his salmon-colored Styrofoam plate heaped with grilled steak and Bea's cannelloni. It is not a suggestion. His father has already started to walk toward the tree.

"Sure," Pete says.

With great effort, his father manages to seat himself cross-legged on the grass.

"Walk in the frigging pool, the doctor says."

"You should."

"Who has time?" he says.

They eat together beside the magnolia, their right and left knees nearly touching, their plates balanced on the insides of their calves. Some distance from them, the others have grouped themselves, the children with Carmen at card tables on the terrace. His mother, Stu, Alexa, and Mary Alice have formed a square in the slanted sunlight in the very center of the lawn. Anthony, Hal, Bill, and Bea recline on the four sides of an old Hudson Bay blanket near his mother's peony bed. They eat propped on their elbows. His mother has brought out books on which to stand drinks in the uneven grass and perhaps, he thinks, to seduce her guests, even one, into borrowing to take home and read.

"Your mother's having a good time today," his father says. He points toward her with his fork, speared with cannelloni.

"How is she?"

His father mooshes the cannelloni piece into the sauce on his plate.

"She's feeling better," he says. "These weird things happen to her, but she doesn't seem to mind. Sometimes she sees people in the room. She was talking to them for a while, but now she pretty much ignores them. . . . How's business?"

"Good. I'm booked into August."

His father grunts.

"I had an offer for the business," Pete says. He cuts a piece from his steak.

"Yeah?" his father says, continuing to eat, the word a little too flat, a little too disinterested.

"Nice piece of change," Pete says.

"Really." Flat. Neutral. His father saws at his meat.

"More than it's worth," Pete says. He notices his father's eyebrows lift a bit.

Phil grunts.

"I was impressed."

He grunts again.

"Why not sell it?" his father says academically. He seems more interested in his food.

Pete senses something switch in his mind. His adrenaline surges. He feels his face flush. In for a dime, in for a dollar. What the fuck?

"Well, I've been thinking about it," he says. "I'd have a fair amount of cash to invest. . . . There's a business for sale here in town. Very successful. Owner wants to retire. Liquor license goes with it."

"Liquor license?"his father says, staring frankly.

Pete cuts through the cannelloni. "It's a gay bar," he says, looking at his father.

"A *what*?!"

"I thought I'd call it . . . 'Flowers'.' "

His father's fork hangs in midair. His mouth opens.

"Be a great investment. I mean, if someone wants to give me all that money for my store? Why the hell not?"

"Jesus fucking Christ!" his father says. He jerks his plate up and spills cannelloni sauce on his pants.

Pete hands him his napkin.

"I'm kidding you, Dad," Pete says. He lays his plate on the grass. "Why did you do that?"

"What?" his father asks, all innocence.

"Send that goon over with a blank check."

His father flushes. "Worth a try," he mutters, sawing through his Styrofoam plate. "Oughta ban this shit," he says, moving food away from the hole he has made.

"I've been thinking, Dad," Pete says, returning to his own food. "About your offer."

"Didn't make one," his father grumbles.

"Sounded like one. At lunch at The Garden? You were going to triple whatever I make now?"

"Maybe you better tell me what you make," his father says, pushing food about.

"I can't do it, Dad."

His father's face sags.

"It has nothing to do with you . . . . And I'm selling my business."

"Thought you liked it," his father says, chewing.

"Not enough anymore."

"How will you live?"

"I'll work it until it's sold."

"What then?"

"I don't know yet. Something new."

His father grunts.

"I do have a counteroffer," Pete says. "I would be willing to consult for you. I can show you how you can be coast to coast within two years for a relatively small increase in your current distribution and advertising costs. You wouldn't have to sell a share of the company outside. . . . I think you had it figured you'd have to?"

"How?" his father says.

"We'll talk about it if you hire me. I'd want a contract."

"How much?"

"I'll do it for nothing. I'll give you the equivalent of one day a week. For two years. It has to be understood that I would be hired as an outside consultant. You have enough vice presidents to do the actual implementation. After two years, you give me a percentage of gross sales west of the Mississippi. It won't be cheap. . . . And you relax your hiring policies."

"What policies?" his father asks defensively.

"To include homosexuals."

His father frowns. He shakes his fork at Pete. "I am an Equal Opportunity Employer."

"Bullshit. I'm surprised you haven't been slapped with a dozen discrimination suits. There is a law in this city against the way you operate."

His father looks up into the copper-bottomed leaves of the magnolia. He sighs.

"You don't want to run the company."

"No."

His father sighs again.

"I'll have to think about it."

» » »

His brother mixes a drink on the terrace.

"Those girls'll wear you out, Stu."

"Naaa," Stu says, pouring gin in his glass. "I love kids. Just can't move as fast as I used to. You want a drink?"

"Got one."

"Your friend's a nice guy," Stu says. "Quick mind," he adds, squeezing a lime slice. "Well spoken."

"He is."

"He likes baseball?"

"I don't know."

"How could you not know a thing like that? Mary Alice says you've been friends a long time?"

Stu twirls his ice cubes with a stirrer. His face and neck are red.

"Five years. He never played baseball. He played soccer in school. I never asked him if he likes baseball. He was pretty good at soccer."

Stu tastes his drink. "I never played soccer." He adds more gin. "You're, um, just friends?"

"I don't know," Pete says, surprised to hear his brother ask.

"You don't know much today. You seem a little spacey, boy. Cheers."

He takes a deep sip from his drink. He waves at the clusters of family in the garden.

"All this making you crazy?"

"A little."

He is touched that his brother would ask. He does not know how to respond to the intimacy. The vocabulary of their adult relationship is limited: the family in generalities, sports, business. He wants to ask Stu why he stays with Alexa.

"Ask Bill if he likes baseball, why don't you? I got some box seats at a good game in Baltimore in a few weeks. A Saturday. We could take the train down. . . . Ask him," he says, pushing his knuckles into Pete's shoulder. "Gotta get back to my fans," he says, nodding at the girls struggling to set up a volleyball net. "Lighten up," he says over his shoulder. "We'll all get used to it." He lifts his hands in the air. He grins. "Haven't got any choice, have we?"

» » »

"Hi," he says.

"Hi," his mother says. She sits at the wooden kitchen table, her feet up on a chair, a bowl of his pudding in her lap. Her turban is slightly askew.

The room is dark, cool.

"You're not supposed to see this," she says, pointing at the bowl with her spoon. "I'm cheating. Want some?"

"God, no," he says. He sits across the table from her.

"It's scrumptious. This is my second," she says. "It's the Decadron. Makes me ravenous . . . How're we doing? They're on a tour of the house, if you wondered. Bill and your sisters. He wanted to see your baby pictures. Just teasing," she says, dipping into the pudding.

"How are we doing?" she says again.

"I don't know," he says. "All right."

"Your father said you made him some sort of offer."

"Yes."

"You didn't do that because you felt you had to, did you?"

"No."

"Curious," she says, licking her spoon.

"What did he think?"

"I don't know. There were no editorial comments. A simple statement. The bourbon is just right in this."

"Where is he?"

"Out in his car. He thinks best in his car."

"Where did he go?"

"Nowhere. He's in the garage. He always goes there when he wants to think about things. He sits in his car. You carried this meringue from your house?"

"Just the egg whites. Carmen whipped them."

"Nice," she says. "Why did you make your father an offer?"

"He needs help. He even hired somebody to buy me out."

"Sounds like him. Generous?"

"Very."

"You went for it?"

"Please."

"Then . . . ?"

"He's stuck. He wants to expand to the West Coast. He doesn't see how he can do it without going public."

"And you know how."

"Yes."

"Why don't you just tell him?"

"He'll enjoy it more if he pays me. Also, I don't think he wants to go it alone."

"And what do you get out of it?"

"If I do it right, a very fat monthly check after two years. And freedom."

"Freedom. Sounds more like indentured servitude to me. I wouldn't work for him. Freedom to do what?"

"Something else."

"What?"

"I'm thinking."

"Good. What about your own business? How can you work for your father and run that? You say you're busy all the time."

"I'm selling my business."

She stops eating, looks at him. "But not to your father."

"No."

"Why sell it?"

"It holds me back."

"From what?"

"From doing anything."

She nods. She licks her spoon.

"I can understand that," she says.

"I'm taking a trip next week."

"I'm appalled. You? In the wedding season?"

"I need to get away. I'll dump it all on Doris. Get her some help. I need to get away for a while."

"Terrain suddenly too flat for you?"

"You could say that."

She looks to her side, the spoon halfway to her mouth. She holds it, poised in the air. She frowns.

"Later," she says.

"What?"

"Not you," she says. She waves the spoon toward the sinks. "Her. Are you wearing cologne?"

"Yes."

"That's what it is," she says, returning to her pudding.

"You want me to move?"

"Of course not. She will," his mother says, indicating the sinks. "Can you imagine me walking by the fragrance counters at Bloomingdale's? Why, they'd have to call for a wagon. Relax, Peter. I'm used to it and you might as well be, too." She scoops a vanilla wafer. "You know, one of these days it'll be that Holy Spirit person showing up for a heart to heart. That'll be a marathon conversation. . . . Back to the Plains states. I've been thinking about our talks. It is none of my business, you know. It's your vehicle. Take it where you like. There are a lot of blissfully happy people in Kansas, for that matter. In the heart of the heart of the country? William Gass, it was . . . And have you read Coover?" she asks. "Wrote a wonderful book about baseball. Did I ever force that on you?"

"No."

"I will . . . Peter, why *didn't* you become a pilot?"

"I don't know," he says. "Fear of flying?"

» » »

The lawn has been set up for croquet. Pete stands with Anthony. They await their turns, tapping the toes of their sneakers with the heads of their mallets. Anthony talks about his desire to open an office. A real office. Nearby, beside the peony bed, Alexa shakes small pieces of paper in Stu's face. Stu appears stricken. Alexa's smile is nasty, vindictive. Pete hears her say to his brother, "And I've been thinking about starting an art collection. I've been thinking I'd start collecting John Singer Sargent."

» » »

The adults, except for Alexa, have gathered in the hall of his parents' house. Pete and Bill hold department-store shopping bags of empty bowls and lidded containers. They are the first to leave.

As Bea squeezes him in her plump, pale-plum-draped arms and whispers in his right ear: "Bring this one *back*," Pete hears in his left ear his father say, "Bill, I enjoyed talking with you. Come back and see us again."

Stu's eyes are bleary, his face is red and puffy. He leans against the paneled wall, holding a fresh gin and tonic.

Behind him, Pete hears Hal say to Mary Alice, "And I think I'll join a gym. Lose some weight. Cut back on all this shit I'm taking."

As he turns, he sees Mary Alice squeeze Hal's hand, sees her struggle with her face. She seems about to cry. He looks away.

His mother is happy, ready to drop. She adjusts the set of her turban with both hands. His father suggests lunch at The Garden as he shakes Pete's hand. Bea scowls. Carmen gives him an uncharacteristic pat on the back and they are out the door.

"Goodbye! Watch out for the muggers! Goodbye," and they are on the front steps. "Goodbye. Nice to meet you, Bill," and they are on the sidewalk, "Bye," and they are at the corner of the garden wall when the heavy front door closes.

They walk up Pine Street. Pete, in the habit of thirty years, looks down at his feet on this block to avoid a glimpse of the corner where the taxi took Cliffie. He smiles absently.

"It was OK," he says with some wonder. "Nobody died . . . not even any real bloodshed."

"I liked it," Bill says. "Your father's a hoot. Called Daddums a 'frigging shit.' "

"In-fucking-credible," Pete says. He sighs.

Their paper bags rattle. Their sneakers make susurrous sounds in the night.

They walk without speaking. In the middle of the Ninth Street block Pete stops at the steps of an antique store and says, "Billy, sit here. Sit down. There's some stuff I need to talk about."

"Oh dear," Bill says. They lay their packages on a marble step and sit beside them knee to knee.

"Listen," Pete says. "About your offer to work for The Empire? . . . I can't do it. I've thought about it. It wouldn't work. It would be bad for us."

"I didn't think you would," Bill says, a little sadly and resigned. "You're right, probably. We'd end up arguing a lot about it. And you'd never feel like it was yours really. You know?"

"Yeah. That's what I thought. I was thinking that."

"Right."

". . . Billy, I decided to take a trip. At two o'clock this morning. I made some plane and hotel reservations. For next Tuesday. A week from tomorrow. To Madagascar. Ten fabulous days and eleven glorious nights."

"In Madagascar."

"Yes."

"Madagascar, Africa."

"Off Africa. It's an island."

"I know the geography."

"I want to listen to the lemurs sing."

"Are you serious?"

"Yes. They sing when they wake up."

"You're going to Madagascar to listen to monkeys."

"Yes. I want to hear them."

"Why? I mean, why next Tuesday?"

"I have a wedding Saturday and it's cheaper to fly on Tuesday."

"I mean why at all."

"I got tested Friday."

"Really . . . For AIDS?"

"Yes."

"You didn't tell me."

"I haven't seen you."

". . . I'm impressed. When do you get the results? Or are the results why you're going to Madagascar?"

"I can get them tomorrow afternoon. First I thought I'd wait until after Madagascar, then I decided I shouldn't be a wimp about it."

"This isn't like you. It's too rational. How come you decided to do this?"

"It's been coming. I've been thinking about things. After I had the test, I went and sat at Woody's a long time. And all the time I was there, I kept thinking I ought to be at the store, I ought to be doing drawings for the Reed wedding, I ought to be on the phone ordering up frangipani, I ought to be trying to find another good designer. And all the time I'm thinking about what I ought to be doing, I'm thinking about the test. I'm thinking that I've got to be HIV positive and what difference, really, will the drawings make, or if the frangipani's unavailable, or if Deirdre Reed snags herself on a pew sconce and falls on her Saint Kitts–tanned face in front of God and three hundred blue bloods? I could be an endangered species. Me."

Pete looks up at the windows of an apartment building across the quiet street.

"And I got to thinking about Madagascar and lemurs. They're endangered, you know. Probably because some of them don't even get *up* until ten in the morning, and you know what they do when they wake up in their trees? They sing, Billy. Across the forest to each other. They have voices like saxophones and bassoons and oboes, and these wonderful songs lift through the trees and fall into the valleys and up the other sides and they don't even know they're endangered.

"Saturday morning my clock radio went off at five A.M.? And what do I hear when *I* wake up? The croaky voice of Stevie Figman telling me that four teenagers on their way home from a prom were killed when their car went through a bridge railing. I said to myself, 'Flowers, you have to get centered. Something is very wrong in your life.' I've been thinking about things. . . . I don't think I'm happy anymore. I mean, I'm not *un*happy. . . . I'm OK. I'm all right. I work. I pay my bills. I work and I pay my bills . . . and I work and I pay my bills."

"It's the American Way, Pete."

"Right. I'm a good American."

Bill nods at Pete. He smiles vaguely. He flips the laces of his large sneakers.

". . . Bill?"

"Pete?"

"You want to go?" Pete says, looking doubtfully over at his friend. "I made the reservations for two."

"For two."

"Yes."

"To go to Madagascar," Bill says. "A week from tomorrow. Just sort of fly off to the other side of Africa like it was Camden, or something. Just the two of us."

"No," Pete says. "No, Billy. Geo and Paul and Gary and Nora. They'll want to go. And you and me. Just the six of us."

Bill grins. "Yeah. It wouldn't be the same without them. . . . You're serious about this."

"Very. I'll even pay for everything."

"What about your business?"

"Doris is going to handle it. She doesn't know it yet. . . . And I'm going to sell it. It's for sale already. I put a sign up yesterday. The business. The apartments. All of it."

"Moving away on top of all of this? Do I hear the foghorns of Seattle in your future?"

"I was hoping we could talk about that. Maybe on the plane back. If it went all right . . . we could look around town maybe? . . . Would you go to Madagascar? Would you think about it? You don't have to tell me now. Just think about it?"

"What would I wear in Madagascar?"

"Ha!" Pete jumps to his feet. He cakewalks down the steps of the antique store. "You're going! Ha! You're going, aren't you?! You are going to go, I can tell! Ha!"

"OK. All right. But I'm not getting up at dawn to hike up some bug-infested jungle mountain to listen to monkeys. . . . And I'm paying my own way."

"No! No." Pete dances around in a little circle. "I'm paying. Ha! And you have to listen to the monkeys once. Just once. Hot damn!

"Come on!" Pete says, pulling on Bill's arm. "Come on. Grab your bag. Get the lead out. Let's go. I got things to do, and you have to start packing!"

"Listen," Bill says as he gets to his feet. "How about if I go with you tomorrow?"

"No . . . No. It's OK. I'll be OK. I'll be fine. Really."

"Listen. I'd like to. Just to be around. I'll wait outside. I'll wait inside the door. I'll just stand inside the door. It'll be better."

"No. I'll be all right. I'll be fine."

"No. I want to go with you. I'll just walk over with you. That's all. Listen to me. It's very scary to go back. I'm going to go. We'll just walk over together. OK?"

"OK," Pete says.

They walk up Pine Street toward Broad. They do not speak. Their shopping bags swing in their hands. Occasionally their shoulders touch accidentally, then they touch occasionally on purpose. Sometimes an arm goes up and a hand pats the middle of a back, or a hand goes up and rests for a few seconds on a shoulder.

They walk for a block.

Bill says, "Your sister Bea's a little eerie."

"What do you mean?"

"She and Mary Alice were showing me the house? We were up in your brother Cliff's old room. I think it was starting to bother Mary Alice, so we were about to leave, and Bea says to me, 'You don't have any bones missing, do you?' How would she know that?"

"What?"

"My ribs. I was born with eleven on one side."

". . . You never told me that."

"Of course I did."

"No, you didn't."

"Well, I did."

"You didn't tell me that."